A
DEADLY
GAME

A DEADLY GAME

a reggie da costa mystery

laraine stephens

LeVel
BEST BOOKS

Historia

For my darling Bob

Praise for A Deadly Game

"Laraine Stephens' third Reggie da Costa novel, *A Deadly Game*, is a delight. Set in 1920s Melbourne, it is a wild ride from beginning to end. Full of exquisite historical detail, flashy real-life characters and an engaging detective in the form of Reggie, it is an entertaining and very interesting historical mystery.

"Historical crime fiction does not get much more enjoyable than this. A terrific, fun read!"—Jeff Popple, Murdermayhemandlongdogs.com

"Author Laraine Stephens has the knack, and the characters, to bring 1920's Melbourne to life. From the seedy back streets, to upper-crust nightclubs, crime reporter Reggie da Costa leads the charge, ably assisted by brother and sister combo Dusty and Ruby, in the third novel in this excellent series."—AustCrimeFiction

New Year's Eve, 1924

It was to be Miss Kitty's last outing for some time, given that it was no longer safe for her to be out in public. She had handed in her resignation, said her farewells, and accepted that going into isolation was the only alternative. But, before she withdrew, she had wanted one last evening, one last chance to let loose and enjoy herself.

The party was being held in a gambling den near the Fitzroy Town Hall, in an area called 'The Narrows,' an assortment of claustrophobic lanes, tired warehouses, cobbled streets, and dingy houses. She was a frequent visitor to that establishment and knew what to expect. All the usual suspects were there, drinking illegal booze, snorting cocaine, gambling, and dancing to a four-piece Dixieland jazz band, watched over by none other than Joseph Theodore Leslie Taylor, alias 'Squizzy,' owner of the establishment.

Miss Kitty enjoyed the atmosphere of Melbourne's underworld, with its smoke-filled rooms, doll-faced girls, and gamblers who played the tables, placed bets on the horses, or watched the shiny pennies spin upwards in a two-up game, betting on the fall of the coins, heads or tails. The clientele of The Narrows was endlessly fascinating to her: petty thieves, gamblers, drug dealers, Squizzy's cronies. Here people lived on the edge, flouting the law, indulging their whims, and surrendering to their addictions. But it was time to take a break from that world and go to ground, because life had become precarious, ever since her fiancé cum protector had died after a knife was plunged into his back.

Miss Kitty knew that she was a contradiction. She was like the penny in a two-up game: heads on one side and tails on the other. On the one hand, she was an intelligent woman who had done well for herself at school with little to no effort, and had never had a problem getting a good job. But there was another side to her: a desire to shrug off her conventional life and live dangerously, associating with an underclass of criminals who made their own rules. It was impossible for her to find a compromise between the two, because both of them gave her pleasure. And she had ensured that each side of her life remained separate from the other. Until now. She had allowed the two to mix, and life had become perilous.

Through the cigarette smoke, Miss Kitty could see Squizzy watching over the proceedings. He was, as usual, dressed as a toff, all five feet two of him. His suit was of the finest quality broadcloth, set off by a silk shirt and patent leather button boots. Diamonds glittered on his fingers and in the pin of his knitted silk tie. He leaned on a silver-knobbed walking stick that had become part of his wardrobe since he was shot in the leg. He saw her watching him and flashed his gold-toothed smile at her. She raised her glass in reply and drained the last of her champagne.

It was time to go. It was late, and the patrons were very drunk. She stood, draping her fur around her shoulders, then made her way through the crowd to the front door, pushing away the lads who desired a kiss or more.

One of Squizzy's henchmen was standing guard at the entrance. 'One moment, Miss Kitty,' he said, opening the door to let her pass through. 'Happy New Year.'

She smiled and pressed a ten-shilling note in his hand. 'Thanks, Les. Look after Squizzy. And yourself.'

It was quiet out in the alley, while up at Gertrude Street one hundred yards away, she could hear the sounds of celebration and the bacchanalian carousing of inebriated revellers greeting the new year. A ginger cat, prowling the laneway, padded up to her and rubbed its neck against her ankles, purring contentedly. She reached down and scratched it behind the ears, then watched it slink away.

The sound of her heels echoed on the cobblestones as she passed the red brick warehouses, dilapidated houses, and corrugated iron fences of this part of town. It was lonely and deserted at this hour. The exception was a sleeping drunk, covered by an old army blanket, who had taken shelter in the doorway of a derelict factory. She stepped around the man, avoiding the empty bottles. As she did, a hand reached out and grabbed her ankle.

She looked down. The blanket had fallen away from the man's head, his face exposed in the half-light of a street lamp. She felt a wave of fear course through her.

'Thought you'd got away from me, did you?' he growled.

She kicked out at him, but his hold on her ankle was strong. His grip tightened, and he pulled her down, down towards him. She lost her footing and landed on her back, her face inches from his. He smiled for the first time, but it was a smile devoid of warmth. From the side of her eye, she had noticed a bottle close to her hand. She stretched backwards to reach it and grabbed the neck, smashing it down on the cobblestones. Then she wheeled it over her head and brought the jagged edge down on his arm.

He yelped, letting her go. Before he could recover, Miss Kitty was on her feet and scrambling down the alley. The bright lights and the sound of laughter and shouting in Gertrude Street beckoned to her, spurring her on. If she could just make it—

Behind her, she could hear the thump, thump of his boots, gaining on her. She cried out, but the only response was the sound of her voice reverberating around the alley.

With only ten yards to go, she stumbled as the heel of her shoe caught in the gap between the cobblestones. Her body landed heavily, and she grimaced in pain.

She heard his voice as he loomed over her. 'You're mine now, Miss Kitty.'

Chapter One

Clutching a glass of Scotch, Reggie da Costa, senior crime reporter for *The Argus*, stood at the window of his rented flat above a grocer's shop while he watched the people hurrying along Swan Street below him. He was looking, rather than seeing, being preoccupied with the events of New Year's Eve the night before. His head still hurt from over-indulgence, which he was trying to offset by using that well-known patent remedy, 'hair of the dog.' The only problem was that the whisky wasn't working. Every time he thought about New Year's Eve, his splitting headache returned.

Reggie's upbringing had been anything but normal. His mother, Mavis, as an innocent young lass of twenty, had fallen in love with a violin-playing Italian who liked the good life but didn't want to pay for it. She had married him, despite the misgivings of her father. When the money ran out during the Depression of the 1890s, Mario da Costa had run off with the maid, leaving Mavis and her thirteen-year-old son destitute and the talk of Brighton society. It was a long hard road back to respectability but, due to the kindness of friends, Mavis and her son had regained their social standing despite a lack of ready money.

Reggie had learned a hard lesson over the years: that no number of bad experiences could deter his mother from falling into the clutches of parasitic men who would blight her life. Mavis seemed to have the knack of attracting the wrong sort. And now there was another contender who had arrived on the scene, ready to take advantage of Mavis da Costa's generosity and naivety by emptying her bank account.

On New Year's Eve, his mother had invited Reggie to accompany her to a matinée at The Athenaeum Theatre, not only to see a performance of 'A Night in Honolulu,' but also to meet her new beau.

That morning, Reggie had inspected the contents of his wardrobe and selected a conservative three-piece suit, in brown houndstooth, featuring the latest wide-cut trousers. Teamed with a cream shirt and gold tie, his attire suggested that he was a man of means; a man who had made his way up in the world; a man who was universally respected. Just the thing to make Mother's new beau realise that he was not to be patronised.

His prized Hupmobile parked close by, Reggie waited outside the theatre, tapping his foot impatiently, anxious for the whole sorry episode to be over. Unsure of the etiquette involved in purchasing tickets for a man he had never met, he decided to wait rather than shell out his hard-earned cash.

Five minutes later, he saw the plump little figure of his mother approaching, a froth of white curls surrounding her rosy-cheeked face. Mavis had dressed with care, wearing a new salmon-coloured satin dress with an abundance of lace on the bodice. Next to her strode a well-dressed man in his mid-forties, at least fifteen years her junior, carrying a black lacquered cane with a brass knob. Reggie's heart sank. With his thick black hair and thin moustache, the newcomer bore an uncanny resemblance to Mario da Costa, Mavis's absent husband. Another philandering, parasitic, money-grabbing, dissolute cad, Reggie thought, ready to take up the mantle of his father, relieving Mavis of whatever cash she had left. It was all Reggie could do to control his emotions.

He accepted the hand that was proffered him and muttered, 'Pleased to meet you' through gritted teeth. Then he kissed his mother on the cheek.

'Happy New Year's Eve,' she said. She gazed up at him with her innocent blue eyes, searching for a sign of approval, which was most definitely beyond him at that moment.

The new beau, aptly named Valentine Peebles, stood aside as Mavis paid for the three of them. His face bore a toothy grin, a fixture on his face every time he looked her way. In the theatre, Mavis sat in the middle between son and beau, turning her head from one to the other throughout the performance.

2

Reggie was horrified to see that Peebles had a firm grip on her hand while his mother looked like she was one step away from heaven.

Mavis had planned for them to have high tea at The Hotel Windsor afterwards, but Reggie had other plans. He told them, feigning disappointment, that he had agreed to attend a New Year's Eve party in Fitzroy and that he couldn't disappoint his host. He neglected to mention that he preferred the company of Melbourne's notorious gangster, Squizzy Taylor, to that of his mother and her new friend.

Peebles looked relieved. Reggie sensed that the new beau wanted him gone, and the sooner, the better. Mavis, happy that she had brought the two most important men in her life together, appeared oblivious to the tension in the air.

'We must do this again sometime,' said Peebles, flashing a winning smile in the direction of Mavis's son.

'Over my dead body,' Reggie muttered under his breath as he walked away.

Later that evening, as the clock ticked past midnight, Reggie welcomed in 1925 at Squizzy Taylor's New Year's Eve party. He showed not one ounce of moderation or restraint, unhappy with the unwelcome development in his mother's social life. Too much hard liquor had encouraged too much gambling, leaving him with an empty wallet and a splitting headache that was assailing him now, on New Year's Day.

Reggie turned away from the window and finished off the last of his Scotch. He wiped his mouth with the back of his hand and glanced around the room, appraising the little improvements he had made in the last year with the approval of his landlady and former neighbour, Dotty Wright. His mood lifted. Despite the constraints of a limited budget, the classy wallpaper in the sitting room, the imitation Persian rugs on the floors, and the stylish, but inexpensive, furniture, reflected his upper-class roots. The one significant modification was the installation of a wall of wardrobes on the landing, to hold his extensive collection of suits, shirts, and shoes.

Reggie considered it fortuitous that when he had needed to move out of the home that he shared with his mother, due to the unwanted return of his philandering and irresponsible father, his friend Dotty had inherited the grocer's shop and needed a tenant for the upstairs dwelling. His new lodgings might not be up to the high standards that he set for himself, but they were cheap and comfortable.

Reggie turned back to the window and watched the pedestrians scurrying along the footpath. The 1st of January 1925 was the beginning of another year. Somewhere, out there, in the city of Melbourne, was another case that he would crack: a story that would go down in the annals of crime. And he was just the person to find it.

A smile spread across his face. His headache miraculously disappeared and, even better, thoughts of Valentine Peebles were extinguished from his mind.

Chapter Two

Ruby Rhodes and her reporter brother rented a single-fronted Victorian timber house in Port Melbourne, not far from the docks of Station Pier. It was a gritty, working-class suburb notable for its warehouses and factories. When the weather was pleasant, Dusty and Ruby would stroll down to the waterfront to watch the ships come in or cargo being unloaded by teams of wharf labourers. They had chosen to live there because it was close to the city, where they both worked, and because it was cheap.

It was nearly dinner time, and Ruby was heating up a pot of stew, while her brother pored over the report that he'd written for *The Truth* newspaper. Will 'Dusty' Rhodes was tall and lean, with large hands and feet. His fair hair grew like a thatch and was at odds with the sparsity of his physical appearance. Wearing a tweed jacket that had seen better days, judging by the patches on the elbows, Dusty's lack of concern with his appearance accorded with his working-class ethos. Although he took his beliefs extremely seriously, often decrying the government's attitude to the working classes, he had a wicked sense of humour and a keen intelligence which allowed him to poke fun at himself, often taking his detractors by surprise.

'Help me, sis. I'm running out of headlines,' said Dusty. 'What do you think? "Naughty Northcote Nellie Nicks Nest Egg."'

'Too much alliteration.'

'You can never have too much alliteration. *The Truth* wouldn't exist without it.'

Ruby smiled. 'I'm sure you'll think of something. You always do. How long have you worked there?'

'Nearly a year. From cub reporter to crime.'

'And now you're moving on to *The Argus*. I'm proud of you.'

'From scandal sheet to respectable Melbourne newspaper by the age of twenty. I'm on my way up.' He pulled a face. 'Will they accept me if they know my true opinions? My socialist affiliations? I might have to lose my by-line "Dusty Rhodes" and become "William Rhodes" instead.'

'Really? How ordinary.' She laughed. 'Be yourself. They gave you the job knowing who you are and where you come from. Don't forget that.'

'That's true. I didn't hide anything. By the way, I'm meeting with my new boss next week. You may have heard of Reggie da Costa?'

Before he could elaborate, there was a knock at the door.

Ruby took off her apron. 'Who would that be at this hour? Dinner-time of all things.'

A policeman was standing on the porch, his helmet under his arm. He shifted from one foot to the other, obviously ill at ease.

'Are you Miss Rhodes?'

'I am. What's this about?'

'My name is Constable Jelley. May I come in, please?'

Ruby stood aside and let the policeman pass into the sitting room.

Hearing voices, Dusty came up from the kitchen, holding a glass of wine.

'Constable Jelley, this is my brother, Will Rhodes,' said Ruby.

Dusty shook hands with the policeman. 'What is it? Has something happened? Have you come to arrest me?' The grin on his face evaporated as he sensed the air of tension emanating from the policeman.

'Perhaps you should both sit down.' The constable waited as they sat on the couch, looking up at him with trepidation. 'A body was recovered south of St Kilda beach last Saturday. Unfortunately, we have reason to believe that it is your sister, Miss Katherine Rhodes.'

* * *

The next few days were a terrible blur for Dusty and Ruby. Seeing their sister, grey and cold, lying on the gurney, a sheet pressed up beneath her chin. The surprised expression on the face of the mortuary assistant when he looked from Ruby's face to Katherine's. Meeting with the funeral home manager and selecting a coffin. Feeling deeply ashamed when they couldn't name one of Katherine's friends or work colleagues who should be asked to the funeral. And sitting in the near-empty church, feeling a distinct sense of regret that they had lost a sister.

The police investigation and the coroner's report confirmed that Katherine's death had been accidental. She had fallen off St Kilda pier, most likely hitting the back of her head against one of the pilings, before drowning in Port Phillip Bay. There was no evidence of foul play. The police had drawn a line in the sand, and that was that.

Chapter Three

Ruby was the sensible one. That's what her mother had said, whereas Katherine, or Kitty as she liked to be called, was impetuous and passionate. Always falling for some boy whom she'd discard, then moving on to the next, with never a regret. Collecting friends like stamps, a talent that Ruby had never been able to master. The twins were like chalk and cheese, except for the startling resemblance between them. Both were green-eyed, tall, and willowy, with long legs and wavy flame-red hair that glowed in the sun. While Ruby had tied hers back in plaits, Katherine wore hers out. Mother said that she did it to attract attention. They were both intelligent, but whereas Ruby was studious, Katherine never took her education seriously. She moved out of home, aged sixteen. Ruby, on the other hand, finished school and became a stenographer and typist. And now, at the age of twenty-five, she was secretary to the boss of a small Melbourne firm.

Dusty had been born five years after the twins. He idolised both, and spent his early life running from one to the other, depending on his mood. If he wanted advice or constancy, it was Ruby whom he sought out, but when it came to fun, Katherine was his destination. She was unpredictable and boisterous, charming when she felt like it, clever with words, a practical joker, encouraging the streak of wildness that ran through Dusty. But, when she left in 1916, and their mother died in the Spanish flu outbreak three years later, it was Ruby who stepped up and became a surrogate mother to him. Within two years, Dusty's grief-stricken father had followed his wife to the grave, leaving the siblings alone to comfort each other.

The War was over, but it continued for the Rhodes children. There was no truce to be had there: Dusty and Ruby formed an alliance against Katherine in her absence, resentful that she had not even returned to the family home for the funerals of their parents. Ruby, in particular, was unforgiving. She dwelled on the fact of her sister's selfishness in not reaching out to help after their deaths. But now, with Katherine gone, Ruby faced the realisation that she would never have the opportunity to mend what had been broken.

* * *

The reading of Katherine Rhodes' last will and testament took place in the offices of Markby and Markby, in Richmond. Mr Frederick Markby, an elderly gent, resplendent in high starched collar, waistcoat, and frock coat straight out of the 1890s, beckoned for Dusty and Ruby to take their seats opposite him on the other side of a large oak desk. It was only as she sat down that Ruby noticed that they were not alone. A man was sitting quietly, his hat in his lap, a few feet from her. He was staring at her intently. A mane of steel-grey hair framed his face, set off by a pair of intense grey eyes. He was a big man in his early fifties.

The solicitor did the introductions and then proceeded to make his preamble before the reading of the will.

'Miss Rhodes. Mr Rhodes. Mr Gascoigne. I have invited you to attend according to the instructions of the late Miss Katherine Ann Rhodes. I was appointed executor of her will. She specifically asked that you all be present.

'The will is straightforward.' He took up the document and read. 'To my sister, Ruby Amelia Rhodes, I leave my house in Richmond and the sum of two hundred and fifty pounds.'

Dusty raised his eyebrows at his sister. 'Who would have known?'

The solicitor shuffled some papers before proceeding. 'I am also instructed to give you a letter.' He handed Ruby an envelope that was addressed to her in Katherine's flowing hand.

He paused, then continued. 'To my brother, William Giles Rhodes, I leave my automobile and the sum of three hundred and fifty pounds.

'To Mr John Gascoigne, I leave the sum of fifty pounds in recognition and appreciation of his friendship and support.'

Gascoigne inclined his head. His voice was deep, his English accent apparent. 'Most generous.'

The solicitor studied them. 'Are there any questions?'

'Katherine owned a house?' Ruby shook her head in disbelief.

'Is there a mortgage?' asked her brother.

'None,' replied the solicitor. 'Miss Rhodes bought it outright a few months ago. My office facilitated the transfer.'

Ruby was incredulous. 'She paid cash? I don't understand. Where did she get all the money from?'

Mr Markby shrugged his shoulders. 'That is not my concern. I looked after the legalities of the transaction, that is all.' He looked at Dusty and Mr Gascoigne. 'Anything else?'

'When was the will drawn up?' asked Dusty.

'On the 1st of November, 1924.'

Dusty scratched his cheek. 'Strange. That's about two months before she died.' He lapsed into silence.

The solicitor closed the file on his desk. 'As there are no more questions, I will bring this meeting to a close,' he said. 'I will be in contact in the near future in regard to final disbursements and the handing over of keys. Now if there is nothing more, my clerk will show you out.'

Ruby and Dusty stood on the steps outside the solicitor's office, lost in thought. In her hand, Ruby clutched the letter that Katherine had written, a letter from the sister who was now dead. A sister to whom she had not spoken in nearly ten years and yet had left her the bulk of her estate. And what was more incredible was that Katherine, whom she assumed had never held a job for more than a few months, should have acquired a significant collection of assets. A house in Richmond. A house that was now hers.

Dusty broke the silence. 'I can't believe this. A car. A house. Money. How could she afford it?'

'I don't know. We haven't seen her for so long. There must be an explanation.'

Behind them, John Gascoigne emerged from the solicitor's office. He stepped down and addressed them.

'I'm glad that I caught you before you left. Please accept my deepest commiserations on the loss of your sister. Katherine mentioned that she had siblings but I must say, Miss Rhodes, that I never knew that one of them was her identical twin. The resemblance between you is startling. If I didn't know otherwise, I'd think—' He recovered, then held out a piece of paper to her. 'Katherine was a friend. We worked together. Here's my address. If either of you have any questions, anything at all, then you can reach me there. I apologise for bothering you in your time of grief.'

Dusty put a hand on his arm. 'Before you go, Mr Gascoigne, where did she work?'

'You don't know? The Museum. In Melbourne. She was my administrative assistant.' He doffed his hat and headed off down the road.

'What a strange man,' commented Dusty, watching him as he walked away. 'He looks like something out of Charles Dickens. That old shiny suit and cravat. All he needs is a top hat. Still, he must have been a good friend to Katherine, if she included him in her will. But I don't understand. Our sister had enough money to invest in a car and a house, with cash to spare, and yet she worked at a museum?'

Ruby nodded. 'What's even more strange is that Katherine wrote a will. She never gave a thought to the future, not in the time I knew her. She was twenty-five, not sixty-five.'

She sighed heavily. She didn't know how to feel. Katherine had left her family behind, cutting off the ties of blood. Normal people felt a sense of loss when their loved ones died, but all Ruby felt was an emptiness. The twin sister she had grown up with, and away from, was gone. Katherine was no longer there to share celebrations, heartache, joy, and sorrow—the essence of life with its ups and downs—once she had packed her bags and left. With her mother gone, it had fallen to Ruby to support her ailing father and her young brother. And those onerous responsibilities had hardened her heart against her twin. Ruby had lost her youth, whilst Katherine, frivolous and impulsive, had left home to pursue a life of self-indulgence. And, in those ten years, she had acquired an opulent lifestyle that Ruby could only dream of, until now.

Chapter Four

It wasn't the sort of house that Ruby had expected Katherine to buy. Very simple. Not ostentatious at all.

The little weatherboard house in Tanner Street, Richmond, was from the 1870s, painted white, with a pretty front porch trimmed with cast iron lacework. The neighbouring homes were a mix of workers' cottages and brick terraces, with small front yards and corrugated iron roofs. Outside, on the street, a few children were playing a game of cricket, using a stick as a bat and a rubbish bin as stumps.

Her brother had dropped her off, promising to return with the rest of her things. Ruby unlocked the front door and stepped inside, placing her suitcases next to the grandfather clock in the entry hall. She experienced an unfamiliar feeling of ownership. This place was to be hers, a house that she had not chosen and didn't know existed, gifted to her by a sister she had been estranged from for years. She sniffed the air; it smelled stuffy and stale after being locked up for months. Moving quickly through the house, she opened the windows and back door to let the fresh air in, getting a feel for the layout as she did so.

Leading off the entry was a sitting room with a decorative fireplace, followed by two adjacent bedrooms, a small bathroom, and a serviceable kitchen across the back. Everything was clean and neat; no sign that the owner's life had been snuffed out suddenly. Windows overlooked a small paved courtyard, which had a shed containing a toilet and laundry, and a gate that gave access to a rear lane. It was all in excellent condition, despite a few straggly weeds that had sprung up between the brick paving.

Ruby strolled back up the hallway and stopped in front of the grandfather clock. She wound the hands to the correct time and set the pendulum in motion, then stepped into the sitting room. It was a welcoming space, the furniture of good quality, with an attractive leather Chesterfield and two matching armchairs, and a small dining setting. Two Chinese vases and a jade cigarette box took pride of place on the mantelpiece.

A few framed photographs were on the oak sideboard. There was one of Katherine dressed for a ball and another of the Rhodes family when she and Katherine were about six. One photograph stood out from the others. Ruby lifted it up and studied it. Katherine's beauty had not diminished as she grew into adulthood. If anything, she was even more striking. She was dressed in a form-fitting sheath dress that showed off her figure, her arm through that of a tall, well-dressed man. His hair was slicked down, and his eyes searched the camera. Most would have regarded him as very handsome, but there was something about the curl of his lip that Ruby didn't like. Katherine's head was turned slightly towards him, her expression revealing undisguised admiration. Ruby put the photograph back in place.

The main bedroom had a Victorian brass double bed with decorative mother-of-pearl inlay, covered by a quilt of pink satin. Next to it was a chest of drawers. In the top one was a selection of silk lingerie, some black and others in the palest pink. Ruby pushed the drawer shut, feeling like a stranger who was intruding on someone else's privacy, examining their possessions without their permission.

The moment passed. She needed to accept the fact that she was the owner of the house now.

Boxes of silk stockings were in the second drawer. Woollen cardigans and jumpers, in a multitude of colours, were folded neatly in the last two. Ruby shook her head in wonder. Some of these must have cost a week's wages.

On racks alongside the skirting board were shoes—flat ones, high heels, sandals, boots—in a range of colours. Ruby counted twenty-two in all. And then there were the hat boxes stacked in a corner, over fifteen of them.

A substantial wardrobe held even more proof that Katherine liked spending money. Dresses, skirts, blouses, evening gowns, sundresses, coats, shawls. All the colours of the rainbow. A dazzling collection of the finest fashions that money could buy. In her twenty-five years, Ruby had never seen anything like this.

The house was a testament to Katherine's success, at least materially. How she had ever managed to afford all of this was beyond Ruby's imagination, unless the man in the photograph had set her up. But the house was in Katherine's name, and the design and furnishings reflected her taste. Always the best.

Someone knocked at the front door. Ruby went out into the hallway. The outline of a woman could be seen standing on the porch.

'Can I help you?' Ruby asked, opening the flyscreen door.

The visitor was in her late thirties, with tired eyes and hands roughened by manual work. She was wearing a worn apron over a simple floral dress. Her hair was wrapped up in a scarf.

She stared at Ruby, dumbstruck, then found her voice. 'Katherine said she had a sister. I didn't expect….' Her voice trailed away.

'I'm Ruby. And you are?'

'Katherine's neighbour, Clarice. I used to clean for her.'

'You know she died?'

Clarice nodded. 'The police came. Asked me questions. I couldn't help them much. I saw her last on New Year's Eve. She came in to wish me a Happy New Year. All dressed up, she was.' Her eyes glistened with tears. 'I was so upset when I heard she'd drowned. Katherine was so beautiful. Like a bright star in the sky. Seeing her, I could dream of what life might have been like.' She wiped away a tear. 'Sorry, Miss. I do go on, don't I?'

She held out a key. 'Katherine gave it to me, to let myself in. I waited after I heard the news. No one came. I hope you don't mind, but after a couple of weeks, I let myself in and cleaned out the kitchen. The food was going rotten. I didn't touch nothing else, Miss Rhodes. Anyway, I thought you might like the key back.'

Ruby took the key and touched Clarice's arm. 'Please, call me Ruby. It was very kind of you to do that. I did wonder about how tidy it was, but I thought perhaps the solicitor had sent someone in.'

'No, them legal people don't do nothing unless they're paid. Anyway, I'll leave you to it. You're moving in?'

'Yes. My brother is helping me. I expect we'll be seeing a bit of each other, Clarice.'

'If you need anything, my old man Fred is home during the day. He works night shifts down at the boot factory. Just holler, and he'll be there.'

She smiled for the first time, which made her look much younger. 'Like I said, Katherine was like a bright star. I'll miss her.'

She turned away and went down the front path, then looked back and waved.

Ruby put the key on the hall table and went back into the bedroom, catching her reflection in the cheval mirror. Without a doubt, she looked like a washed-out version of her sister, with her artificial silk blouse in coral and cream stripes and pale grey skirt. So dull compared to Katherine's fashionable and striking wardrobe. Clarice would have noticed it, and the photographs on the sideboard confirmed it. But it went deeper than a choice of clothing. Somehow, Ruby could never radiate personality like her sister did. Katherine had a talent for drawing people in, she thought.

'And I don't,' she whispered.

She couldn't pin down the exact moment when she had felt this way, but it was from a young age. As a mature woman, she knew that it was ridiculous to envy her sister. She had worked hard to make something of herself, using her intellect and those under-rated qualities of diligence, conscientiousness, and attention to detail. Her employer made it clear that she was valued, but the fact was that she had envied her sister's lust for life and her popularity.

'Enough of this,' she said aloud, turning away from the mirror. 'Stop dwelling on what you will never be.'

Ruby entered the second bedroom, where she found an iron bedstead, side table, empty wardrobe, and two trunks. In the corner was her father's oak rolltop desk. Katherine had specifically asked for it after their father's death, sending a stranger to collect it. Inside, on a spike, were bills and invoices, waiting to be paid and filed. She gathered them up and put them in an envelope, intending to deal with them later.

Over the next hour, Ruby moved Katherine's possessions from the main bedroom into the spare one, carefully folding away the clothing in the trunks and hanging up the dresses in the wardrobe. She couldn't give them away, not yet. Deep down, she wanted the tangible reminders of the twin sister she had lost; it was as if some part of herself would disappear if she disposed of Katherine's belongings. It was complicated, she knew, but then anything to do with Katherine had always been complicated.

As Ruby finished clearing out the wardrobe, she noticed a box on the top shelf. She sat on the bed and emptied the contents into her lap. There were some lovely pieces of costume jewellery, in the Egyptian style, including a twist-curled bangle resembling a snake and a necklace made of turquoise and glass beads, with a pendant in the shape of a pharaoh's head. The discovery of King Tutankhamun's tomb, three years earlier, had unleashed a fascination with all things Egyptian, in clothing, jewellery, furniture, and decoration. Apart from the jewellery inspired by treasures found in the pharaoh's burial chamber, Katherine had gathered together an impressive collection of earrings, bracelets, necklaces, and headpieces, made of crystal, pearl, and rhinestones, some of which looked expensive.

Beneath them all, wrapped in tissue paper, was a brooch in the shape of a scarab beetle. Ruby placed it against her blouse. It was deliciously exotic. When she was young, she had taken trinkets and baubles from her mother's dressing-table and worn them around the house. It had been her one weakness: her admiration for finely crafted jewellery. But neither she nor her mother had been able to afford anything, other than imitations and paste. She placed the jewellery back in the box and returned it to the shelf, then went back to the sitting room, where she poured herself a sherry from the fine crystal decanter on the sideboard.

As she settled herself on the couch, she asked herself the question: How could Katherine have acquired all of this on the wages of a museum assistant?

Chapter Five

Notwithstanding the setbacks of his childhood, Reggie da Costa had managed to claw his way up from office boy at *The Argus* to that of senior crime reporter, celebrated for his way with words, his investigative skills, and his uncanny knack of being in the right place at the right time. His fortuitous discovery of the body of Cornelius Stout, in what was dubbed 'The Basement Murder,' and his role in tracking down the guilty party in the grisly case of 'The Death Mask Murders,' had brought Reggie kudos and respect, even from those who sought to break the law.

Within the ranks of criminals, he was accepted, not only because he could be trusted to keep confidences, but also because he enjoyed the company of those who were his 'bread and butter.' Reggie could be seen frequenting the bars and gambling dens of Melbourne's underworld, soaking up the atmosphere and recreating them in print, making the gangsters' lairs infinitely more appealing and less sordid than they were in real life. He gave gang leaders the notoriety they craved, and encouraged others to cooperate with him, in the knowledge that he could destroy reputations with a few well-chosen taps on his typewriter's keys.

In short, Reggie was at the top of his game. Only recently, his sub-editor and immediate boss had promised him an assistant, a junior crime reporter, to share the load, because crime in Melbourne was a lucrative and booming business.

Reggie had interviewed a few likely lads and narrowed the field down to two: a cub reporter from *The Kangaroo Island Courier*, who had recently moved from Adelaide, and Dusty Rhodes, of Melbourne's scandal sheet, *The*

Truth. Both were worthy candidates to learn from Reggie, but the young South Australian slipped up badly when he was asked about his ambitions.

'I want to be a senior crime reporter, Mr da Costa. I want to be just like you.'

Anyone with an ounce of sense would have known that such a declaration was anathema to Reggie's ears. There was only one senior crime reporter at *The Argus*, and that was he.

Dusty Rhodes, on the other hand, had the credentials, having spent nearly a year learning on the job and refining his talents. He had a flair for language, he expressed a desire to learn from the master himself, Reggie da Costa, and he was keen and conscientious. His one weakness was his appearance. In Reggie's view, he looked a mess. However, this was perhaps due to his working-class roots and socialist leanings, the latter reminding Reggie of himself when he was young. With no legitimate reason as to why he should not be offered the position, apart from his poor dress sense, Dusty was to become a member of *The Argus*'s crime desk, conditional on approval from the boss.

'Are there any stories that you are pursuing at *The Truth*?' Reggie had asked him at the interview.

'There's talk on the street that a Labor Party official is bribing people to join the Party. In return, these new members are expected to support the nomination of a selected candidate.'

Reggie nodded. 'The buying of political influence.'

'That's right. Once that candidate is elected to parliament, they're under the control of their proposer.'

'Interesting,' commented Reggie. 'If you were offered the job here, would you follow this up?'

'Definitely. I have some leads. No one else at *The Truth* is interested in this.'

'Good lad. The job is yours, as far as I'm concerned. You'll get a letter in the mail shortly.'

* * *

19

Reggie was working at his desk on Tuesday morning. The newsroom was a hive of activity as the deadline for the next day's newspaper drew near. The clatter of typewriters, the hum of conversation, phones ringing, the office boy running from one desk to another to collect stories for the typesetter or the editors, these distractions were all around him, but he was adept at blocking out the noise when he needed to concentrate. And he was giving his full attention to the seed of a story that promised much, if he could just find the evidence.

Back in 1922, Reggie had scooped the other daily newspapers by revealing that a new drug, cocaine, had entered the illegal drug market. His disclosures had forced the police to acknowledge that the 'snow habit' had reached Melbourne. Reggie's research revealed that cocaine, morphine, and other opiates had been used widely in the Great War, a fact that was not well known by the general public. Interviews with ex-soldiers and eyewitness accounts confirmed that servicemen, both English and Australian, had been supplied with drugs, both for medicinal use and as an escape from the terrifying reality of modern warfare. What amazed him was that the top brass had shown little concern for the drugs' addictive qualities or the effects that they might have on soldiers in the field of battle.

The war had ended, but the use of drugs by servicemen had continued back in Melbourne. A new market opened up for bootleggers, street traders, and unethical pharmacists: cocaine. And it didn't stop there. Prostitutes and criminals had also become ready purchasers of 'snow.' With alcohol unavailable after six o'clock because the hotels were shut, inner-city dwellers turned to cocaine.

Now, three years later, Reggie noticed that there had been a spate of robberies in recent months, with cocaine being targeted in each case, along with cash. Businesses in King Street and Bourke Street in Melbourne, the National Drug Company warehouse in Russell Street, as well as chemist shops in Prahran, Carlton, and Richmond, had been robbed. The break-ins were well-executed, and there were few clues left behind for the police to investigate.

Reggie had a hunch that there must be one organised force at work behind the thefts, rather than being the disparate actions of a variety of gangs. His previous contact in the Criminal Investigation Branch, Detective Sergeant Mick O'Flanagan, had retired, replaced by his old friend, Detective Sergeant Clary Blain.

'It looks like a professional job,' Clary told Reggie. 'Unfortunately, we have nothing to investigate. No one's talking.'

There wasn't one gang leader that Reggie knew who could pull this off. Squizzy Taylor was too disorganised. Horace Striker had the brains but was more interested in gambling, booze, and prostitution. Henry Stokes, the 'Two-Up King of Melbourne,' appeared reluctant to venture into the drug scene. Who was responsible for the robberies? It was an intriguing question, and one that Reggie hoped to answer.

Chapter Six

It was Sunday. Ruby was cleaning out the kitchen cupboards of her new home when she heard a car pull up outside. It was Dusty, driving Katherine's Australian Six automobile. She wiped her hands on her apron and went out onto the porch to greet him.

'The last of your things,' he said, indicating the boxes he was carrying. He paused and looked back at his acquisition. 'Isn't she beautiful? Immaculate tan paintwork. Rolls Royce-style radiator. Split windscreen. Fold-down hood. Six cylinders. Top speed of forty miles per hour. Thank God I learned to drive.'

Ruby laughed. 'You sound besotted.'

'I am.' Dusty nodded towards the house. 'How are you settling in?'

'I feel like I'm surrounded by Katherine. The way that she decorated the house. Her choice in furniture. Her clothes. You have to see it.'

He put the boxes down in the hallway and did a quick tour of the house, his eyes widening as he went from room to room.

'She really did have money. There's even a hot water service! How could she afford all this?'

'Come and look at her clothes. They're worth a small fortune on their own.'

In the second bedroom, she opened the wardrobe and showed him Katherine's collection of elegant and fashionable dresses, skirts, and blouses in vibrant colours, made of the best quality fabrics.

'And there's hats and shoes too. Furs. And jewellery.'

'But she worked in a *museum*.'

'That's what I can't come to terms with. She was an administrative assistant, not married to some bloke on Nob Hill.'

'Are you sure you want to live here, in Katherine's house?'

'I'm sure. It will set me up for good, and it's near to shops and the train.'

In fact, she had considered the same question only the night before, and had decided that she wanted to stay. Unspoken was her fear that the sale of the house would forever erase any tangible reminders of Katherine, and she didn't want that to happen.

Ruby cast around in her mind for something to lighten the conversation. 'Her taste in jewellery is unusual. Tutankhamun has a lot to answer for.'

'It's all the rage. You find Egyptian motifs on everything these days. Some of my friends have held Egyptian-themed parties. And don't forget she worked in a museum. She must have liked old stuff.'

'Dusty, why won't you move out of Port Melbourne and live here with me?'

He smiled. 'I'm nearly twenty-one years old. The fact is that I'm too old to live with my sister. Anyway, I've taken in a boarder. He's my replacement at *The Truth*.' He clicked his fingers. 'I can see the headline now: "Does Dusty Stay Put in Port?"'

'More likely, "Dusty Gathers Dust Staying Put in Port."'

Her brother chuckled. 'You could get a job at my old newspaper.'

'If you change your mind—'

'I know. But I'm happy where I am. And now I have a motorcar, I can visit you anytime.' He checked his watch. 'I'll have a better look around next time. We need to get going. The constable is meeting us at the St Kilda pier in forty-five minutes.'

* * *

Dusty glanced at Ruby as they travelled down Punt Road towards St Kilda Junction. She looked pale, he thought, her flame-coloured hair hidden beneath her broad-brimmed straw hat. Her light grey and white checked summer dress looked fresh, but did little to relieve the lack of colour in her

23

cheeks. If only she would make more of herself, for she was a very attractive woman beneath the sober apparel. And, more to the point, he knew that beneath the self-effacing and reticent exterior, beat the heart of a woman whose intelligence and thoughtful personality were under-appreciated due to her shy and solitary lifestyle. A night out dancing would do her a world of good.

But today was not the right time to broach those subjects because the constable, who had broken the news of Katherine's death to them, would be waiting at the pier to show them where Katherine had drowned.

Dusty still wondered whether moving into Katherine's house was a good idea and whether a fresh start in a different house would be better for her state of mind. But Ruby was pragmatic: it was hard to argue with the logic behind her decision. And, due to the fact that she had helped raise him, he tended to defer to her opinions.

Once they reached St Kilda Junction and passed the imposing edifice of the Grand Junction Hotel, they turned into Fitzroy Street. It was the first week of February, a hot summer's day, and everyone was out enjoying the sunshine. Being a Sunday, the road was crammed with automobiles, tramcars, cyclists, pedestrians, and horse-drawn buggies. Dusty had folded back the hood on the Australian Six, allowing the breeze to cool them as they drove at a sedate pace towards the beach. At The Esplanade, they turned left and parked not far from the pier.

On the other side of the road, the blue-green waters of Port Phillip Bay glinted in the sunshine, as the seagulls wheeled overhead and fishing boats bobbed up and down on the choppy waves. The St Kilda pier extended out into the Bay, splitting the beach in two, one section stretching north towards the city of Melbourne and the other south towards the pretty seaside suburbs of Elwood, Brighton, and Black Rock. Children paddled in the shallows while families relaxed on the sands, enjoying the fresh air and balmy weather of the last month of summer.

Dusty and Ruby crossed the road and waited beneath the weatherboard shelter that was situated at the entrance to the pier. Soon, they saw a policeman heading their way.

'Constable Jelley, thank you for meeting us,' said Dusty.

The policeman, a young man in his twenties, nodded his head. 'Miss Rhodes. Mr Rhodes. If you'll follow me, I'll show you where we found your sister's possessions.'

The pier was broad, one side bounded by wooden railings while the other was open, with large white-painted bollards to allow boats to dock. Between the posts, fishermen sat contentedly, their lines dangling over the edge into the water below. At the end of the pier was an attractive two-storey pavilion which served refreshments to visitors.

Jelley paused, pointing to a spot a few yards away from the building. 'Miss Rhodes' handbag was found there,' he said.

The constable stepped back, letting them move in front of him. 'Your sister, she must have overbalanced, there being no railing.'

Ruby looked over the edge, staring down into the dark shadowy waters which swirled around the pilings.

'It's not such a big drop,' she said. 'It's deep water, but Katherine could swim. Why wouldn't she swim?'

'She drowned, Miss Rhodes. She hit her head in the fall. There was water in her lungs. Perhaps she had a bit too much to drink? It was New Year's Eve.'

'Why would she come to St Kilda pier? How would she have got here?'

'Unfortunately, we don't know.'

'Who found her bag?' asked Dusty.

'A fisherman. Around ten o'clock on New Year's Day. He handed it into the police station. It wasn't till two days later that her body washed up about five hundred yards down the beach.' He pointed in the direction of Elwood, to the south. 'The tide must have taken her.'

Dusty turned to Ruby. 'Are you alright?'

She shrugged her shoulders, her face pale. 'It makes no sense.'

'Did you interview any of the workers at the kiosk?' asked Dusty, glancing back at the weatherboard pavilion.

'It wasn't seen as necessary. It was an accident.'

Ruby looked over the edge. 'Would she have—?'

'No,' replied the constable. 'It would have been instantaneous. She never would have felt a thing.'

The policeman checked his watch. 'I have to go now. My deepest condolences. If there's anything I can do—'

'You've been very kind. Thank you.'

'I meant to tell you that her possessions are ready to be collected. Or we can post them to you if it's more convenient. Let me know.'

They watched as he walked away. Dusty felt a deep sadness as he considered his older sister's last moments. Despite the constable's assurances, he knew that drowning would not be a pleasant way to die. Ruby, standing next to him, strangled a sob, then unleashed a flood of tears.

'I'll never have the chance—'

'What?'

'To say I'm sorry.'

'You have nothing to apologise for.' He drew her to him and kissed the top of her head.

She looked up at him with sorrowful eyes. 'I do.'

'Let's get a cup of tea. The kiosk is open.'

'I'd rather go home.'

'If that's what you want.'

As they turned to leave, they heard a voice. 'Excuse me!' A man had come out of the pavilion. He was wearing an apron and mopping his brow with a checked handkerchief. 'I saw you with the copper. Is it something to do with the young lady that drowned?'

Dusty nodded.

'I run this place.' He cocked his head towards the pavilion. 'You see, I was here early New Year's Day cleaning up after a party. About five o'clock it was. I saw a couple walking down the pier.'

'A man and a woman?' asked Ruby.

'That's right. They were standing under one of the lamps. She was a real looker. Evening dress. Fur. Drunk, I reckon. The bloke was holding her up. I thought they'd had a bit of a night out, if you know what I mean. I looked for them a while later, but they were gone. Didn't think too much of it till I saw you with the copper.'

'Could you describe the man? Tall? Short?'

'Truth is, I didn't take much notice of him.'

'Did she look anything like me?' asked Ruby.

The man studied her. 'Hard to say. But she did have red hair.'

Chapter Seven

R uby worked at Smith and Sons, a furniture factory in Carlton, on the northern edge of the city, only walking distance from the Melbourne Museum. It was disconcerting knowing that she could have stepped inside and made that first move towards reconciliation. Perhaps things might have worked out differently. Perhaps Katherine wouldn't be dead now. It was awful to think about it. But although nothing could change the past, she could try to uncover if someone were responsible for her sister's death. Given what the man at the pavilion had told them, she wanted to know about Katherine's last hours and with whom she'd spent them. John Gascoigne seemed to be a logical first choice if she were to start her enquiries, being a friend and work colleague of hers.

She entered the museum through the Russell Street entrance and felt the temperature drop. It had been a long time since her last visit as a young child, tugging excitedly on the arm of her father while Katherine pulled on the other, as they went from one exhibit to another. It didn't surprise her that her twin had decided to work here, given how taken she was by the place as a child. Her bookshelf had been full of books about weird and wonderful animals and descriptions of ancient civilisations. But those times were over now, and Katherine was gone.

It was with different eyes that Ruby now viewed the place. McCoy Hall, the main exhibition space of the museum, was lit by a series of skylights, illuminating a range of wild animals saved from decay by the work of the taxidermist. The lions, elephants, coyotes, wild boar, and bears no longer thrilled her, as they once had. Cold glass eyes peered out from rigid and lifeless bodies, stuck in time. They smelled dusty and stale. She looked away, unnerved.

On the other side of the main space, Ruby saw John Gascoigne striding towards her. He was a striking man, about six feet tall and with a barrel chest. His mane of steel grey hair was brushed back from his face, while dark bristly eyebrows settled above a pair of intense grey eyes. The shininess of his plain black suit indicated that it had seen better days.

'Miss Rhodes.' He shook her hand firmly. 'I thought you might have forgotten me.' He ran his eyes over her. 'I can't believe how much you resemble Katherine. It's astonishing.'

Ruby felt distinctly uncomfortable. She was only too aware that she was at a disadvantage in any comparison. Her sister had been stylish and sparkling, even in her teens, making the most of her looks and sense of fashion. She, on the other hand, dressed in a utilitarian sort of way. Although her suit was well-cut, it was brown. Rather than making the most of her crowning glory as Katherine had done, she had drawn her thick and wavy red hair back into a bun at the nape of her neck. No rouge or foundation enhanced her face, apart from the subdued lipstick, which was her one concession to makeup. Sometimes she wondered if she'd chosen to present herself in that way to differentiate herself from her sister, but she didn't want to dwell on that, particularly not now. She concentrated instead on the reasons that had brought her here.

'I'm on my lunch break. I was hoping to have a quick chat with you. Is this a convenient time?' she asked.

'I can take a few minutes. There's my office. We won't be disturbed.'

She followed him into a room off McCoy Hall. He offered her a chair, then sat on the edge of the desk, facing her. She noticed that the cuffs of his white shirt were frayed.

'It's nice to see you again. You look well,' he said.

'Thank you.'

'How are you coping?'

'I'm fine.'

'Are you settling in well to your new home?'

29

Ruby thought before she answered. 'It's not really mine. I suppose it will be, in time.'

Gascoigne went silent.

Ruby looked down at her hands, then raised her eyes to his. 'If I may be blunt, I'm not very good at social chit-chat.'

'Then why are you here, Miss Rhodes?'

'I want to know more about Katherine. You were her friend and colleague. How long did you know her?'

'About two years. We needed an administrative assistant. She applied and got the job. She was bright and intelligent. She was good at her work. Everything came easily to her.'

'Was your relationship purely work-related?'

Gascoigne looked startled. 'You are blunt. There was nearly thirty years' difference in age between us. I was old enough to be her father. She leaned on me for advice, but there was nothing more than that. Just friendship. And an appreciation of history and the importance of museums in our society.'

Ruby took a deep breath. 'I appreciate your candour, Mr Gascoigne. I don't know how much she confided in you. About me. The fact is that we didn't get on. She pleased herself and never seemed the least interested in a relationship that was enduring. Including one with her family.'

'That sounds rather harsh, Miss Rhodes. I always found Katherine to be good company.'

'She left me to care for my sick father and younger brother. Perhaps you might understand my feelings if you were treated that way. She didn't even come to our parents' funerals.'

'I'm sorry to hear that you suffered. In Katherine's defence, I believe that she was remorseful. She once confided in me that she felt too much time had passed to make it up with you.'

'She said that?'

'It's true. I asked her once about her family, and she said that she hadn't seen you for years. She didn't elaborate on why and I didn't ask. I thought that would be intrusive. In her last few months, she showed a greater maturity. There was still the vivaciousness and love of attention, but she had times when she was more introspective. I believe that she was keen to see you.'

'Perhaps. But she didn't. And now she's left us with a lot of questions.' She crossed her arms in front of her. 'The fact is that reliving this business with Katherine is difficult for me. She fell off a pier and drowned. What was she doing on St Kilda pier that morning? And who was the man with her? And where did she get the money to buy a house and a car? I need to find out.' Ruby looked at her watch. 'I have to get back to work. I'm sorry to have taken up so much of your time.'

Gascoigne followed her out of the office. As she was about to go, he touched her arm. 'Let's meet again. Not here. We need to talk further. There's something I have to tell you. About Katherine.'

Chapter Eight

Felix Messenger was sitting in his Ford Model T motorcar outside Katherine Rhodes' house in Tanner Street, waiting for its owner to return home. An employee of the Federal Trade and Customs Department, Felix preferred to call himself an investigator rather than a Customs officer, which implied a higher status amongst the hierarchy that policed the importation of illegal goods. His boss was the Comptroller-General of Customs, Robert McKeeman Oakley, whose position he coveted. One day, he swore, it would be his.

Felix stared out of the window at the white weatherboard cottage. It was such a pity that the woman hadn't been home when he first called. He was keen to secure her cooperation in shutting down the trade in illegal antiquities, and he needed her to make it happen. Whether she did it of her own free will, or by being blackmailed into it, was immaterial to Felix. He was in no mood to show any latitude to those whom he could use for his own ends.

Only that morning, he had argued with one of his work colleagues, Jim Claxon, who policed the drug trade.

'Still keeping your hands clean, Messenger? You're an old relic, you know, like that stuff you stop getting into the country. Look at you. The same brown suit, white shirt, and brown tie every day. No wife. No friends.'

'My choice, Claxon. It keeps my mind firmly on the job. No distractions.'

'You're as bent as those you prosecute. Anything to secure a conviction. And what's worse is that you're not averse to informing on your fellow officers if it means there's something in it for you.'

Messenger turned on him. 'I do that to root out the dead wood. You know as well as I do that some of yours are on the take. I don't care what people say about me. You need to be tough in this business, if you want to get on.'

Claxon leaned in, his eyes narrowed. 'You know what they say about you, behind your back? Someone *should* shoot the messenger. Trouble is, we don't know if they're joking.'

Felix scowled. 'I get results. What I do is better than mixing with the dregs of society in an opium den.'

That was one area of Customs work that Felix disliked intensely: trying to stem the trade in opium. Contraband regulations had been tightened up as a result of the Opium Convention in Geneva, but tins of the stuff were still arriving undetected on steamer ships or in suitcases. If found, the drug was burned in the presence of Customs officers but, for the rest, illicit opium was being sold on the streets for ten pounds per tin. He would do anything to avoid what Claxon and his team had to do: tedious searches of ships and their crews, and interviews with an underclass of criminals and drug fiends in filthy hovels and drug dens. Although Felix liked convictions, he didn't like to get his hands dirty.

Antiquities were his area of expertise. Felix believed that the gangs of Richmond and Fitzroy were behind much of the illegal trade and that their influence was growing. He needed someone on the inside, someone who could feed him information on the middlemen who were receiving valuable artefacts from overseas contacts, and were making a tidy profit selling their ill-gotten gains to private collectors in Melbourne.

He had briefly considered going undercover, having features that were so nondescript that anyone who was asked to describe him was hard-pressed to find something significant to mention. The addition of a moustache or a wig or spectacles might be enough to transform him into a completely different person, but Felix had no desire to put his own life at risk. Far better to find a 'patsy' who would suffer the consequences if things went awry.

He needed someone who would not arouse suspicion and who had access to those in high places, someone who could ferret out the incriminating evidence that he needed to blow the illegal trade in relics apart.

Some months ago, he had been given a name. He had made initial contact, found the target to be uncooperative, and had thus spent considerable time gathering incriminating evidence against her. But, when he was finally ready to pounce, the woman had disappeared from view. Four months later, he had tracked her down, and now he was ready to force her hand. Miss Kitty was her name.

* * *

Felix Messenger watched as a tan Australian Six pulled into the curb on the other side of the street. A woman waved as the man drove off, then crossed in front of his car and opened the gate. Felix smiled grimly to himself. It was Katherine Rhodes, otherwise known as 'Miss Kitty.'

She was dressed conservatively, in a pale blue blouse and a pleated grey skirt, not her usual attire. But there was no doubt that she was the same person he had met with months ago and who had refused to cooperate. Well, he was ready to show her who was in charge now.

He got out of the car and walked up the path, greeting the woman as she was unlocking the front door.

'Good evening, Miss Rhodes,' he said, doffing his hat. 'No doubt, this is a surprise?'

The smile left her face. 'I don't believe I know you.'

'Of course, you do.'

She pulled the key out of the lock and faced him. 'I have no idea who you are, Mr—'

'Messenger. We've met before. I interviewed you before Christmas.' He had to admire her composure. 'You remember me, of course?'

She shook her head. 'You must be mistaken. I've never met you. Now, if you don't mind, please leave.' She turned to unlock the door.

'Not so fast,' he said, grabbing her arm.

'How dare you. Let go of me, or I'll scream.'

'If you want to play it that way.' He took out his identification card and waved it in front of her. 'Customs Investigator Felix Messenger. Department of Trade and Customs. We have a lot to talk about.'

She shook her head. 'We have nothing to talk about.' She pulled away from him. 'Go away.'

'You have been consorting with the likes of Squizzy Taylor and Horace Striker. You've been seen in gambling dens and social clubs associating with low-life scum. Don't play the innocent with me.' He shook his finger at her. 'You'll either help me with my enquiries or I'll find something to charge you with.'

A shocked look flickered across her face. His words had had an effect, he realised. But then she recovered and folded her arms in front of her.

'I am secretary to the managing director of Smith and Sons in Melbourne. I have no idea what you're talking about. Quite frankly, you have the wrong person.'

Messenger was nonplussed. She was one tough sheila and, if he didn't know better, he would have thought that he'd made a mistake.

'Miss Katherine Rhodes. I advise you to cooperate with the Department of Customs.'

The woman turned on him. 'I am Ruby Rhodes, not Katherine. My sister is dead. What she did when she was alive has nothing to do with me.'

The Customs officer took a step back. Then he laughed. 'Next you're going to tell me that you're her identical twin.'

'Exactly. Now leave, if there's nothing further.'

'I am an officer of the Crown, madam. Show me proof of identity.'

She glared at him, then reached into her handbag and handed over her passbook from the State Savings Bank of Victoria.

Messenger studied it carefully, and then her. He was shaken. 'You really are her twin? When did she die?'

'Over two months ago.'

'How did she die?'

Ruby gave him an angry stare. 'She drowned, if you must know. Now, give me back my passbook and go.'

The Customs officer nodded. He doffed his hat. 'I'll need to speak to you again.'

Ruby ignored him and walked into the house, shutting the door behind her.

Messenger stood, collecting his thoughts. 'Bugger me. That's a turn-up for the books.'

Chapter Nine

Once inside, Ruby collapsed into an armchair and hid her face in her hands. She was shocked and horrified by what the Customs officer had just told her. What if there were some truth to his claims? Had her sister been a gambler? Had she been mixing with criminals and profiting from that association? She'd read about Squizzy Taylor and Horace Striker in the newspapers. Their reputations were terrible. Only last year, Squizzy had been accused of driving a car which killed a woman as she was alighting from a tram. Not to mention his association with jury-fixing, brothels, illicit liquor, and illegal gambling. And Horace Striker had been mentioned in two of Dusty's *Truth* articles about Melbourne's criminal underworld. Surely the Customs officer was exaggerating?

She raised her head and looked around her. The house, the car, the cash: all displays of material success. Shoes, hats, silk stockings, and fashionable garments were not the wardrobe of an administrative assistant. There was no way that Katherine could have afforded all of this without being involved in some sort of illegal activity. But how could she find out the truth?

Her eyes rested on the envelope propped against a vase on the sideboard. Inside was Katherine's letter, still unread, delivered to Ruby by the solicitor at the reading of the will. Ruby had been waiting for the right moment. And that time had come.

She took it down and tore it open. Inside was a single sheet, written in Katherine's flowing hand, dated about six weeks before her death. Ruby took a deep breath and started to read:

November 13, 1924

My dear Ruby,

If you are reading this, then it means I'm dead. I've been playing a deadly game.

I want you to know that I love you and always have, and that I regret that we never mended our relationship. In recent months I have thought about you a lot and wanted to contact you but, unlike you, I do not have that strength of character.

We are so different, you and I. We look the same, we even sound the same, but our personalities could not be more contradictory. I have always envied you. I suppose you are finding that hard to believe, but it is the truth. You had the courage to deal with Mum's death and look after Dad and Dusty when I could not. Strangely, Death doesn't scare me anymore, even though I believe it is close.

The fact is that I have got myself into trouble. I always went too far in everything, played it too hard, thinking that I could get away with it. But you pay for that, in the end, as I have discovered.

Please forgive me as I forgive you. We both made mistakes. For my part, I should have come back when you needed me, instead of indulging myself. It's too late now to change the past.

I hope that the house brings you happiness. It has been a sanctuary to me but I suspect that will be short-lived.

Give my love to Dusty. Tell him that I wish I'd been a better sister to him.

Your loving sister,
Katherine.

Postscript: Do you remember what fun we had leaving secret messages for each other? I hope you do.

She let the letter fall to the floor. Katherine's words hit her hard. Coming on the back of Felix Messenger's harsh assessment of her sister, the letter appeared to confirm his comments. It raised questions, rather than providing answers. What on earth had Katherine been involved in? What had scared her so? Predicting her own death was the stuff of 'penny dreadfuls,' and yet, she had been right. And what did she mean by the postscript? It seemed strangely out of place, given the serious nature of Katherine's message.

Her references to the past and family didn't fit with the person Ruby had known all those years ago. It had always been clear that Katherine lacked concern for others and self-reflection, but her letter indicated a change of heart. Perhaps circumstances had made her reconsider the past; with her life in jeopardy, her recognition of her shortcomings had been brought into sharp focus.

Why did she refer to her home as a sanctuary? A sanctuary from what? In Ruby's view, Katherine's choice of neighbourhood was odd. She had done well in a material sense and could have afforded to live in a 'better' area. And yet, she had chosen to live in a working-class suburb full of factory workers, odd-job men, and labourers. There were pockets of wealth in Richmond, but they were few and far between. At the other extreme, there was grinding poverty, where families lived in the slums and eked out a hand-to-mouth existence.

From the outside, there was nothing to indicate that Katherine's cottage was any different from those of her neighbours. It was a neat and tidy weatherboard, surrounded by houses of a similar ilk, some rundown, some in better condition but, in the main, unremarkable. Just the place, one would have said, to hide away, or as others might say, hide in plain view. And that's when it hit her that Katherine's home, like her furnishings and clothing, had been well-chosen too.

Chapter Ten

It was hot and sultry in the busy city of Melbourne, the summer intense before the change of seasons. The air was heavy with humidity as a fierce sun beat down relentlessly from a cloudless sky, the asphalt roads absorbing the heat. Trams trundled up and down Swanston Street, the main thoroughfare, their metal wheels squealing against the tracks as though protesting, while horse-drawn buggies laboured alongside them. A dray, laden with beer barrels, lumbered past, pulled by a team of sweating horses. Melbourne was usually a lively cacophony of sounds and smells—horns tooting, tram bells ringing, car engines roaring, pedestrians scurrying along the footpaths or stopping to chat animatedly—but the city was sluggish this day, full of weary people sweltering in the sultriness beneath a southern sun, dragging their feet as they trudged past.

Oblivious to the prevailing mood, Dusty Rhodes was carefree as he strolled along Swanston Street. He was buoyed by the reaction to his final story for *The Truth*, about an unfaithful husband in his seventies, Elias Budd, who had been caught out in a hotel with his mistress. Dusty's headline—'An Ancient's Amorous Antics Nipped in the Budd'—had been a triumph of brevity and wit, it was agreed.

The last hour had been spent sharing a beer or two or three with his reporter colleagues in the newsroom, before collecting his belongings from his desk and storing them in the boot of the Australian Six. He had felt a strange mixture of regret and elation, leaving behind a room full of eccentric and unpredictable *Truth* journalists for the more decorous and respectable offices of *The Argus*, where he hoped to make his mark and learn from that most celebrated of crime reporters, Reggie da Costa.

Dusty crossed over the Bourke Street intersection and continued up to Franklin Street, where he turned left. Ahead was Mac's Hotel, a two-storey bluestone building with an impressive iron verandah, dating from the time of the gold rushes. It was here that he and Ruby had arranged to meet up with John Gascoigne.

Glancing in through the window of the public bar, Dusty could see that many of the drinkers were already looking the worse for wear, despite there being an hour left of drinking time. Dusty liked a beer himself but had never subscribed to the 'six o'clock swill,' where patrons overindulged before the hotel shut its doors. His father had been too keen to walk that road after his wife's death, drinking until the publican turned him out onto the street.

He looked around to see Gascoigne crossing Franklin Street, heading his way. Although he had only met him once before—at the reading of the will—it wasn't easy to forget that big frame set off by a mane of grey hair.

They shook hands, Gascoigne's grip firm and confident.

'I thought we'd have a quick beer in the bar before Ruby arrives,' suggested Dusty.

Gascoigne mopped his brow with a handkerchief. 'Good idea.'

They went into the public bar and found stools at the counter. Dusty ordered a couple of beers and handed one to Gascoigne.

'How's work?' he asked.

'Quite busy. We've had a bequest from one of our patrons, recently deceased. We'll be using the money to add to our Egyptian collection.' He looked around him, his eyes watchful, then focused on his companion. 'I believe you're a reporter.'

'That's right. I finished up at *The Truth* this afternoon.'

Gascoigne snorted. 'Hardly a quality newspaper. Too much prying into people's lives for my liking.'

Dusty had heard it all before, having been with the newspaper for nearly a year. He sighed inwardly, bored at the thought of the conversation that was to come. At least this would be the last time, now that he was moving on to a 'respectable' newspaper. In Dusty's view, there was an element of snobbery in the way people derided *The Truth*, with Gascoigne just another middle-class prig staking his claim to the high moral ground. The working classes, traditional readers of the newspaper, didn't pretend to be something they weren't. They were honest, unlike the Gascoignes of this world, who read *The Truth* on the sly and were too embarrassed to admit it.

'I don't deny that there's gossip,' Dusty said, 'but we do shine a light on corruption which the more *reputable* newspapers seem to be afraid to do.'

'Rubbish. I saw one of your recent articles: "Pornic Perverts. Lewd Lechery Lauded in Little Lon." Complete trash.'

Dusty chuckled. 'So you do read it after all. See beyond the headline, Mr Gascoigne. Little Lonsdale Street is still a corrupt neighbourhood. *The Truth* managed to close down Madame Brussels' brothels earlier this century. But the shops selling bootleg liquor and the opium dens haven't gone away completely. We draw attention to them in the hope things will change.'

'Public spirited. Definitely.' Gascoigne's voice dripped with sarcasm.

'Let's beg to differ,' said Dusty, growing impatient. 'I don't want to discuss the ethics of newspapers.'

'That's just as well.' Gascoigne downed his beer. 'It must be about Katherine then.' He beckoned to the barman for another. 'What's on your mind?'

'I was hoping that you can help me with my sister, Ruby.'

Gascoigne's tone became more conciliatory. 'And what would that be?'

'She seems to think that Katherine's death was no accident.'

'She implied as much. But what's that got to do with me?'

'Help me convince her to let sleeping dogs lie. She'll get herself into trouble if she tries to track down Katherine's supposed killer.'

'You don't believe she was murdered?'

'I'm not convinced that she was, no.'

Gascoigne frowned. 'It's really none of my business.'

'Perhaps as a token of your friendship with Katherine, you could help her twin sister? Give it some thought, please?' Dusty looked at the clock on the wall. He drained his glass and set it on the counter. 'Time to meet Ruby.'

* * *

Ruby had been sitting at a table in the Ladies' Lounge for about ten minutes, waiting for Dusty and Gascoigne to join her. She glanced around her, still rankling from the fact that the bartender had been reluctant to serve a woman on her own, until she had explained that her brother and a friend were joining her. However, it was a lovely old pub, with its dark wooden architraves and skirting boards, exposed brick and bluestone walls, and polished floorboards.

She tapped her foot, trying to relax. Her brother had said that he wanted a bit of time with Katherine's former colleague, suggesting that Gascoigne might open up about her activities if they were alone. Ruby didn't believe him. She thought that he had an ulterior motive in wanting to talk to Gascoigne and that it involved her. Dusty tended to be over-protective of her, despite the fact that he was much younger, and she thought that it might have something to do with her questioning the manner of Katherine's death.

She was impatient too, eager to hear what Gascoigne had meant when he said, 'There's something I have to tell you. About Katherine.' She wondered if he were going to confirm what she had heard from Felix Messenger.

Ruby sipped a Sherry Cobbler. Seated near her were three women and two men, chatting contentedly. They looked right at home. Completely relaxed. That was something that she envied in others: the ability to fit in and to make easy conversation. She swirled the liquid in her glass and sighed. Katherine is so good with people, and I'm not, she thought.

She caught herself in the lie. Katherine was dead. Despite that salient fact, she couldn't escape Katherine. Living in her house, surrounded by reminders of her twin sister, Ruby couldn't let her go. Even in death, Katherine consumed her thoughts. How had she died? Who killed her and why?

She became aware of someone addressing her. She looked up. It was John Gascoigne. She noted the shiny black suit, grimy collar, and frayed cuffs. It appeared that money was still short, despite the £50 from Katherine.

'I can't believe how much you resemble her,' he said, putting his beer on the table as he pulled up a chair opposite her. 'It's uncanny.'

Ruby nodded, unsmiling. 'People used to say that we sounded the same; even had the same laugh.'

'She was stunning, your sister. Lit up a room.' He took a swig of his beer.

Dusty joined them and gave his sister a kiss on the cheek. 'Sorry to keep you waiting. Mr Gascoigne and I were talking about the ethics of the press.'

'Really? That's what you were talking about?' Ruby smirked, then took a sip of her Sherry Cobbler. 'What is this place?'

Gascoigne leaned forward, his eyes shining. 'It's the oldest hotel in Melbourne. 1853. Built during the gold rushes. Out the back was a stable that could hold one hundred horses.'

'You obviously love history, Mr Gascoigne.'

'I work in a museum. It's a prerequisite.'

'And Katherine. Did she love history?' Ruby asked, watching him closely.

'I believe she did. She was a passionate woman who loved life.'

'Can I be frank, Mr Gascoigne?' asked Ruby, putting her glass on the table. 'I'm not here to talk about Katherine's social life or her vibrant personality. I want to know what she actually did to make so much money. She worked at a museum. She was an assistant. And then there's the letter from Katherine saying she was in trouble. That she feared for her life.'

'Please stop this,' Dusty said. 'You need to let this go.'

Ruby was defiant. 'I want to know who was threatening her. Mr Gascoigne is my best hope of finding that out.'

Gascoigne rubbed his chin, his eyes narrowing. 'I wanted to spare you, Miss Rhodes, but it appears that you won't be content until you know the truth.'

'And that would be?'

'Ruby,' said Dusty, interrupting, 'this will not make things better.'

'It can't be any worse,' she replied grimly. 'My sister is known to Customs for leading a life in the shadows. She was no Miss Goody Two Shoes, I know that, but to find out that she's been associating with the gangs? It's heart-breaking.'

Gascoigne stared into his glass, swirling around the liquid, then he placed it on the table in front of him.

'If I tell you, perhaps you'll forget all about this business.'

'Then tell me.'

'There was a side to Katherine that she kept hidden. A secret life. She didn't want me to know about it, but I found out after she died.' He paused, considering his next words. 'Working at the museum made her realise that there was money to be made from antiquities. We had suppliers in the Middle East that we dealt with legally. They had licences from the government to supply us with cultural property, but I think she saw an opportunity. In theory, any discoveries are the property of the Egyptian government. In practice, poverty-stricken locals loot the temples and tombs and sell their finds to dealers, bypassing the authorities.

'After Katherine died, a letter came addressed to her. I opened it. It was from a dealer in Cairo. He was offering her goods that would be smuggled into Australia. She was to find markets for them. In return, she'd receive a cut of the profits.'

'That sounds dangerous,' said Dusty.

'It certainly is.' Gascoigne drained his beer. 'Her clients could hardly be described as "law-abiding citizens." And if the authorities caught her, she'd go to jail.'

He pushed his empty glass aside. 'Your sister was too smart for her own good. She liked money. She'd come into work wearing a new dress, her hair in the latest style, red lipstick, silk stockings. She was a good-looking woman, and she used it to get what she wanted. I'll be blunt. I think she got greedy. She bit the hand that fed her, and the hand slapped her down.'

'Are you talking about her death?' asked Ruby.

Gascoigne shook his head. 'I don't know about that. I didn't have anything to do with *them*, the bad men that she'd got herself mixed up with. It was what she told me about a month before she died. She said that she had to leave the museum and hide herself away. She didn't go into details, but she was scared. Of whom, I don't know. I told her to go to the police, but she was too afraid. I don't know what she'd got caught up in, but I do know that she feared for her life. She said that she'd come back in a year, if she were still alive. *Still alive*. That's what she said. I think differently.'

'What do you mean?'

'I don't believe that she was killed. I think she couldn't cope with the pressure. She panicked. Took her own life. That's what I think.'

Ruby shook her head. 'I find that hard to believe. Katherine loved life. She would never have killed herself. And recently, we discovered that Katherine was seen with a man on St Kilda pier on the day of her death.'

'Any idea who he was?'

'No.'

'Have you spoken to the police?'

'They're not interested.'

'And with good reason, Ruby,' interjected Dusty, 'because it's all speculation. There's no evidence that she was murdered.'

'Listen to your brother, Miss Rhodes.' Gascoigne leaned forward, his grey eyes focused on her. 'You need to forget about this. Even if I'm wrong about Katherine killing herself, it's a fact that she was terrified of something or someone. If she was killed by the gangs, think what danger you're putting yourself in.'

Ruby took a deep breath. 'I know what you're saying is right. I know it's dangerous, but I'm still determined to find the answer, no matter what the cost. These gangs. Where can I find them?'

Dusty broke in again. 'That's crazy talk, Ruby. You don't want to know them. Squizzy Taylor and Horace Striker are dangerous. They're unpredictable. There are no rules. I write about them, and I know them. They don't respect authority. They bribe the police, fix juries, anything to avoid going to prison. Cocaine, opium, alcohol, prostitution, fixing horse races, gambling. Whatever will bring in the money. Each year they become more violent. You have no idea what you're dealing with. Take our advice and forget this.'

John Gascoigne shook his finger at her. 'Stay away from the gangs, Miss Rhodes. Let this go. Katherine was afraid and it's likely that she killed herself. That's the truth. If you meddle, you'll end up like your sister. Dead.'

Chapter Eleven

It was Saturday evening, and Reggie was standing at the window overlooking Swan Street. He was in a quandary. The invitation that he held in his hand was for Dusty Rhodes' 21st Birthday celebration, to be held at the Wattle Path Palais de Danse, a St Kilda landmark situated on the Upper Esplanade overlooking the beach. He had been there a couple of times and enjoyed himself, because of the attractive young lady that had accompanied him and, also, because he loved to dance. But that lady was gone, and he was uncertain whether he wanted to attend an event where he knew almost no one, except the guest of honour.

Dusty Rhodes had been employed at *The Argus* for over a week now. Reggie had to admit that his new protégé was settling in well, but he still had a lot to learn, as well as a lot to unlearn, from his days at *The Truth*. The two newspapers were as different as chalk and cheese, not only in the type of stories they printed, but also in the behaviour of their reporters. The latter were a wild lot, keeping late hours, carousing, and drinking prolifically. Unconventional, to say the least. Not like those from Melbourne's premier newspaper.

Dusty had struggled at first to adapt to a different style of reporting, learning to eschew the more salacious gossip and scandalous news offerings for the more sober tone of the respected and reliable *Argus*. But, with Reggie's guidance and his frequent use of a red pen correcting Dusty's articles, the new recruit was making headway.

Reggie liked Dusty. He was not conventional; his socialist leanings reminded Reggie of his own youthful embrace of Mother Russia. Furthermore, he was quick on the uptake and ready to take advice. And there was no doubt as to his admiration for Reggie da Costa. How could he not, Reggie asked himself, reflecting on his own illustrious career. His investigations into the Death Mask Murders of 1918 and the Basement Murder in 1923 had made him a household name in Melbourne and, indeed, Victoria.

Dusty would be devastated if his mentor did not attend his birthday celebration, of that Reggie was sure. He must go. And there was another reason to attend, a better one. It would give him the chance to wear the latest acquisition to his wardrobe: a grey check evening suit with shiny silver lapels, white waistcoat, and white bow tie, teamed with grey and white two-tone shoes.

He washed and shaved, then trimmed his 'Ronald Colman' moustache. After brushing his hair with a pair of silver brushes and smoothing it down with a dab of Brilliantine, Reggie stepped back and regarded himself in the mirror. Those specks of grey in his sideburns certainly made him look distinguished. But would there be any attractive young women at the Wattle Path tonight who would appreciate a well-groomed and experienced man of the world, such as he?

Reggie slipped out of his robe and began to dress. His crisp white shirt under the satin waistcoat teamed well with the silver grey of his suit. His tailor had skilfully cut the trousers and jacket to enhance the best of his physique and hide the thickening of his waistline. He straightened his bow tie and looked at himself in the full-length mirror. Perfection.

Reggie's new automobile was parked out in the back laneway. It had been a Christmas present to himself, trading in his two-seater Citroen 5CV 'Torpedo' tourer, with its four-cylinder engine, pale yellow boat-tail, and black mudguards, for the dramatic, stylish and flamboyant Hupmobile Series R Special Roadster. Wire wheels had set him back an extra twenty-five quid, but they looked well with the whitewall tyres, he thought. The motorcar was 'forest-green' in colour, with black fenders, top, and interior. It was the personification of the Twenties to Reggie, and now that he was closing in on forty years of age, he liked to think of himself as a man of his times.

Seated behind the wheel, he pressed the starter button, and the automobile roared into life. Reggie released the brake, and the Hupmobile surged forward.

Soon he was travelling down Punt Road at a respectable thirty-five miles per hour towards the beachside suburb of St Kilda, where the Wattle Path Palais de Danse was situated. Perhaps, just perhaps, he might meet the woman of his dreams: rich, beautiful, and compliant, but time had taught Reggie da Costa that this was becoming an increasingly unlikely possibility.

* * *

Meanwhile, about two miles away, Ruby Rhodes was awaiting the arrival of her brother, who was driving her to his birthday party. Ruby had tried to make her excuses for not going: 'I'm not good with people,' 'I won't fit in,' and 'I have nothing to wear,' but Dusty had insisted. She was his sister after all, and it would not be the same without her. His friends would be there, he told her, along with some of his colleagues from *The Argus* and *The Truth*. She would enjoy herself, he assured her, although she had her doubts.

Earlier that evening, she stood in front of her open wardrobe, which revealed a dispiriting lack of possibilities. The dress code was formal, which limited her choices. She took out the navy dress with the cream collar and bow and placed it against her, staring at her reflection in the mirror. It looked rather drab, she thought. There was the black one with the lace on the bodice. It was the right length, but she hadn't got around to repairing the rip where it had caught on a wooden seat. And there wasn't time for that now. There was her nice sensible grey suit for weddings and funerals, but it wasn't suitable for a dance. The fact was that she'd never had to bother with cocktail dresses much, given that she rarely went out.

Katherine's wardrobe. She thought of all those beautiful dresses hanging up in the next room and was tempted. Ruby walked into the spare bedroom and opened the wardrobe. An abundance of possibilities confronted her. Dresses in different hues and colours; a treasure trove of choices. She couldn't help herself. She pushed her hands in amongst them, feeling the caress of the fabrics and catching the slight fragrance of Katherine's perfume, which still clung to them. Her head swum with giddy delight.

She pulled away. 'I can't do it,' she whispered. 'They're Katherine's, not mine.'

Returning to her bedroom, she took the navy dress off its coat hanger and slipped it on. She looked at herself in the mirror and was reasonably satisfied with the result, although she guessed that Dusty would be disappointed that she hadn't made enough of an effort to dress for the occasion.

She powdered her face, added a touch of lipstick, tied her hair back into the usual bun at the nape of her neck, and studied her appearance again. Perhaps she should make a concession by adding something extra from Katherine's jewellery box?

Back in the spare room, she spilled the contents onto the bed, then selected a Spanish comb set with jade and brilliants and fixed it into place above the bun. She stood back and appraised her appearance in the mirror. The dress looked plain. Perhaps that scarab beetle brooch would give it a lift? She pinned it into place on the bodice. It caught the eye, distracting from the ordinariness of her dress. She gathered the jewellery together and put the box back in the wardrobe, then collected her coat and handbag.

Out in the hallway, she waited nervously for Dusty's arrival. Events like these always made her feel like a square peg in a round hole but, perhaps tonight, she would fit in.

Chapter Twelve

The Wattle Path Palais de Danse & Café was another world to Ruby. She had never seen anything like it before, as she and Dusty paused on the threshold and stared at the mass of people in front of them. Wattle Path boasted the largest dance floor in Australia, which appeared, at first glance, to be full. The interiors were magnificent, featuring decorative murals and panels.

'This will be fun,' said Dusty, taking her hand and guiding her towards one of the dining balconies, where they were to meet his friends.

On the way, they passed an illuminated soda fountain almost thirty feet long, with sixteen syrup pumps gushing a dazzling variety of drinks. Men in evening suits and women dressed in their finery promenaded down the side of the hall, or paused to watch the more accomplished dancers go through their paces. Up on the stage, Harry Yerkes' Flotilla Dance Band was playing 'Blue Lagoon.'

'There's someone I'd like you to meet,' said Dusty, heading towards a small group of people who were congregating together. He smoothed his hair and straightened his bow tie.

'Not John Gascoigne?' asked Ruby, smirking.

Dusty snorted. 'Much nicer.'

He led her over to a young woman and introduced them to each other.

'Toula, this is my sister Ruby.'

Ruby smiled. 'Toula. That's an unusual name.'

'My mother is Greek, my father Australian. It was my grandmother's name.'

'How nice. And quite exotic, too,' commented Ruby.

Toula was a pretty lass with large dark eyes and short black hair, cut in a fashionable bob. Her silver dress was embellished with embroidery, with two long tassels falling from the waistband to the hemline. She had a slim, almost boyish figure which did justice to her stylish outfit.

'I didn't know Dusty had a sister,' she said, looking Ruby up and down. 'I must say that's a lovely brooch. Where on earth did you get it?'

Ruby fingered the scarab, feeling rather self-conscious. 'Just something I found.'

'My aunt would love that. She likes good jewellery, particularly in the Egyptian style.'

The introductions continued as the party-goers arrived, about twenty in all. Some were couples, some had come alone, but soon most of them had either gone in search of a drink or downstairs to the dance floor, leaving Ruby alone.

A latecomer had arrived. He was beautifully attired in a striking dinner suit, the like of which Ruby had never seen. Grey check, almost silver. His hair shone like ebony, and his moustache reminded her of one of the silent movie stars, whose name she could never remember. It was hard to believe that her Dusty, inclined to be rather shabby if the truth be told, could be friends with this sartorially elegant man.

She stepped forward and introduced herself, feeling that she should do the honours in the absence of her brother.

'I'm Ruby Rhodes, Dusty's sister. He's dancing, otherwise, he'd be here to welcome you.'

'Reggie da Costa, from *The Argus*.'

Ruby smiled. 'You're Dusty's boss. He's spoken about you. He said you've been very helpful getting him settled in.'

Reggie smiled, showing a sparkling set of white teeth beneath the black line of his moustache. 'It's a different world from that of *The Truth*. Quite an adjustment, actually.'

'Particularly the headlines, don't you think?' asked Ruby. 'Dusty was proud of his use of alliteration. One of his best was "Lashings of Liquor in

Little Lonsdale Lane."

Reggie snorted. 'It's the staple of any newspaperman. People like it. But no, you don't get a lot of that at *The Argus*.'

'I'm glad he's working at a more reputable newspaper.'

'We all have to start somewhere. I have a colleague. His first posting was a country newspaper, *The St Arnaud Mercury*. He told me that his first headline was "Sheep Farmer Fleeced by Con Man."'

Ruby laughed. This man was more amusing than his appearance suggested. Clothes might make the man, but this one had a way with words.

As if divining her thoughts, he added, 'Words are the tools of our trade. We use them to communicate, to entertain, and to sell newspapers.'

Ruby nodded and rested against the balcony rail, looking down on the dancers. Below them, Dusty and Toula were engaged in an enthusiastic and energetic Charleston.

'I must say that your brooch is very beautiful,' commented Reggie, pointing at the scarab beetle pinned to Ruby's dress.

'You're not the first to mention it tonight. It's just costume jewellery.'

'Looks expensive to me. I have excellent taste.'

Ruby touched the brooch tentatively. 'I did think it looked exotic, but I doubt—'

The Flotilla Band started playing a favourite of Ruby's, distracting her. It was 'Stumbling.' She swayed gently to the music.

'Would you like to dance, Miss Rhodes?' said Reggie holding out his hand to her.

'I haven't danced for a while.'

'Follow me. I'll show you how.'

Ruby touched her hair self-consciously. 'Perhaps. Just this once.'

They walked down the stairs and made their way onto the dance floor. At first, Ruby felt only too aware of the fact that she was out of practice, if she excluded the times when she danced to the gramophone in the privacy of her own sitting room. But Reggie was obviously an expert dancer and led her well, so that she soon relaxed into the foxtrot. She had a chance to study him up close and thought him very good-looking. But he was out of her class. He was so confident, so self-assured, and she wasn't. She felt dowdy, despite her best efforts. It came into her mind that Katherine, with her vibrant personality and fashionable clothes, would have been completely at ease at the Wattle Path dancing with this man.

Her partner was apparently enjoying himself, moving well to the music and casting admiring glances at some of the more attractive women who glided by. And yet he didn't completely neglect her, occasionally leaning forward and making some observation about the band, or some couple nearby, or his new colleague, Dusty.

Over to her left, she could see Dusty and Toula dancing together. It was obvious from the look on her brother's face that he was besotted with the young lady, although she looked more in control of her feelings than did her partner. Dusty glanced their way, a big smile on his face as he recognised his mentor. He raised a hand to acknowledge Reggie, then turned back to Toula.

As the band finished its set, the dance floor emptied. Ruby and Reggie worked their way through the scrum of people who were trying to find a table or who were intent on buying drinks. As they reached the staircase leading to the balcony, Ruby was bumped aside by a well-dressed gent who was in pursuit of a pretty girl in red.

'Watch out!' yelled Reggie after him, as Ruby lay sprawled on the floor.

The man turned and glared at him, and then continued on his way down the side of the hall.

'Have you hurt yourself?' Reggie asked, helping Ruby to her feet.

'I'm fine,' she replied, smoothing her dress. 'Thank you.'

Reggie was scowling. He seemed unnecessarily riled by what had happened.

'Is something wrong?' she asked him. 'I'm fine, really.'

'I know him. The man who knocked you over. He's a friend of my mother's. Valentine Peebles.'

A sour expression still on his face, he took her arm, and they ascended the stairs to the balcony where the party-goers had assembled.

While champagne corks popped and toasts were made in honour of

Dusty's birthday, Ruby noticed that Reggie was looking increasingly out of sorts. As some of the party returned to the dance floor, he announced that he had to leave, due to commitments in the morning. Ruby, too, was eager to go. It had been a big night, and she was tired. She mentioned it to her brother, but Dusty had other ideas about taking her home. He was keen to stay on and celebrate, and spend time with Toula.

'Reggie will take you home,' he suggested. 'He won't mind.'

Ruby blushed. 'I couldn't ask him.'

Brushing off her objections, Dusty approached his colleague and whispered in his ear. Ruby was mortified when she saw Reggie glance her way; he didn't look too pleased at the prospect. But he had no choice, given that it would have been rude to refuse. Ruby, embarrassed and feeling awkward, followed the crime reporter out to his automobile.

At first, there was little conversation on the drive home from St Kilda to Richmond. Reggie kept his eyes on the road and did little to acknowledge his passenger. Ruby felt obliged to apologise for the imposition.

'I really am sorry about this,' she said. 'Dusty should never have asked you.'

He shook his head. 'It's not far from my place.'

'As I said, he should never have asked you.'

'Don't worry. It's nothing to do with you.'

Ruby attempted to ease the tension between them. 'This is a lovely car,' she commented. 'I don't think I've driven in one before.'

He glanced sideways at her, pleased with her response. 'It's a Hupmobile Series R Special Roadster. Four-cylinder, three-speed transmission, with a top speed of thirty-five miles per hour.'

'Really? Just right for a crime reporter.'

Reggie visibly relaxed. 'You'd be surprised what I keep in the boot. And it's not a dead body.'

Ruby laughed. 'What is it?'

'My reporter's kit,' he replied, his eyes on her again. 'Keeps me ahead of the press pack.'

'Tell me about it. It sounds interesting.'

'There's the necessities: a typewriter and blank paper for typing up reports on the fly, some spare notebooks, and a camera and film in case my photographer can't make it.'

'That sounds sensible,' commented Ruby.

Reggie continued, warming to his theme. 'I do stakeouts, you see, involving long hours, so whisky, cigarettes, and the latest copy of the *Victoria Police Gazette* help me pass the time. If I'm out overnight, there's a change of clothing and a shaving kit handy, not to mention gumboots, a raincoat, and umbrella in case of rain.'

'I'm impressed. You're very professional.'

Reggie nodded. 'I am, indeed, but I've been doing this for a long time. But there's more. In my business, you need to grease the occasional palm, if you want information. I have tickets to sporting events, films, shows, and dances.'

'I hope Dusty is taking notes.'

'I believe he's started putting his together. Your brother has potential.'

By the time he finished speaking, they'd drawn up outside her house in Tanner Street.

'Perhaps I could offer you a cup of tea or something stronger, to thank you?' Ruby asked him.

Reggie looked at his watch and shrugged his shoulders. 'It's still early. A glass of red wine wouldn't go astray. You do have wine?'

'Of course.'

He followed her into the house and raised his eyebrows as he glanced into the sitting room.

'Very nice. I didn't expect this.'

'It was my sister's house. She died on New Year's Eve.'

'Dusty did mention it. What did she do for a living?'

'Administrative assistant at the Melbourne Museum.'

'Really?'

Ruby watched as his gaze moved from the grandfather clock to the leather Chesterfield, to the Chinese vases, and then on to the crystal decanter on the oak sideboard.

'I'll pour you a drink,' she said. 'Make yourself comfortable.'

When she returned with a bottle and two glasses, she found Reggie standing next to the sideboard, one of the photographs in his hand. It was of Katherine on the arm of the flashily dressed man.

'She's beautiful, isn't she? We were identical twins, but I suppose that's not so obvious.'

'The similarity is undeniable. It's just a question of taste.'

She flinched at his comment, but didn't respond. It was the truth, after all. She poured the wine and handed him a glass. He'd put down the photograph, but was still staring at it.

'I don't know who her beau was,' she added, watching him. 'I never met him.'

'I know who he was. He was also her fiancé if the ring on her finger is any indication.'

'She was engaged? I didn't notice that. So, who is he?'

'Stanley Duggan.' Reggie took a sip from his glass and raised an eyebrow. 'Not a bad drop.' Then he added, 'You've heard of Horace Striker?'

Ruby nodded. 'I've read about him in the papers.'

He pointed at the man in the photograph. 'That was his nephew. Heir apparent to a gambling empire. Died in an alley in September. The police are no closer to finding the culprit.'

Ruby blanched. 'My sister was mixing with types like that?'

'I'm afraid so.' Reggie shook his head. 'Stanley was six-foot-two of pure intimidating muscle. He had these cold blue eyes and a lop-sided smile, which was frankly off-putting. He learned everything he knew at Striker's knee. When he was younger, he invested in a property deal that went belly-up. The coppers even suspected him of the murder of Cornelius Stout, the man who'd talked him into it. Uncle Horace bailed him out, and became his mentor and benefactor.'

He looked back at the photograph. 'I half-expected that Stanley would go out in a blaze of glory: a shootout with a rival gang or hanging at the end of a rope, but not in a Fitzroy alley with a knife in his back.'

'That's awful.'

'It's a surprise to think that he was engaged to your sister. I have to wonder whether she knew what she was getting herself into. Dangerous company.'

Ruby took a seat on the couch. 'Can I tell you something? Something private?'

Reggie sat down. 'Of course.'

'The police say my sister drowned on New Year's Eve. I don't believe that she did. I think that she was pushed into the water.'

'What's your evidence?'

'Not a lot, admittedly. She was last seen with a man on St Kilda pier just before she died. Then there's the coroner's report. They found a bump on the back of her head, but said that it was probably a result of the fall.'

'As you say, not a lot of evidence. What do the police say?'

'They're not interested.'

Reggie smiled. 'Forget it, Miss Rhodes. You've done well inheriting this house. Very well, indeed. My advice would be to accept what you've been given and get on with your life. One thing I'll grant you, your sister was mixing with criminals and, judging by this house, she was benefitting from that association. Most probably, Stanley Duggan was supplementing her income.'

He checked his watch. 'I must go.' He noticed that she was looking dejected. 'I will say this. If you do find anything to support your theory, you can contact me through Dusty. Or telephone *The Argus* and ask for the crime desk.'

He drained the rest of his glass and stood up. 'Goodnight, Miss Rhodes. Enjoy your good fortune.'

Chapter Thirteen

Squizzy Taylor and Horace Striker controlled much of Melbourne's trade in bootleg liquor and cocaine, as well as overseeing most of the illegal gambling dens in Richmond and Fitzroy. When 'Long Harry' Slater, all seventeen stone and six-foot-three inches of him, was gunned down by Henry Stokes, it was Horace Striker who took control of Slater's patch in Fitzroy, whilst keeping his headquarters in the seedy back lanes of Richmond.

To Felix Messenger, it was Striker who posed the bigger threat to law enforcement. Squizzy was vulgar and conceited, enjoying the publicity that he generated. His loud clothing and posturing aped the American bootleggers that he so admired. He was like an annoying buzzing little fly that needed swatting.

Horace Striker, on the other hand, was self-disciplined and focused. He had been born into poverty but had clawed his way up through the ranks, using his natural intelligence, animal cunning, and business acumen. Felix found him a difficult adversary. Striker eschewed the limelight, the tentacles of his influence extending into the upper levels of Melbourne's political and legal classes. Bribery and blackmail were the tools of Striker's trade, and Messenger was having difficulty finding his Achilles heel.

Horace Striker inhabited a nondescript brick terrace off Shamrock Street. He was protected by two bodyguards, both Scots, nicknamed Burke and Hare, after the two grave robbers who killed innocent victims and sold their bodies to the Edinburgh Medical College for dissection. They were the reason that Messenger had never got past the front door. He was of the belief that Striker was hosting private collectors at his social clubs, providing them with the opportunity to acquire treasures smuggled into the country, thus breaking the law. If he could plant someone in Striker's circle, he could get the information that he needed to make arrests.

Katherine Rhodes, or Miss Kitty as she was known, was the perfect option. She had been the fiancée of Striker's nephew and, as such, was trusted to keep his secrets. Through his contacts and those he leaned on, Messenger had discovered that Miss Kitty was involved in small-scale fraud, importing modest amounts of antiquities without declaring them and lining her own pockets with the profits. Shutting her down would not stop the traffic, but prosecuting those who received such goods would send a strong message that Customs was aggressively pursuing wrong-doers. Felix wasn't above blackmailing her into cooperating with him. But now she was dead, and that avenue was closed.

Or was it?

Close scrutiny of Katherine Rhodes' activities had revealed that she had drawn a line between her public and private lives, using the moniker 'Miss Kitty' in criminal circles and 'Katherine' in her job at the Melbourne Museum. Consequently, there were few people who knew that Miss Kitty and Katherine Rhodes were one and the same person. And, furthermore, Messenger's intensive inquiries had failed to uncover the fact that Miss Kitty had an identical twin.

According to his contacts in Melbourne's netherworld, the prevailing opinion was that Miss Kitty had gone into isolation, the result of feeling threatened by forces greater than she. What those forces were, was unknown, but there was the belief that the murder of her beau, Stanley Duggan, was somehow connected. Opinions varied about where she'd gone. Interstate? Overseas? Her purchase of the house in Richmond had gone unnoticed. It had taken weeks for Felix to track her down.

The newspapers had not identified her either when they reported on the finding of a woman's body south of St Kilda beach; a drowning was of little or no public interest and thus had only garnered a couple of lines on the bottom of page five.

A brilliant idea had come to him, as he drove home from work one evening. If it were assumed that Miss Kitty had gone into exile, why not bring her back in the form of her identical twin sister, Ruby? If he could coerce her into cooperating, he could use her to infiltrate Horace Striker's criminal empire and, hopefully, expose those who dabbled in the trade in illegal antiquities. The plan wasn't fully formed, but it had potential. As usual, he kept his stratagem to himself. If it failed, and Ruby was hurt in the process, no one would know that it was his idea.

And thus, about two weeks after his first visit, he arrived unannounced on Ruby Rhodes' doorstep again, hoping to take her off-guard.

* * *

The day had been one of those last hurrahs of a Melbourne summer, common in early March. The sun had been unrelenting, beating down from a cloudless sky. The air had been thick and damp, cloying in its humidity. Felix Messenger took off his hat and wiped the sweat from his brow. His shirt was sticking to him beneath the thick serge of his brown suit jacket. He rapped on the front door.

'It's you again, Mr Messenger.' Ruby pushed open the flyscreen door.

'Miss Rhodes, may I come in? Just for a few minutes?'

'I'm busy,' she said, barring the doorway.

'Very well. We'll talk out here.'

He studied Ruby intently, looking her up and down. It would only take a few minutes to transform Ruby into her sister. A slash of lipstick, the skills of a hairdresser, and some fashionable clothes would do the trick. No one would be able to pick the difference between them. If he could persuade her—

'Has anything occurred to you which might help me in my investigation?' he asked.

'As I told you last time, I haven't seen Katherine in years.'

'Have you come across anything of interest?' He looked past her down the hallway. 'Anything at all would be helpful.'

'I don't know what you're referring to.'

'Documents? A list of her associates?'

She shook her head. 'It's hot, Mr Messenger, and I'm not in the mood for conversation.'

'Perhaps you would allow me to have a look around?' Messenger took a step forward, but Ruby was having none of it.

'No. You do not have my permission.' She stepped down onto the porch and shut the door behind her.

Felix changed tack. 'I'm sorry to have offended you. It was terrible that your sister died in such a tragic accident.'

'If it were an accident.'

Felix's ears pricked up. 'You think someone was responsible for her death?'

'I do.'

'Do you have someone in mind? I can help you if you tell me a name.'

She ran her fingers through her hair and looked past him onto the street. 'I don't know, but I intend to find out, somehow.'

Felix's mind was working fast. He sensed an opportunity. 'Perhaps we can help each other. You believe that someone murdered your sister. I want to close down the black market in antiquities.' He smoothed the brim of his hat. 'If I could explain. Your resemblance to your sister is remarkable. If you changed your hair, dressed more like her, no one would know the difference.'

Her eyes focused back onto his face, more alert this time. 'Why would I do that?'

'To help the Australian Government. Your civic duty, no less.'

'What are you suggesting?'

'We have conclusive evidence that your sister was involved in smuggling antiquities into Australia. If she was murdered, it is likely that one of her associates was the killer. My suggestion is that you go undercover. Pretend to be your sister. Go to the places where she went. Find out what she was doing and who she dealt with. Then give me the information so that I can prosecute those who are defrauding the government.'

She frowned. 'How will that help me find her killer?'

'As I said, he had to be in her social circles. She must have upset someone to end up dead.'

She leaned forward. 'I think you should leave.'

'Miss Rhodes. I'm finding your attitude most perverse. I am an officer of the Crown. It is your duty to assist me.'

She flushed, her voice rising. 'Just to remind you, I'm a law-abiding woman. You're asking me to associate with criminals. I have no idea what Katherine was doing, and it appears that you don't either, otherwise, you'd be more specific.' She stepped forward, face to face with him. 'You should go now.'

Messenger put on his hat, disgruntled. 'This isn't the last you've seen of me. We will meet again soon.' He walked down the path and opened the gate, then turned and wagged his finger at her. 'One last word, Miss Rhodes. Your sister mixed with criminals. You can clear her name if you help me. And, if you cooperate, the Department will protect you.'

She followed him and shut the gate. He walked around the rear of his Model T Ford, then stopped, staring down at the back wheel.

'Bloody hell,' he muttered.

'What is it?' she asked, leaning against the gate.

'Someone's dented the mudguard.' He frowned and shook his head in disgust, then glared at her.

He took his handkerchief out and wiped the back of his neck. What a hopeless day, he thought to himself. It's bloody hot, this woman won't play my game, *and* now someone's damaged my car.

Chapter Fourteen

Clad in her nightie, Ruby stood in the courtyard behind her house, staring up into the blackness of the sky. She couldn't sleep, weighed down as she was by Felix Messenger's words. The night was still and silent, but the sluggish damp air and distant flashes of lightning promised a coming storm. The weather had always affected her moods, those days when leaden clouds hung heavy, threatening to soak the earth, or the wind howled and moaned around the walls of the house, or when sharp icy hail that sounded like a drum roll launched its rat-a-tat against the windows. She was tempted to stay and watch the storm break, but it was almost midnight, and she had to go to work in the morning.

Ruby went inside and splashed her face with water, then wandered off to bed. Feeling over-tired and lethargic, she lay down on top of the bedclothes and closed her eyes, but sleep remained elusive.

The thunder rumbled, its volume increasing as it drew nearer, intruding into her uneasy slumber. She twisted and turned, changed position, dozed. At last, she got up and opened the window, but there was barely a breeze to ruffle the curtain or to relieve the tedium of the night. She fluffed up her pillows and sat up in bed, surrendering to the thoughts that she had suppressed earlier that evening.

The Customs officer had unnerved her, with his veiled threats and slurs on her sister's character. Gangs, gambling dens, illegal booze, smuggling. And Reggie da Costa had identified Katherine's fiancé as being the nephew of an infamous gangster. What did Ruby know or understand about a life that revolved around that? And was it her responsibility to make atonement for Katherine's crimes? If she had wanted to disbelieve Messenger, she could not, for John Gascoigne had offered confirmation of his claims, with his comments about Middle Eastern middlemen, emphasising yet again that Katherine had a secret life alien to Ruby's.

The thunder came again, and lightning flashed through the thin gauze of the curtain. The wind was rising, a low moan growing in volume. Not long now till the storm would break, and the rain would bring relief. She tried to clear her mind, but unwanted thoughts persisted, like the mosquito that was buzzing above her head. What should she do about Katherine? Find her killer? But how? Imitate her, as Messenger suggested?

She had to stop this. Her mind resembled a hamster on a wheel, thoughts running faster and faster, getting more muddled and growing out of proportion to the realities of the situation.

Ruby sat on the edge of the bed. Perhaps a cup of tea might calm her racing mind. She was reaching for her dressing gown when she heard the wind come up. At the same time, the gate to the courtyard slammed.

'I could have sworn I shut it,' she muttered, wrapping her dressing gown around her.

She padded down the hallway towards the kitchen, fatigued at the thought that she was going to have to brave the elements to shut the gate.

The lightning flashed, illuminating the interior of the house. Thunder clapped overhead, a precursor to the drenching that was to come.

The blind on the large window overlooking the courtyard was down. As she stepped into the kitchen, the gate banged again. She approached the back door but stopped in her tracks as an unfamiliar sound reached her ears. Not the pitter-patter of rain against the window or the moan of the wind, but something curious, unidentifiable. It came again. Someone or something was scratching the window. High-pitched. Putting her teeth on edge. She tensed, holding her breath, her heart thumping. There it was again.

Ruby withdrew a large carving knife from the knife block near the stove. She clutched it in her right hand. The ring-pull of the roller blind dangled in front of her. She counted slowly, trying to calm herself. She raised the knife, then leaned forward and pushed down on the ring-pull with her left index finger. The blind clattered up the window.

A piercing screech rent the air.

A jet-black tomcat, yellow eyes gleaming in the darkness, with its back arched and its fur standing on end, bared its fangs at her. It leaped off the window ledge onto the brick-paved courtyard. As the rain pelted down, the cat disappeared over the side fence.

Ruby staggered backwards, dropping the knife, torn between stunned surprise and hysterical laughter. It had been a cat. Nothing more. She closed her eyes, chiding herself for being so open to suggestion.

As her breathing slowed, she stared out into the darkened courtyard, the brick paving wet and shiny. The gate, still visible through the driving rain, was swinging back and forth in the wind. She stepped out into the yard, her dressing gown soaked in seconds. The thunder boomed, and lightning split the night sky, too close for comfort.

As she ran to the gate, her foot kicked something solid. She looked down. The lightning flashed again, picking out the shape of a crowbar. She reached down and clasped it in her hand, then pushed the gate wide open and walked out into the laneway.

Ruby stopped dead. About twenty yards further down stood a man dressed in a dark overcoat, rain running off the brim of his hat. He was watching her, she could tell, although his face was hidden. Ruby's dressing gown was saturated, sticking to her, while rivulets of water ran down her hair and dripped onto the ground. She couldn't move, her eyes fixed on him as she clutched the crowbar, while he stood guard at the other end of the laneway. The driving rain was the only barrier between them, as they faced off against each other. Although it felt like minutes, afterwards she realised that it was mere seconds that they held each other's gaze.

He took one step forward. Lightning illuminated the sky; thunder cracked overhead. The crowbar dropped from Ruby's hand, clanging loudly on the bluestones, breaking the spell.

The man backed up, touched the brim of his hat as if in farewell, and walked to the end of the alley. He stood for a moment looking back at her, then disappeared from view into the adjoining street.

Ruby stood staring after him, water streaming down her face. Another crack of thunder and she came to her senses, staring up as the lightning flashed again. She backed up into the courtyard and bolted the gate behind her, then leaned up against it, breathing heavily.

Back in the kitchen, she stared at the water pooling at her feet, dripping from her sodden clothes. A shiver passed through her, alerting her to the chill that was creeping into her bones. She pulled down the blind and slipped out of her nightie and dressing gown, letting them fall to the floor. Taking two towels from the linen press, she dried herself off, then wrapped one around her hair.

Later, dressed in clean pyjamas, Ruby poured herself a sherry and settled herself down at the kitchen table. In the darkness and alone, she went into shock, violent shudders passing through her body. Her imagination roamed free, throwing up awful visions of what might have happened to her. What if she hadn't slept badly? What if the gate hadn't slammed? What if she hadn't heard the cat?

Finally, she pulled herself together and checked that all the doors and windows were locked. She was safe, she told herself. But what should she do now, at three o'clock in the morning? She downed the sherry and refilled the glass. Dutch courage. Her mind moved on. She was thinking clearly now. She ticked off the possibilities. Did this have anything to do with Katherine? Was it a disgruntled client looking for something? Perhaps someone from the list of associates that Felix Messenger had been talking about? Or was it a prowler, and she was his random victim?

The storm passed. The clock above the stove ticked on. It was after four. She was growing numb with cold. Taking a blanket from the bed, Ruby wrapped it around herself, and lay down on the Chesterfield in the sitting room. The sound of a door slamming made her jump. It was her neighbour, Fred, heading out to work the early shift at the factory. Shortly after, the nightman's cart went past, the sound of the horse's hooves clip-clopping along Tanner Street. The world was waking up for the day.

Ruby turned on the lamp and tried to read, but the meaning of the words escaped her. Sometime around dawn, as the sun's rays emerged from behind the workers' cottages, exhaustion got the better of her, and she fell into a deep sleep.

Chapter Fifteen

For once, Ruby found her work at Smith and Sons dragged.

When her alarm had gone off at six, she had arisen from the couch, stiff and exhausted. She had a wash then dressed, trying to summon up the energy to eat breakfast. However, curiosity drove her out into the lane. She was shocked to find that the crowbar was gone. Had the prowler returned to reclaim it, or had an opportunistic street urchin carried it away?

Inside again, she forced herself to eat breakfast while she considered her situation. The mystery surrounding her sister's death wasn't going away, what with midnight visitors, Katherine's unexplained wealth, and Customs officers harassing her. The question mark around Katherine's death needed to be solved, and there was only one person who was motivated to do that. Not the police. Not her brother. Only herself.

At work, she tried hard to concentrate on her job, typing up orders and sending off invoices, but at times she found herself staring into space, reliving the events of the previous night. Mr Smith interrupted one of her reveries and asked if there was anything wrong. She gave him a brief account of her encounter with the prowler and was surprised by his response.

'Go to the police station, Ruby,' he urged her. 'Go now. You need to report it.'

'You're so kind to me,' she replied. 'I feel like I've been nothing but trouble over the last two months.'

'You've had a lot to deal with. And you never let us down. Now, go.'

* * *

At the police station, she received a different reception from that of her boss. A bored sergeant listened half-heartedly to her account of the previous night's visitor.

'You're letting your imagination get the better of you,' he said, doodling on a piece of paper. 'It was probably a drifter looking for food or easy money. There's no proof he was going to break into your house.'

'What about the crowbar?'

'He didn't break in, though, did he?'

'No, but what if he had?'

'That would be a different matter, miss. Anyway, the crowbar's gone.' He looked up and studied her. 'I'll tell you what I think. You ladies read a few too many of those trashy novels. I know what that can do to you when you're sitting there alone at night. Maybe it was a possum, or the trees looked like a man. When you calm down a bit, you'll realise that I'm right.'

'I'm not some sort of over-imaginative person,' she retorted. 'There are no trees. It's a laneway. You think I don't know the difference between a man and a possum? You think I'm imagining this?'

'Now, miss, you're being emotional. I'll write up a report, alright?' He took some notes and smiled at her. 'That's done. If you are afraid, why don't you pack a bag and stay with a friend or relative for a few days? Or if you want to stay at home, lock yourself in at night and you'll be as safe as houses. Now go home and have a nice cuppa tea.'

It was on the tip of her tongue to tell him what she thought of him, but what use would that be? He'd still do nothing. As she left the police station, she looked back. The sergeant was screwing up the report and throwing it into the rubbish bin. She shrugged her shoulders and headed back to work, angry and frustrated.

'Go home, Ruby,' said her boss. 'Get some sleep. I'll see you tomorrow.'

She was packing up her desk when one of the typists came up to her.

'I meant to tell you. A man rang while you were out. He left a message. Is he a secret admirer?'

'Who was it?' she asked.

'He said that his name was Felix Messenger. He told me to tell you that

70

he'd be back to see you soon.'

Ruby frowned. The perfect end to a terrible twenty-four hours.

* * *

Now, at home, with the dinner dishes washed and put away, Ruby thought about the typist's words. A message from a secret admirer. A message from a Messenger. And then her mind ticked over to something that had been nagging at her, subconsciously.

A message. A secret message. In her letter, Katherine had alluded to the secret messages that they had exchanged when they were young:

'Do you remember what fun we had leaving secret messages for each other? I hope you do.'

At the time, the postscript had struck her as being out of place, given the general tone of the letter. Why mention something like that? She thought back to the past when they'd been about ten years old. The twins had found a loose board in their bedroom and levered it up, then placed a tin box between the joists to hold their notes to each other. Their private hiding place was undetectable once the board was put back into position and covered with a rug. From then on, secret messages passed between them that only they would read and understand. Secret messages left in a spot beneath the floorboards. Was her sister telling her something from the grave?

What if Katherine had hidden away something incriminating in this house? Was it what Felix Messenger had been seeking? Was it the reason for the late-night visit of the mysterious man in the lane? More importantly, whatever was hidden might explain what Katherine was referring to when she said:

'I've been playing a deadly game ... I have got myself into trouble.'

Not knowing if it were a book, documents, or photographs made it difficult. But the first place to look was under the floorboards. She went through each room methodically, pulling away the rugs, walking slowly across the floor, listening for a creak, looking for a gap in the boards, anything that might indicate that a hidden cache lay underneath. The sitting room, bedroom, and hallway yielded no result. The kitchen floor was covered with linoleum. That left the second bedroom.

She entered the room and looked around, studying the floor. To her right, the iron bedstead sat out from the wall, leaving a few feet on each side. Opposite it was the wardrobe and the trunks stacked on top of each other behind the door. There was no rug. She got down on her hands and knees, looking for a gap between the floorboards. Nothing.

'You're imagining things,' she said aloud. 'Katherine was being sentimental. There's no secret message.'

But then Ruby noticed that there was a board peeking out from under the bed, that wasn't flush with the adjacent one. She pushed the bed across towards the window. The board was about two feet long and four inches wide. Oddly, another three the same size lay parallel with the first, cut to match. It was a small trapdoor, concealed beneath the bed.

She went out to the kitchen and took a knife from the drawer, then returned to the room. Getting down on her hands and knees, she saw a few scratch marks at the end of one of the middle boards and inserted the knife tip in the space between it and the next one along.

'I don't believe it.'

The four boards lifted out as one, leaving a neatly cut hole in the floor. She looked down into the cavity and saw the glint of metal: the handle of a silver box. She removed it and placed it on the floor in front of her. The container was relatively new but dusty, around twelve inches long by ten inches wide, and six inches deep, and it was quite heavy. There was no lock, just a latch to release the lid. Ruby hesitated, then flicked it open.

Inside, on the top, was a small pile of documents—invoices and receipts—fastened together with a paper clip. She thumbed through them, giving each a cursory glance. Bills for a vase. A bracelet. A statuette. Some of the amounts were substantial.

Beneath them was a leather-bound notebook. She flipped through the pages. There were names and addresses, the former unfamiliar to her. But, looking closer, she realised that it wasn't an address book at all, but more a record of clients. There were columns for the date of purchase, the name and address of the buyer, brief descriptions of what had been sold, and the amounts involved. The suburbs were upper-class: East Melbourne, Brighton, and Toorak. The dates went back two years, and, in most cases, Katherine had placed ticks next to the names. Payment received perhaps? Or goods delivered?

This was the proof that John Gascoigne had been right. Katherine was using the museum as a front for receiving illegally obtained antiquities. It was clear that what Ruby had in her hands were the details of Katherine's clients.

Of one thing Ruby was sure: Felix Messenger would be keen to get his hands on the notebook. It would give him the names of private collectors who had avoided paying import duties so that they might possess some of the Middle East's most sought-after treasures at cheaper prices. In his hands, that notebook would be clear evidence that Katherine was dishonest, culpable in the eyes of the law.

Putting the notebook aside, she reached into the box and removed the last item: a canvas bag. She opened it and gasped. Inside was money, lots of it. She upturned the bag and let the notes fall to the floor. In front of her was more money than she'd ever seen in her life. Hundred-pound notes. Fifty-pound notes. Tenners and fivers.

She put the money back in the bag, then took it into the kitchen. She emptied it onto the table and felt a chill go through her. It was all too much. The house. Katherine's double life. Her death. And now a bundle of cash. She put the kettle on to boil, and while she was waiting, she put the notes into piles. Slowly she counted them and then sat back, staring in disbelief at the fortune that lay in front of her: £7,855.

The kettle was boiling, steam pouring from its spout. She glanced over, hardly registering, then, as if in a daze, turned the gas off. All interest in a soothing cup of tea had passed. She returned the money to the box, under the invoices and notebook. Then she placed the box back inside the floor cavity, covered it with the boards, and shifted the bed back into position.

Returning to the sitting room, Ruby sank into the leather cushions of the Chesterfield and put her head in her hands. There was no doubt that her sister had been involved in shady deals. How else to explain a stack of money hidden away from prying eyes beneath the floor of the house, and not in a bank?

When she considered her discovery, she realised that it wasn't the wad of cash or the invoices and receipts that were important. The notebook was the key. Such a list was evidence that could be used against those engaged in the black market. Someone might even risk breaking into Katherine's house in an attempt to find it. And then she wondered if Katherine might have been blackmailing someone, someone who might have committed murder to silence her.

Who were these clients of hers? Ruby didn't know them, but someone else might. Perhaps their names would be familiar to John Gascoigne? Perhaps those people were connected to the museum? Donors or philanthropists? She shook her head. Now she was being naïve.

What about her reporter brother? Could she confide in him? But she knew him well enough to know what he would say. Destroy the notebook or hand it over to the police. If she burned the notebook, there would be no resolution to finding Katherine's killer. And she wasn't confident that the police would go any further than tracking down Katherine's clients and prosecuting them, rather than opening an inquiry into her death.

There was one last possibility: Reggie da Costa. Crime reporter for *The Argus*. If the people named in the notebook were involved in illegal activities, he would know, just as he had recognised Stanley Duggan in the photograph. He had said that if any evidence emerged to support her theory that her sister's death was not an accident, he was prepared to look at it. Perhaps she should hold him to his promise?

Ruby went out into the kitchen and put the kettle on the hob again. She felt better now, given that she had a plan. Taking her cup of tea to the sitting room, she slipped her shoes off and sat with her feet up on the leather Chesterfield. On the sideboard was the photograph of her twin sister.

'What were you doing?' she asked Katherine. 'Why would someone kill you?' She waited, but there was only silence. 'Tell me, Katherine, should I destroy the notebook?'

A voice in her head answered her. 'You know you can't, Ruby, because you owe me.'

Chapter Sixteen

Reggie parked his car outside Ruby's house. He rubbed his chin. Perhaps he shouldn't have offered to find her sister's supposed killer? Perhaps he'd been hasty, given that he was sceptical that such a person existed. Still, this was why he was ahead of the press pack, because of his uncanny knack of keeping his ear to the ground and following hunches. He suspected that this would be a waste of time, but she was Dusty's sister, and that counted for something.

He got out of the automobile and wiped an errant spot of dirt off the side panel with his handkerchief. How he loved his new car. A Hupmobile Series R Special Roadster. He said it aloud; it sounded so good. It had cost him nearly £470, not including the trade-in and, even then, it was worth every penny.

On the porch, he glanced at his reflection in the window, pleased to see that his suit still looked freshly pressed after a day at work. He licked his fingers and smoothed his hair, then knocked on the door and stood back, waiting.

He could hear footsteps coming down the hallway, and then the door opened. Ruby was the picture of respectability, in her grey skirt, pale pink blouse, and sensible black shoes. She was nice, quite friendly really, and seemed intelligent, but that was as far as it went. She had all the attributes of a beautiful young woman—she couldn't be more than mid-twenties—and yet she chose to conceal her charms behind a façade of dreary garments that were more suited to an elderly maiden aunt. What a waste. Even her glorious flame-red hair was hidden away in a bun at the nape of her neck. It was a shame that Dusty couldn't talk sense to her, but then he was no picture either. What had their parents been thinking, bringing their children up to look like that?

Reggie had never had that problem, fortunately. Mother had always insisted that he make the best of himself, which had been easy given that he was blessed with aristocratic and classic features, as well as a manly physique. Impeccable taste had been the icing on the cake.

'Please come in, Mr da Costa,' Ruby said, standing aside.

'Reggie, call me Reggie.'

'Then you must call me Ruby. I hope it wasn't too much of a liberty inviting you here.'

'Not at all,' he said as he followed her through into the sitting room.

'I'll make us some tea, and then I'll tell you why I've asked you here.'

Over the next half-hour, Ruby shared her concerns about Katherine's double life: her work at the Melbourne Museum, which gave her a respectable front, and then that other side, where she associated with people like Stanley Duggan. According to Ruby, there were question marks over her so-called accidental death, the identity of the man who had accompanied her to the pier, the unwillingness of the police to open an investigation, and lastly, and most importantly, the letter that she had penned to Ruby before her death, with its cryptic postscript.

'I think she was killed, but no one believes me. Even Dusty is sceptical. He doesn't want me to get in over my head, but how can I ignore this? John Gascoigne was her boss at the museum. He says she was mixed up in the black market and that she was so distraught that she killed herself, but that's out of character. Admittedly, I haven't seen her in ten years, but that doesn't fit with the person I knew. And then there was the other night when someone tried to break into my house. At least, I think he did.'

Reggie raised an eyebrow. 'What happened?'

She described her encounter with the man in the laneway, and how the crowbar had disappeared by morning.

'You can't be sure that your house was the target. Did you report it to the police?'

'I did, but they said I was imagining things.'

Reggie shook his head. 'They're overworked. Gangs, illegal liquor, gambling, drugs. It's no excuse, but that's what it comes down to. Is there anything here that might interest a thief?'

'Not anything of mine. But Katherine had some very nice jewellery and furs.'

'Nothing else?'

She paused.

'You're not telling me everything, are you, Ruby?'

'There's the notebook.'

'The notebook?' he asked.

'Katherine had hidden it away.'

'What made you look for it?'

'A Customs officer came here looking for Katherine.'

'Felix Messenger. Brown suit, white shirt, brown tie? No taste?' Reggie pulled a face.

'That's him. How did you know?'

'Educated guess. He delights in making a nuisance of himself.'

'He thought I was Katherine at first. He accused me of being involved with the gangs. He's been here twice now. He wanted to search the house. I told him to go away. After my midnight visitor came, I decided to have a look myself.'

'And that's when you found the notebook? Would you like to show it to me?'

'Give me a moment.'

'Of course.'

Shortly after, Reggie thumbed through the pages, studying the names carefully. He looked up.

'What did Dusty say about this?'

Ruby blushed. 'He doesn't know.'

'What else doesn't he know?'

'About Felix Messenger. The prowler. Stanley Duggan.'

'I think you're being very unwise. He is your next of kin, the head of the family, in a manner of speaking. He should know what is going on in your life.'

She met his look. 'I'll consider it.' She pointed at the notebook. 'Do you know any of them?'

His expression was thoughtful. 'Louie "The Lip" Lippmann. Joe Calypso. Eddie Ling. Fencers of stolen goods. Interesting that she should know them.' He shrugged his shoulders. 'Look at this.' He pointed at a couple of entries. 'John "Doughy" Baker. Jimmy O'Callaghan. Minor players in prostitution, but known to like the finer things of life. William Hind. Francis Wishaw. Made their money in speculation. Upper-class, but there's a slight stench of villainy that drifts around them, although nothing that can be proven.'

'What about the rest?'

'Names I don't know. Classy suburbs, though.' He turned a page. 'Now, this one's interesting. Toby Swithins. Likes to be known as "Mayor" Swithins, even though it's been a while since he held that position on the Collingwood City Council. He's a big shot in the Labor Party.'

'What do you think Katherine was doing?'

'At a guess, I'd say this is a record of transactions. She lists her clients, contact addresses, the date and cost of purchases, and her suppliers. The nature of the goods makes me wonder. Do you mind showing me that brooch of yours again? And any other pieces like it?'

Ruby went back into the spare bedroom and brought out the jewellery box, which she was now keeping under the floor. She emptied it out on the table. Reggie leaned across and picked up the bangle shaped like a snake, then the turquoise necklace with the pharaoh's head pendant and, finally, the scarab brooch.

'Interesting,' was all he said.

'Are they real?' she asked.

'We should find out. I know just the man who can help us. An old friend of mine. I consulted with him on the Death Mask Murders case. Dr Silas Bacon. He used to work at the Melbourne Museum, as did your sister. Perhaps she knew him?'

'I don't know. When would we see him?'

'Are you free next Sunday afternoon? I'll pick you up about two o'clock. I'll let Silas know we're coming.' Reggie checked his watch. 'It's been a long day. Must go.' He put on his hat.

Ruby leaned against the door jamb, looking troubled. 'What do you think? Am I imagining things?'

Reggie smoothed his moustache. 'I feel like there's more to this than meets the eye. Your sister was certainly mixed up in something questionable. Whether it caused her death, I don't know, but I'd certainly like to find out.'

As Reggie started his car, he wondered what else Miss Rhodes had found in that house. He sensed there was more to the story than she was telling him. From Dusty's account of the family, their sister Katherine had been a free spirit, fashionable and sophisticated, but there appeared to be a criminal side to the young woman's personality. His reporter's nose had picked up the scent of a scoop, one that promised to blow the lid on Melbourne's underworld: a tale of smuggling, deceit, ill-gotten gains and, with a bit of luck, a killing rather than an accidental death. But for now, he would keep such thoughts to himself.

Chapter Seventeen

Ruby had heard that bad things came in groups of three but, until it happened to her, she had never really believed it.

It had begun with her decision to 'spill the beans' to Dusty after dinner, on the advice of Reggie.

Her brother had been less than impressed, to put it mildly. When she had confessed the rest of it—the midnight prowler, Felix Messenger's visits and his suggestion that she impersonate Miss Kitty, the money and the notebook under the floor, as well as Katherine's engagement to Stanley Duggan—he became even more emphatic that she should leave things be, and not get swept up by forces beyond her control.

'I'm shocked that my own sister would be involved in that,' he said, frowning and shaking his head. 'Katherine was playing a deadly game. Customs was after her too. It looks like you were right. Someone killed her. And that's a good reason not to get involved. What did Reggie say? He didn't encourage you?'

'He didn't commit himself, one way or the other,' she admitted. She looked at him defiantly. 'I have to keep going with this, Dusty. I have to know.'

Despite his pleas and arguments to rethink her intention, he could not convince her.

He ran his fingers through his hair. 'You can't pretend to be Miss Kitty. You're nothing like her. And you have no idea what you're getting yourself into. If you are so pig-headed, then you need to see something. Perhaps it will make you see sense. Put on your coat and come with me.'

She followed him out to the car. It was getting dark, and a thin mist of drizzle was settling over the laneways of Richmond.

Dusty drove in silence up Tanner Street, resisting Ruby's attempts to engage him in conversation. Not even compliments about his Australian Six automobile could distract him. It was clear to her that he was serious about making her change her mind, but where he was taking her was a mystery.

Crossing into Wellington Parade, Ruby realised that Melbourne was their destination and, sure enough, Dusty made the turn into Spring Street, heading north.

'Come on, Dusty,' she pleaded, 'this isn't like you. Tell me what this is about.'

Her brother remained tight-lipped until they reached Lonsdale Street.

'If you want to play games, you may as well see a sample of what you're going to face. Welcome to "Little Lon."'

'This is a notorious red-light area, Ruby. Full of vice, poverty, and crime. It was home to Madame Brussels and her brothels late last century. *Truth* called her the "Queen of Harlotry." There are still streetwalkers here, but a lot have moved to The Narrows, where Squizzy Taylor holds court. But you can still find gambling, cocaine, illegal liquor, and opium dens if you want to.'

The rain was steady now, giving the area a slimy, washed-out look. Water poured down rusting gutters, pooling between the bluestones, streaming into the drains. They cruised past neglected timber and brick cottages, squalid shopfronts, and boot factories, and did a circuit of the block bounded by Lonsdale, Exhibition, La Trobe, and Spring Streets.

The pungent smell of onions, urine, and beer wafted in through the open window. Filthy laneways were strewn with timber crates, broken bottles, and rubbish. Cats prowled, slinking along the edges of the alleys, sniffing out vermin. Two prostitutes, in cheap and gaudy dresses, strutted past, drenched and bedraggled, but oblivious to the falling rain. One of them made a lewd sign at Ruby, then laughed loudly at her reaction. In an alley, two men were fighting, watched on by a motley collection of louts and drunks, swearing and yelling abuse and encouragement. An old man was propped up in a doorway, sitting on a wooden crate, an empty gin bottle in his lap, while an opportunistic street urchin, dressed in a worn and patched coat, checked his pockets for coins. A door opened, and a man and a woman, drug-addled, staggered out into the feeble light of a street lamp, looking dazed and confused.

Dusty pulled into the curb and faced her. 'It's not safe here. Don't you understand? And it will be worse in Fitzroy. These people were raised on the street. They know it. They know how to survive here. You don't. You'd be like a newborn babe in the jungle if you go there. I'll be reading about you in the obituaries.'

'It's you who don't understand, Dusty. I need to find out what happened to Katherine.'

'I didn't expect you to be so naïve, Ruby. Let the police do it.'

'You know they don't care.'

Dusty shook his head. 'Nobody will be able to help you if you end up in the clutches of the gangs. Or any private collectors that she might have cheated. Please, don't do this.'

The drive home was silent, the tension between them palpable. And when Dusty walked her up to the front door, he held her by both her arms and looked into her eyes, his face troubled.

'You're determined, aren't you.' It wasn't a question, but a statement of fact. 'I'll be moving in for a little while. Tomorrow, in fact. If you won't see sense, then I'll try to protect you. But I don't approve of this.'

She had never had to endure the censure of her brother before. He had left her without his usual farewell hug and kiss on the cheek.

If that was not bad enough, worse was to come.

Chapter Eighteen

I t was after six o'clock, two nights later, when Ruby stepped down from the train at Richmond railway station. She turned up the collar of her coat and walked down the ramp. It had been a busy day at work, requiring her to catch up on a backlog of orders from the previous month. The sun had set, and the street lights reflected a feeble glow off the wet concrete roads. As she strolled home, she wondered how much longer she would have to endure Dusty's stony silence. He was still angry with her, refusing to discuss the rights or wrongs of her course of action. In many ways, it stung her more than if they had argued.

As she approached her house, she saw that the porch light was on. Dusty must be home, she thought. Perhaps tonight, relations between them might thaw a little after a good dinner.

When she opened the gate, she was surprised to see a man standing next to the front door. It was John Gascoigne in his trademark black suit and white shirt. She quickened her pace.

'Where's Dusty?' she asked, glancing past him through the open front door.

'There's been an incident,' he said, removing his hat. 'Your brother's been assaulted.'

Ruby rushed past him into the house, Gascoigne following her.

'Where is he? What happened?'

'He's not here. An ambulance took him to hospital. I found him unconscious in the hallway. Someone knocked him out.'

The sitting room was a mess. The couch had been upended, and the underside of the upholstery ripped open, the stuffing strewn across the floor. The drawers of the sideboard had been systematically pulled out, spilling their contents. Books lay open on the rug, while soot from the fireplace spotted the polished boards. A large vase had been smashed against the brick hearth.

Tears pricked Ruby's eyes as she picked her way amongst the wreckage of the once beautifully decorated living room. She wiped them away with her handkerchief, then went into the bedroom. The mattress had been pushed off the bed; the wardrobe shifted from the wall; her clothes lying in a tangle on the floor.

Gascoigne's voice came from behind her. 'They were looking for something.'

She turned and nodded. 'But there's nothing to find.'

In the spare room, the thief had been similarly thorough. Letters, documents, and bills from the rolltop desk were scattered across the floorboards. Katherine's dresses had been pushed to one side, exposing the back of the wardrobe.

'A common thief. Looking for money and jewellery, Miss Rhodes. Thank God you weren't home.'

'But Dusty was. Where is he?'

'The Melbourne Hospital. I've called the police already, so you don't have to worry about that tonight.'

She smiled at him weakly. 'I am grateful. Thank you.'

'Do you notice anything missing?'

'I can't tell you yet. It's such a mess.'

'Do you think they were after something in particular?'

Ruby glanced Gascoigne's way. 'Why do you ask?'

'I've been thinking about Katherine. She told me that she was keeping a diary. I was wondering if it might hold incriminating evidence against the people she dealt with.'

'A diary? No, I haven't found one.'

Gascoigne nodded. 'Can I help you clean up?'

'I'll do it tomorrow. I need to see Dusty.'

85

'I'll take you.'

'No need. His car is outside, so I'll drive there myself.'

'Do you want me to come?'

'You've done enough, Mr Gascoigne.'

'John. Call me John. By the way, the thief got in through a side window. I've fixed it as best I could, while I was waiting for you to come home. You should be safe until you get it repaired properly.'

'I'm very grateful. For everything.' She paused. 'You never told me. Why were you here?'

'I decided to come and see you after work; see how you were settling in. You're Katherine's sister, after all.' He ran his hand through his mane of grey hair. 'It was around five o'clock when I got here, and then I realised that the front door was open. I went in and found your brother lying on the floor. I'm glad I came when I did, otherwise—'

'I hate to think. I must be on my way, John. Thank you again. I'll contact you soon.'

Gascoigne shook her hand. 'Look after yourself. If there's anything I can do, let me know.'

Ruby watched him get into his automobile and drive away, then went into the spare room and checked under the loose boards. The box was still in place.

With one last look at the house, she locked the front door, then climbed into Dusty's Australian Six and pressed her foot on the starter button.

Chapter Nineteen

Misfortune had not finished with Ruby Rhodes, for a third turn of events was waiting for her the next afternoon, which would set her on a course that would change her life irrevocably.

It had been the most terrible day, one which had put her emotions into a spin. After a short visit to the hospital, where Dusty lay unconscious, she had gone to work, then attended an interview with the police. She had no idea who might have broken into the house and attacked her brother, she told them. The thought crossed her mind that she should share with them her fears about Katherine's involvement with the gangs, but she kept that to herself, given that she had no firm evidence that it was the reason for the attempted burglary.

Returning to the hospital later that afternoon, she stopped at the kiosk, realising that she hadn't eaten all day, and bought a bun and a cup of tea from one of the volunteers. Then she climbed the stairs to the third floor and checked in at the nurses' station, where she was directed to Dusty's new ward on one of the balconies overlooking the street.

'We're heavily overcrowded,' said the nurse apologetically, 'and Mr Rhodes is no longer regarded as being in danger. He regained consciousness earlier this afternoon. He's now sleeping.'

Dusty was sharing the balcony with other patients, their beds lined up with their feet facing out towards the balcony rail. Blinds had been set up to give them protection from the wind and weather, but Ruby thought the conditions were terrible. Her brother deserved better, but there was nothing she could do about it. As it was, Dusty was not aware of his changed circumstances and slept soundly while she sat by his bedside.

As Ruby watched over him, she felt remorse that he should be here, in hospital. If she had been willing to listen to reason, he would never have moved into her home, feeling that it was his duty to protect her. And, as such, he would not have been targeted by the burglar. A daytime robbery, when the occupant was supposed to have been at work, and the house was empty, was what the thief had anticipated, not the unexpected arrival of her brother. It was her fault. She felt her resolution wavering as to whether she should track down Katherine's killer.

Ruby leaned over and kissed Dusty on the cheek. 'I love you,' she whispered. 'I'll see you tomorrow.'

* * *

Later, as she parked the Australian Six outside her house, she heard a tap on the window. She groaned at the sight of Felix Messenger, in his customary brown suit, standing beside the car.

'I'm tired,' she said, as she stepped onto the road and walked around the rear of the automobile, Messenger following her.

'We need to talk,' he said enigmatically.

'Then you'll have to talk now on the street. I'm not letting you into my house.'

'I heard it was broken into. Your brother was attacked when he came home early.'

She nodded, trying to avoid prolonging the conversation. It made her weary thinking about it.

Messenger plied her with questions. What were they looking for? Had she found the proof that her sister was consorting with criminals? Did she notice anything missing?

'I have no idea,' she replied. 'Nothing seems to have been taken. Please leave me alone. I have to clean up the house.'

He wasn't finished. 'That can wait. Do you still plan to go through with our agreement to expose your sister's clients?'

She stopped and stared at him, her face blank. 'What agreement?'

He was becoming increasingly agitated. 'Her list. Have you found the list?' he insisted.

She was tempted to go inside and give him the notebook, so that he might leave her alone, but something about his manner provoked her. 'I don't know of any such list. And, if I did, why should I help you?'

Messenger shook his finger at her, his face flushed. 'Because I have proof, unassailable proof, that your sister was up to her neck in the black market, selling antiquities to the highest bidder. You have refused to help me, so you leave me with no choice. I will bring your non-compliance to the attention of my bosses and make sure that your sister's name is dragged through the gutter. I will make sure that the press hears about her dirty dealings, mixing with the scum of Melbourne society and defrauding the Commonwealth of thousands of pounds. You and your brother will suffer by association.'

She stared at him in horror. 'How dare you threaten me!'

Messenger's voice was thick with menace. 'I will do whatever it takes to rid this country of the carrion crows that feast off it. If someone suffers in the execution of my duty, that is not my problem.'

Ruby's eyes glistened with tears. 'You can't do this to me and Dusty. We've done nothing wrong.'

He took a step forward. 'All I need are the names of those who are breaking the law. Don't you understand plain English?'

She recoiled. 'There is no list, so how can I give you names?'

'You're the spitting image of your sister. No one seems to know she's dead, so take on her identity. Pretend to be Miss Kitty.'

'That's ridiculous. I'd be putting myself in danger. Why can't *you* find them?'

'My dear little lady,' he spluttered. 'I would never get past the front door. I am with His Majesty's Customs Department. I am an officer of the King.'

'You intend to blacken my dead sister's reputation when she can't defend herself?'

'That's right. At last, you're starting to understand. It's the only way to stop the trade and put these people in prison, where they belong.'

He leaned forward, his face inches from hers, and held out a card. 'Here is my telephone number. You have two weeks to think about this. If I don't hear from you, you know what to expect. I will ruin you. You *and* your brother. That I can promise you.'

Chapter Twenty

With an eclectic array of interests, from phrenology, to taxidermy, to natural history and anatomy, Dr Silas Bacon was a most unusual man, analytical and detached in his demeanour. He was, in his own words, a scientist and, as such, valued rationality and logic in his dealings with the human race. In his long career, he had been a medical doctor, a wax modeller and, in his later years, an administrator of the Melbourne Museum, whose employment he had left just two years before.

Surprisingly, perhaps, Silas had been instrumental in solving the Death Mask Murders case, along with Reggie da Costa, although there had been little recognition of this fact. But this was not something that bothered Silas, for he was not a vain man or one who sought publicity. He was content with his lot in life, as long as he could pursue his hobbies.

His most recent obsession was archaeology, fostered by the excavations of tombs in Egypt and the need for the museum's collection to reflect the public's enthusiasm for all things Egyptian.

In appearance, Silas was unusual as well, with his big ears and broad forehead, which were at odds with his slight build. He lived in a small terrace house in Napier Street, Fitzroy, between the footwear factory and the Presbyterian Church.

When Ruby Rhodes and Reggie da Costa visited that Sunday, Silas was sitting in the kitchen with his nose in a journal. He had quite forgotten that he was expecting visitors, and looked up, surprised, when he heard the knock on the door.

'Reggie, my friend,' he said, greeting him. 'This is such a pleasure.'

'It's been a while, Silas. I'd like you to meet a friend of mine, Miss Rhodes.'

Bacon nodded at her. 'You've interrupted me reading a most interesting article in the latest issue of *The Journal of Egyptian Archaeology*. It's about the mouse in Egyptian medicine. It appears that the Ancient Egyptians believed that the mouse was a spontaneous product of the mud after each Nile inundation. Fascinating.'

'Indeed,' replied Reggie, raising an eyebrow. 'I hope that you can spare us a few moments. We've come here on a quest for information, which I'm sure you can provide.'

Silas looked from one to the other. 'If I can. Follow me.'

Once they were seated around the kitchen table, Reggie began. 'It concerns Miss Rhodes' twin sister. She worked at the Melbourne Museum. Perhaps you knew her? Katherine Rhodes.'

Silas shook his head. 'I retired in March 1923. She would have been under the direction of my successor, Mr Gascoigne. He was appointed in February 1923. There was a brief crossover period when I instructed him in the Melbourne Museum's procedures and practices. Miss Rhodes must have been employed after that.'

'I'm surprised that you retired, Silas,' said Reggie. 'You loved your job.'

'I did. However, the public was obsessed with Egyptian archaeology, which meant that the museum had to alter its focus away from natural history. I studied hard and tried to acquire the requisite knowledge. In fact, I thought things were going well until the museum's administrators decided to appoint Mr Gascoigne. His credentials eclipsed mine. He'd worked under Sir Jeffrey Smythe at the British Museum, and was looking for a position in Australia. Unfortunately, the board decided it was time for me to go.'

'I'm sorry to hear that, Dr Bacon,' commented Ruby, glancing at the magazine open on the table. 'It seems that you haven't lost your interest in Ancient Egypt.'

'Indeed, no.' Silas smiled, tapping the journal with a long thin finger. 'I've made a precise study of the contents of Tutankhamun's tomb, the work of Howard Carter and Lord Carnarvon, and Ancient Egyptian archaeology and mythology in general.' He gave a disparaging smile. 'As with most things, I've become obsessed.

'Before we continue, perhaps I could offer you some cake and tea?'

Shortly after, Silas sat back, observing his two guests. 'Now, what brings you here today?'

Reggie put aside his cup and saucer. 'As I said, it concerns Ruby's sister, Katherine. It appears that Miss Rhodes was involved in a smuggling operation, using the museum as a front.'

The little man frowned. 'That would never have happened in my day. How do you know this?'

Ruby spoke up. 'I've come into possession of a notebook. It details transactions. It lists the goods and their purchasers. On face value, it appears that my sister was selling antiquities to private collectors. Large amounts of money were involved.'

'Why have you come to me? This is police business. I can't help you with that.'

'Ruby has some jewellery that belonged to her sister. I think it might be valuable,' Reggie explained. 'Would you mind taking a look at it?'

Silas shook his head. 'I am not a jeweller.'

Reggie leaned forward. 'It's not ordinary jewellery, Silas.'

'Please, take a look, Dr Bacon.' Ruby took the jewellery box from her bag and lay the contents on the table.

'Goodness me,' said Silas, staring at the array in front of him. 'I'll need my loupe and scales.'

Crossing the room, he took a small black magnifying glass from a box on the shelf above the stove, and a set of brass scales from the window ledge, and placed them on the table in front of him. He fitted the magnifier against his right eye socket and picked up the snake-like bangle, studying it from different angles. Silently, he laid it on the scales and adjusted the weights, then gently placed the bangle back on the table. He turned his attention to the pharaoh's head pendant, which was suspended from a necklace of turquoise and glass beads. Under the magnifier, he inspected the gemstones carefully, then scrutinised the intricate carving of the pendant. As before, he weighed it then placed it beside the bangle.

He grunted. 'Interesting.'

Next was an anklet made of glistening black and white beads, inlaid with diamond-shaped insets of gold. Ruby and Reggie watched on as Silas examined it meticulously.

He removed the eyeglass. 'This looks like alabaster and obsidian,' he said. 'Some of it is cloisonné.'

He bounced it gently in his hand, nodded his head as if confirming a thought, then sat it on the scales. As with the others, he put it aside.

A pair of golden earrings, engraved with a cartouche, received only a passing glance.

'Costume jewellery.'

Lastly, Silas unwrapped the scarab beetle brooch from its tissue paper. He inserted the magnifier and studied the object. He looked up, his face aghast. The loupe dropped into his lap.

'My goodness.'

The moment passed; Silas's analytical and calm gaze was restored. He replaced the magnifier and picked up the brooch again, treating it with a reverence that had been missing with the others. He turned it over, examining the gems and their settings, the inscriptions on the metal, and the overall design. Silas shook his head, removed the loupe, and placed the brooch gently on the set of scales, adjusting the weights till they were in balance.

He raised his eyes to his companions, noting the expectant looks on their faces.

'Well?' asked Reggie.

'The pick of the bunch. An incredible piece.' He took it up again and held it up to the light. 'Pectoral scarab. Gold, lapis lazuli, and carnelian, depicting the scarab beetle, Kheperu, the solar disk, Ra, and the crescent, Neb.'

Ruby shook her head. 'What does that mean?'

Silas looked at Ruby steadily. 'Together they form Tutankhamun's throne name, Nebkheperura.'

Ruby was stunned. 'Are you saying that it's real?'

'If I'm not wrong, your brooch dates from around 1300 B.C. The bangles. The necklace. The anklet. All from Ancient Egyptian times. I couldn't even guess what they would be worth.'

'I thought so,' said Reggie, smoothing his moustache. 'I know these things. And if Katherine stole the brooch from a client, that would be motivation enough to kill her.'

Ruby sat back in shock, looking from Reggie to Silas. 'What was Katherine involved in?'

Silas replaced the brooch and steepled his fingers in front of his face. 'At a guess, I'd say Reggie is right. Your sister was involved in smuggling Egyptian antiquities.' He sat back. 'I'll make us a second cup of tea, and then I'll tell you how this situation came to be.'

Seated at the kitchen table again, Silas explained how the changes to the laws covering excavations of Egyptian tombs had led to a trade in antiquities, illegal in the eyes of the Egyptian government. Nine months before the discovery of King Tutankhamun's tomb in 1922, Egypt had gained independence from the United Kingdom, and proceeded to take control over existing antiquities laws.

'It had a devastating effect on archaeologists like Howard Carter and those who funded the excavations, such as Lord Carnarvon. The government tore up the agreement that said they would split the finds fifty-fifty with the excavator. Egypt claimed it all. Nothing was to leave the country, at least not legally, without their permission.

'There was still enthusiasm worldwide. Even Australia has its own branch of the Egypt Exploration Society. They contributed funds to excavate Tell el-Amarna. That's where the Pharaoh Akhenaten and his queen, Nefertiti, were buried.'

Reggie nodded. 'Parents of King Tut.'

'Quite right,' agreed Silas. 'The Society hoped that some of the treasures from the tombs would find their way to Sydney. Two cases of antiquities did arrive this month. You could say they were disappointed. The sole of a sandal, a bronze needle, a fragment of pottery. You understand? Most of the important relics were seized by the Egyptian Department of Antiquities.'

Ruby shook her head in dismay. 'So, what you're saying is that the actions of the Egyptian government brought about a black market in antiquities, and my sister took advantage of this?'

'That's what it looks like.' Silas sipped the last of his tea. 'There are private collectors who will pay anything to get their hands on select pieces from the tombs. I know that from experience. When I was at the museum, I received some improper communications from people asking for my "cooperation." Of course, I destroyed their letters. These same people may have reached out to your sister who, I regret to say, was not as ethical as one might hope for. This is pure speculation, of course, something I usually abhor.'

'But it makes sense,' added Reggie.

Ruby nodded her head. 'Mr Messenger from Customs said as much. He said she was mixing with the wrong people: gangs and collectors. Avoiding paying duty on imports. A black market in antiquities.'

'Do you mind me asking a question, Miss Rhodes? You speak of your sister in the past tense. Am I to assume that she has died?'

'Very perceptive, Dr Bacon. You see, Katherine was killed on New Year's Eve. The police believe it was an accident, but I know better now.'

'One has to wonder how she came into possession of this jewellery,' said Reggie. 'Perhaps she cheated some of these private collectors out of their treasures. And then she went into hiding when she thought they might catch up with her.'

'I have to ask,' said Silas. 'Did Mr Gascoigne know about this?'

'I've spoken to him. He says that he found out after she died,' explained Ruby.

Silas put his cup down. 'I wonder. You have priceless antiquities in your possession, Miss Rhodes. Treasures that belong to the Egyptian people.'

'What should I do?' she asked him.

'Take them to the police,' he replied.

'But then, I'll have to explain everything. Katherine's role in this. And that I'm her twin sister.'

'I can understand your reluctance to reveal her criminal activities,' said Reggie. 'But what does it matter if people know that you're Katherine's twin?'

She stared at Silas, then at Reggie. 'You see, that way, I'll never find out who killed her.'

'How would you anyway?' asked Reggie, watching her closely.

'Felix Messenger had this idea. Pretend I'm Katherine and find her killer.'

Silas gaped at the suggestion. Reggie, in contrast, showed no such misgiving. He smiled, nodded, and smoothed his moustache. 'A stroke of genius. And I'm just the man to help you.'

Chapter Twenty-One

In the waiting room of the Melbourne Hospital later that day, Ruby put her visit to Dr Silas Bacon out of her mind and mulled over what the doctor had just told her. It would be a few days before they could be sure that Dusty would fully recover, but there were signs of improvement. He was awake and responding to stimuli, aware of where he was and what had happened to him. A short visit would be allowed, as long as Ruby did not tire him out.

'You can go in, Miss Rhodes.'

She followed the nurse out onto the balcony. Dusty sat propped up against the pillows, his face pale, his fair hair, thick and tousled. A bandage was wrapped around his head. He opened his eyes and gave her a feeble smile. Ruby took his hand and squeezed it.

'How are you?' she asked.

Dusty sighed. 'A bit groggy.'

'This is awful, being out here.'

'I don't mind it. When the blind is up, you have something to look at, instead of a wall. And the fresh air is good for you.'

'Still—'

'Don't worry about me.'

She shrugged her shoulders, unconvinced. 'Do you remember anything?'

'Not much. I came home early to pick up some notes. For a report. I went in and saw stuff on the floor. And then something hit me. That's all I know. He must have been behind the door.'

'You didn't see anyone?'

'No.'

Her eyes filled with tears. 'I'm so sorry, Dusty. This is my fault. I should have talked you out of moving in with me.' Her voice broke. 'I could have lost you.'

Dusty squeezed her hand. 'It was my decision. By the way, how did I get here?'

'It was John Gascoigne's doing. He found you and called an ambulance. Lucky that he turned up when he did.'

'I underestimated him.' He fixed Ruby with a weary look. 'I assume that you're leaving this Katherine business alone now?'

'We'll talk about it another time. My focus is on seeing you get better.' She kissed him on the forehead. 'You need to rest. I should go.'

Dusty rallied, despite his fatigue. 'Speak to Reggie. Tell him what's happened. Ask him from me if he'll keep an eye on—'

As he spoke, his eyes rolled up into his head, and he began to convulse.

'Nurse! Someone help him!'

* * *

It was hours later that Ruby left the hospital, exhausted. She had been told to stay in the waiting room while the doctors worked on him. Finally, a doctor approached her.

'Your brother has stabilised,' he told her. 'He'll need to be moved so that we can keep him under close observation. His stay with us will be longer than we planned. The danger has passed, though, we believe.'

'Can I see him again?'

'One last look. You are still welcome to visit him tomorrow, a brief visit, but please don't upset him in any way. Keep him calm.'

'Of course. Is there a chance that you may have to operate?'

'If the convulsions occur again, we may have to look at the options. Let's hope that won't be necessary. He sustained a small hairline fracture of the skull in the attack. It may have caused a superficial bleed to the brain, hence the seizures. However, medication seems to have done the trick.'

She was allowed a couple of minutes with Dusty before she left. The fairness of his hair accentuated the pallor of his face, but he looked to be in a restful sleep, and his breathing was regular. She sat next to his bed and took his hand in hers.

'I'm sorry, Dusty, but I can't give this up. I'll find Katherine's killer, and I'll make sure that whoever did this to you will be brought to justice too.'

Chapter Twenty-Two

Determined to make a name for himself as a crime reporter, Reggie had immersed himself in Melbourne's underworld, studying the players that made up the gangs, making contacts within the police, political parties, union leaders, and criminal classes. In some respects, he was not unlike the crime bosses themselves. Horace Striker, Squizzy Taylor, Long Harry Slater, and Henry Stokes needed a network of informants and associates, as he did. In their case, it was to avoid prosecution and expand their empires, whereas Reggie was interested in obtaining insider information that would flesh out his stories.

Intrigued by Ruby's suggestion that she would assume her sister's identity in order to track down Katherine's killer, Reggie realised that his association with Melbourne's gang leaders could be useful. Over the next few days, he considered the strategies that would be required to facilitate Ruby's transformation into Miss Kitty. She would need a mentor, he told her on the telephone, someone who would smooth her way into the murky social milieu of her twin sister.

He met Ruby after work one day, outside Smith and Sons. As they strolled down Swanston Street towards the railway station, he outlined his plan to her.

'I'm an acquaintance of Horace Striker,' he explained. 'I believe that he's the logical person for you to contact.'

'But he's a gangster,' Ruby protested. 'He's in all the papers.'

'I understand your reluctance, but it's crucial that you have someone from that world to ease you in. Remember that Katherine was engaged to his nephew. If anyone is going to look kindly on your quest, it will be Striker. But, if I introduce you to him, it will be up to you to gain his trust. It won't be easy. You need to give him a reason to help you find your sister's killer, because you can't do this without his help. He will give you access to the clubs she attended and the people she knew.'

'Will you come with me to these places?'

'If I can, I will, but I think you should rely on Striker first. Only he can give your impersonation legitimacy. Miss Kitty was Stanley's fiancé, so Horace knew her well. If he doesn't support you, you may as well forget this little charade, because you will be putting yourself in danger otherwise.'

Ruby had looked at him, her eyes wide. 'I never thought of that. I thought that I could turn up looking like her and things would be fine.'

Reggie shook his head. 'You told me that you haven't seen Katherine for ten years. You were children then. You don't know how she lived her life, whom she liked, whom she hated, what she did. You have a wardrobe of clothes, nothing more. You need someone who knew her well. Someone like Horace Striker. If I know anything about him, I know that he is perceptive. He looks for strengths and weaknesses in people and knows what makes them tick. Don't ever underestimate him. I did once, and I paid the price. If he says something, he means it.'

'Do you think I can do this?'

'I don't know, but I admire your spirit. Not a lot of women would do what you're planning on doing. It's admirable.' His voice softened. 'One thing, Ruby. If you can't win over Striker, you should forget about this. It's a deadly game that you'll be playing.'

* * *

The following Sunday, Reggie parked the Hupmobile in Shamrock Street, a few houses down from Horace Striker's residence.

'Ready?' he asked her.

She nodded, trying not to show her nervousness. 'As ready as I ever will be.'

'Good girl. Have you thought about what you're going to say to him?'

'I have.'

'Let's go then.'

Approaching the house, Ruby was aware of being watched. The curtain shifted, and a thin man, with a bloodless face and red, cropped hair, emerged from the doorway. He took one look at the crime reporter and then inspected Ruby with cool, green eyes.

'Wait here,' he said, in a broad Scottish accent. The door closed behind him.

* * *

Horace Striker was sitting at his desk in his office, contemplating the future. It had taken him nearly six months to overcome the grief and rage he felt after his nephew's murder. But now he was ready to move on and reassert himself in Melbourne's underworld.

Without Stanley, Horace's succession plan was in disarray. Stanley Duggan had been his protégé and heir apparent. Striker had invested a lot of time and energy into his nephew's education. He had taught him much: how to read people and judge the truth or falsehood of the claims they made; how to deal with those who challenged him; how to punish those who let him down or double-crossed him; how to use his influence to ensure that decisions—from councils, lawmakers, and politicians—feathered his rapidly growing nest; how to insure himself against police interference. And, most importantly, Uncle Horace showed Stanley that everyone was susceptible to bribery or blackmail. Everyone had something to hide, if you looked closely enough. Everyone could be bought off.

News of Stanley's death had filled him with despair and sorrow, as well as an overriding desire to wreak revenge on the man who had plunged a knife into his nephew's back. His response was rapid. His minions were sent out into the brothels, gambling dens, and liquor shops of Melbourne, their ears pricked for whispers of who had done the deed. They leaned on sources, threatened and cajoled, but the overwhelming response was silence and, in particular, shock that anyone could be so foolish as to provoke Horace Striker.

As time passed, Horace bunkered down in his Shamrock Street premises, anger eating away at him. The crimson velvet curtains, the flocked wallpaper, and the heavy mahogany furniture seemed to weigh him down and made him feel claustrophobic. It was dark and depressing. At the suggestion of one of his sisters, he decided to redecorate. It would lift his spirits and give him a fresh start, she said. Art Deco was the latest thing. It was the 1920s, after all.

Out went the trappings of yesteryear, Victorian England, and the War. In came imported furniture from France, made of burl walnut and maple, inlaid with ivory, brass, and mother-of-pearl, as well as ornaments and wall posters that complemented the new look. The only concession Horace made to the past was to keep his desk. It was a magnificent piece of mahogany with a leather top, solid and substantial. It gave the message that, although Striker was forging a new path, he still had ties to the past.

His surroundings inspired him. Now was the time to expand into new revenue sources, he decided. Cocaine, prostitution, alcohol, and gambling were lucrative, but Horace wanted to be where the power really was: in government. Imagine how much easier things would be if he could influence the lawmakers by becoming one of them himself, or by installing a proxy who would do his bidding? He already had contacts within political ranks and amongst the authorities who enforced the laws. But if he could inveigle his way in, the tentacles of his power would extend far beyond what they did now. For the first time in months, a smile spread slowly across his face.

The smile faded. Stanley was not there to share his vision for the future. He looked around him, and his eyes narrowed. His fists clenched subconsciously. The decor of his residence might have changed, but there was one thing that never would: his desire to inflict a slow and agonisingly painful death on the person who had taken his nephew's life. It would be a long and excruciating journey to the Gates of Hell, of that, he would make certain.

His reverie was interrupted by a knock at the door.

CHAPTER TWENTY-TWO

'Come in.'

The pale-faced Scot, known as Hare, stood in the doorway. 'Mr Striker. Reggie da Costa is outside with a lady. They want to see you.'

Striker raised an eyebrow. 'You look like you've seen a ghost.'

'I think you'll feel the same way, sir.'

* * *

Shortly after, Hare stood at the door, beckoning for Ruby and Reggie to come inside. Too late now to change your mind, Ruby told herself. She smoothed down the front of her sensible green dress and followed him in.

Horace Striker was nothing like what Ruby expected. Tall, lean, clean-shaven, with grey streaked hair, recently trimmed. He was well-dressed, in a sharply-cut grey suit and shiny two-tone shoes. His face was strong, with an aquiline nose, piercing brown eyes, and a long face, with high cheekbones. For his age, which she estimated to be early fifties, he was in good shape and was quite handsome, if in a rather daunting way.

He stood in front of his desk, ignoring Reggie, making it obvious that he was appraising her. Ruby felt that it was some sort of test, designed to assert his authority and ascertain the character of the person with whom he was dealing. She was determined to withstand his gaze, even though inside, she was quaking with fear. As the seconds ticked by, she kept her nerve and felt relieved when he finally spoke.

'I don't believe we've met.' He had a deep, sonorous voice.

'I'm Ruby Rhodes, Mr Striker. Katherine's twin sister.'

There was the slightest raising of one of his eyebrows.

'Please sit down, Miss Rhodes.' He motioned to a chair. 'You too, Reggie.'

'Thank you for seeing me,' she said.

Striker paused, then sat on the edge of his desk, staring down at her. He shifted his gaze to Reggie and leaned down towards him.

'You haven't lost your sense of style. Nice suit,' he commented, rubbing the material of Reggie's collar between his fingers.

Reggie didn't blink. 'Zink and Sons. Oxford Street, Sydney.'

The reporter was doing his best to appear nonchalant, but Ruby sensed that he was uncomfortable under Striker's gaze.

The gangster sat back. 'I saw you at my club recently. The Stockade. You looked like you were enjoying yourself.'

'A bit of gambling in good company. Nothing wrong with that.'

'Indeed. It's been a couple of years since we've spoken, hasn't it? That was in a back alley in Richmond, I believe? I hope my boys didn't inflict permanent damage on you?'

Reggie stared back at him, defiantly. 'I was fine, thanks.'

'I'm glad you learned your lesson. I don't like my privacy being invaded by the press. I suggest that you remember that. Now what can I do for you two today?'

'Miss Rhodes needs to chat with you. She has a problem, and I thought that you'd be the best person to see.' He stood, glancing down at Ruby. 'I'll leave you two together. I'll be outside.'

Striker nodded. 'Hare will show you out. Watch yourself, Reggie.'

The door closed behind them. Ruby looked up at Striker, aware that it was now up to her to plead her case. She took a deep breath. 'You knew my sister.'

Horace nodded. 'Your resemblance to Kitty is striking.'

'That's as far as it goes,' she replied. 'Katherine and I shared little apart from our appearance.'

'You're direct, if nothing else.' He scraped his chin with a manicured fingernail. 'Which leads me to the question, Miss Rhodes. Why are you here?'

Ruby had expected the question, and had thought long and hard as to what her answer would be. And now, faced with Horace Striker, she realised that her prepared answer would not suffice. This man would not accept falsehoods and fabrication. Although his speech was uneducated, she could tell that there was a keen intelligence at work. His own appearance was fastidious, his manner calculated and considered, and his environment reflective of a man who appreciated the finer things of life. Indeed, the furnishings of his office surprised her. She had not expected a gangster to

106

like Art Deco. From her reading of the newspapers and her conversations with Dusty, she had assumed that such people had basic tastes and interests: women, gambling, money, and booze. It was clear, within the first few minutes of her time with Horace Striker, that he was a man to be reckoned with.

'I'll try to answer your question, Mr Striker. My reason for seeing you is complicated. I'll begin by saying that I am not satisfied that Katherine died accidentally. Someone killed her. She wrote me a letter before she died, telling me that she was in trouble. I've since discovered that she was smuggling Egyptian antiquities into the country and selling them for inflated profits. I believe it likely that she upset someone in the process, and that she was murdered. I can think of no other answer.'

'You don't believe that she drowned?'

Ruby shook her head.

'Then why not go to the police?'

'I've tried. They're not interested.'

'What do you want from me?'

'I was hoping that you could help me find her killer. I know that she was engaged to your nephew and that he was killed too.'

Striker raised his eyebrows. 'You're different from most people I know. You say what you think.' He reached for a photograph on his desk and turned it so that Ruby could see. 'This was my nephew, Stanley. He was special to me. He was family. Sharp as a tack. I could trust him. In my business, you can't underestimate trust. He was going to inherit all this. But someone snuffed out his life.'

His voice faltered. He put the photograph back in its place, then recovered himself. 'I find it hard to talk about this. My nephew loved your sister. She was high-spirited and enjoyed life. I liked her. Up till today, I didn't know she had an identical twin.'

Striker rubbed his chin. 'Now, what proof do you have that she was deliberately killed, apart from this letter that you're talking about?'

'The day that she drowned, she was seen with a man on St Kilda pier.'

'Interesting, but not conclusive. What else?'

'She could swim, for one. For another, two weeks ago, a prowler was in the laneway behind my house in the early morning. Only ten days ago, my house—her house—was ransacked and my brother bashed.'

'What do you think they were looking for?'

'Maybe some of the items that Katherine had smuggled into the country. Or perhaps the list of her clients that she'd hidden away. It seems that she was leading a double life. On the one hand, she worked at the museum, an administrative assistant, leading an apparently conventional existence. But there was another side to her, a wild side, mixing with people like—'

She hesitated.

'Like me,' said Striker, finishing her sentence for her. 'She may have been wild, but she was never stupid.'

He looked thoughtful. 'Stanley *and* Kitty. It makes me wonder if the two deaths are connected.'

'It's possible,' replied Ruby. 'Rather a coincidence otherwise, their deaths being only four months apart. Perhaps your nephew protected her, and then he was gone? For whatever reason, she gave up her job, one that she loved, and hid herself away. She talked of dying.'

'This is most concerning, Miss Rhodes. She never confided in me that she feared for her life, but then I hardly saw her after Stanley died. She reminded me too much of what I had lost.'

Striker studied her intently. 'You were estranged from your sister?'

Ruby nodded, trying not to be overawed by this intimidating man, who seemed to be able to read her so well. 'She left home at sixteen. Never came back, not even when Mum and Dad died. I haven't seen her for years. You could call it a breakdown in our relationship, one that I'll never get a chance to repair.'

'I sense that you regret something? You want to make up for the past?'

Ruby held his gaze. 'There's truth to that. I don't want to go into details, but I did the wrong thing by Katherine, a long time ago. I owe her. I intend to impersonate her and find her killer. That will go some way to making recompense.'

'You're an interesting woman, Miss Rhodes. I suppose you want me to help you?'

'We are in a similar situation, Mr Striker. We have both lost family members through the actions of others. If there is a link, and we were able to find out who killed Stanley and Katherine, then I think we would find some sort of comfort knowing that the perpetrator is in the hands of the police.'

'I would resolve things differently, Miss Rhodes. In my business, it's important to send out messages.'

'What sort of messages?'

'I think I'll spare you the details.'

Ruby winced. 'Perhaps you should. However, there's something you can help me with, if you decide to do so. If I'm to impersonate Katherine, I can deal with the superficial details of hair and dress. But there's more to her than that. I don't know the places she frequented, or the people she mixed with.'

'You want me to help you become Miss Kitty?'

'In a word, yes. There's so much I don't know about her. What she liked to talk about. What she liked to do. Even her tastes in food and drink. It's nearly ten years since I spent time with her. I have to be able to fool people into believing I'm her.'

She twisted her hands in her lap. 'It's shocking, isn't it? Here I am, her twin sister, admitting that I know nothing about her.'

Striker moved to his chair behind the desk. 'You're a very different personality from Kitty. She was very outgoing. She was impulsive; she enjoyed life. To coin a phrase used by Stanley, she lit up a room.'

'And I don't.'

Striker held up his hands in front of him. 'I meant no criticism. All I'm saying is that her manner was different, and that's something you would need to mimic.'

Ruby nodded, her eyes searching his face. 'I understand the enormity of the task. I still don't know if you're prepared to help me.'

'You interest me, Miss Rhodes, and most people don't. I accept what you tell me on face value, but I feel that you're keeping something from me. No doubt, I'll learn what it is in good time.'

'So, will you help me?'

Striker nodded. 'If it helps find Kitty's killer, then it will be worth it, and the idea of a little distraction in my business is quite attractive. And it might lead to my nephew's murderer, given that I've exhausted all possibilities there. I'll indulge you for now, and we'll see how we go.'

Ruby smiled bleakly, trying to suppress a rising feeling of consternation. 'Thank you. When will we start with my—'

'Education? Why not now?'

'What about Reggie? He's waiting for me.'

'He can leave. I'll get Hare to drive you home.'

* * *

It was a strange and exhausting way to spend a Sunday. Over the next hour, Ruby was given an insight into the life of Melbourne's underworld: the main players, their petty rivalries, their main sources of income, the ethos of each gang, and where they were primarily based. Fortunately, Ruby was blessed with a retentive memory, a characteristic that would come in handy in the future.

Once the subject of the gangs was dealt with, Horace moved on to Miss Kitty, as she was called in his circles.

'Why did she call herself that?' asked Ruby.

Striker paused. 'That's a good question. I think that it gave her status as well as distance. She set herself apart from the people she mixed with by being known as *Miss* Kitty, rather than plain Kitty. If she did lead a double life, as you suggest, then it gave her a separate identity. No one ever referred to her surname. Or called her Katherine. I doubt anyone ever knew it. Apart from me and Stanley.'

It appeared that Mr Striker was a keen student of human nature and was very observant when it came to analysing the personalities and peccadilloes of those he associated with. And that included Katherine. In fact, he told Ruby that he lived by the mantra: 'If you know your enemy as well as you know yourself, you will be victorious.' She found him to be a most unusual gangster.

Burke and Hare, his private bodyguards, were invited in. They participated in the briefing, adding their perspective to a general picture of how Miss Kitty behaved in public, and how she treated people. According to her three tutors, Ruby was fortunate to both look and sound like her sister; the timbre of her voice and her laugh were the same. But the main sticking point was whether Ruby could project Kitty's *joie de vivre*, given that she tended to be reserved and serious.

It was fortunate that Katherine's taste in food and drink was unexceptional, as was Ruby's, although Katherine did love the occasional glass of French champagne. She enjoyed a bet on the horses, loved dancing the Charleston, and preferred the films of Rudolph Valentino, Charlie Chaplin, and Gloria Swanson.

Ruby's first public outing as Miss Kitty, the following Saturday, would be a test of whether she could apply her new-found knowledge of Katherine's mannerisms, interests, and personal habits in a practical way. It was generally agreed that the biggest hurdle would be meeting people that Katherine knew, but whom Ruby did not. Horace promised that he and his men would do their best to cover for her, but warned her that she would have to use her own ingenuity as well. One mistake could be fatal, if others discovered the truth.

Chapter Twenty-Three

It was Saturday night, and Ruby was ready. Soon Horace Striker would be arriving to take her to one of his more salubrious venues in Richmond, a gambling den that catered to the upper classes. It would herald the beginning of her quest to find Katherine's killer and, possibly, Dusty's attacker. Her protector would be a gambler, a drug dealer, a brothel owner, and, most probably, a murderer: in the person of Horace Striker. And yet, strangely, after an afternoon in his company, she felt that she could trust him.

Ruby had found a box of cosmetics in a drawer. Using her sister's photographs as a guide, she had replicated her makeup, after going through the painful process of plucking her eyebrows. Her freckles disappeared beneath an application of foundation and the liberal use of a powder puff, while her lovely green eyes were accentuated after she'd outlined them using a kohl pencil and dusted her eyelids with brown eye shadow, achieving a soft smoky look. In a small dish, she prepared a mix of Vaseline and soot and applied it to her eyelashes, making them appear thicker and longer. Next came rouge, in a warm and glowing tone that gave a flush to her cheeks. The finishing touch was when she shaped her lips into a cupid's bow, as was the fashion, using a bright red lipstick.

She looked through the wide selection of dresses in Katherine's wardrobe, searching for one that might suit the occasion and, more importantly, be more her style. There was a lovely crimson dress, but it had a plunging neckline. A midnight blue frock, with silver buttons and handkerchief hem, was made of the finest silk and would cling too much for her liking. She took a jade green, short-sleeved crepe de chine dress off its coat hanger and held it up against her. The bodice had decorative pin tucks and a low Peter Pan collar. The dropped waist featured a wide belt in the same material, set off by a smart ribbon rosette. The skirt was a wafting mix of draperies that fell to mid-calf. Compared to most of Katherine's dresses, it was relatively modest.

Ruby slipped off her dress and put it on, fastening it at the back. Her figure was almost the same as Katherine's, if slightly less voluptuous, but the dress was an almost perfect fit.

There was still the question of her hair. Judging by the photographs, Katherine had worn hers short, either crimped or in a bob. At this stage, Ruby had no desire to sacrifice her crowning glory to catch a killer. At least, not yet. Instead, she found a silver turban in one of the hat boxes and slid it over her head, pushing her hair up underneath it. Then she slipped on a pair of silver shoes and selected a black chiffon evening coat from the wardrobe.

Ruby took a deep breath and stood in front of the cheval mirror. She drew in a breath. Staring back at her was beautiful, exotic Katherine; dowdy, conventional Ruby was nowhere to be seen. And then it struck her. Cloaking her true self in the garb of another might give her an excuse to be someone different tonight. Maybe, just this once, she could break out of her demure, strait-laced self, and be a little unconventional. She banished the idea. Such thoughts were not helpful, because although she could not be Ruby, she couldn't be anyone else but Miss Kitty.

* * *

As the grandfather clock struck eight, there was a knock on the door.

Hare, dressed impeccably in a black tuxedo, was waiting on the doorstep. Usually expressionless, a glimmer of a smile passed over his face as he took in the changes to her appearance.

'Miss Rhodes. Mr Striker is waiting for you in the car,' he said in his distinct Scottish brogue.

'You look very nice, Mr Hare.'

'Thank you. As do you, Miss Rhodes. And you're welcome to call me Hare.'

Parked on the road, underneath the street lamp, was an immaculate Daimler, deep crimson in colour, with highly polished black mudguards and chrome headlights. In the back was Horace Striker, with Burke up front as the driver. Hare opened the door for Ruby, and she climbed in, then he returned to his seat next to Burke. Striker tapped the window with his cane, and the car pulled away from the curb.

'Miss Rhodes, you look very beautiful.'

'Thank you, Mr Striker,' she said, blushing. She cast her eyes around, keen to change the subject. 'This is a wonderful car.'

Horace smiled. 'Special order with Daimler. King George has something similar. As you may have guessed, I value quality.' He paused, looking at her intently in the half-light. 'Are you feeling nervous?'

Ruby nodded. 'I am. I don't know how convincing I will be.'

'You've certainly passed the test as regards appearance. I would never have guessed that it wasn't Kitty sitting here next to me. I remind you that you have me for support.'

'I appreciate that.'

'Are you prepared to meet some of Miss Kitty's clients tonight? They will be there, and no doubt, they will be eager to see you.'

'I've memorised Katherine's list. I know what they bought, how much they paid, and when the transaction occurred.'

'Excellent. I like people with initiative and attention to detail. But you might still find yourself in danger. If her killer is there, the witness to her death, they will question who you really are. It's a deadly game you're playing, Miss Rhodes.'

He saw her flinch, and he touched her arm. 'However, I seriously doubt whether anyone who attends tonight is responsible for Kitty's death, but you never know. You can stop this now. We can take you home.'

'My brother is in hospital. I might be the one who is attacked next time. I could sell the house and move away, but I ask myself why I should. I'm damned if I'm going to change my life because of them.' Her eyes shone in the darkness.

'Strong words, Miss Rhodes. Good for you.' He looked at her thoughtfully. 'You mentioned your brother yesterday. Would I know him?'

'You might. He's a reporter.'

'Not Dusty Rhodes of *The Truth*?'

'He's now with *The Argus*. Does that bother you?'

'It adds an extra dimension, but I have little to fear from him.'

'I didn't think you would.' She sighed. 'There's one problem that I've been thinking about. What do I say if people ask me where I've been for the past few months?'

'Say that you needed time away from Melbourne to recover from Stanley's death. Say that you were staying at my retreat in Daylesford. It's a farmhouse on ten acres. No one goes there but me.'

'Thank you, Mr Striker.'

'Kitty called me Horace.'

'Thank you, Horace.' She nodded towards the driver's seat. 'What about Burke and Hare? They won't tell anyone what I'm doing?'

Striker's eyes narrowed. 'They know to keep their mouths shut.'

He lapsed into silence, his eyes straight ahead. They turned into a laneway not far from St Ignatius' Church on Richmond Hill, and pulled up outside a nondescript building, the doorway guarded by two burly men. One stepped forward and opened the door.

'Mr Striker.' He almost saluted as the gangster emerged from the Daimler. Horace turned and offered his hand to Ruby.

'Miss Kitty. Welcome to The Stockade.'

She stepped down, then gave Striker a dazzling smile. 'Thank you, Horace. It's nice to be back.'

They walked into the foyer, depositing their coats in a small cloakroom. Ruby took Horace's arm, passing two doormen who held open the impressive double doors that offered entry to the social club.

The noise was what struck Ruby first. Laughter, the babble of voices, the sound of a band playing, and the raucous hubbub of people mingling together were in direct contrast to the silence of the street. A haze of smoke

115

hung in the air, as men sucked on cigarettes while expensively attired women brandished champagne glasses.

Ruby looked at Horace Striker, her eyebrows raised.

'It's always like this,' he said, noting her reaction. 'People wanting to let off steam. They drink too much, laugh too much, gamble too much. But it's money in my pockets so why deprive them of what they enjoy? We do control it. By invitation only. If you become unpleasant, we show you the door.

'Come with me and I'll show you around.'

The building had originally been a warehouse built in the 1870s. Its exposed red brick walls rose over two storeys, with large skylights in the ceiling, the original simplicity of the design expensively remodelled in recent years to create a series of smaller, more intimate rooms off the main one. The central space was dominated by a large bar, behind which five bartenders were serving up cocktails, popping champagne corks, mixing drinks, pouring beers. Men and women, dressed to impress, chattered and laughed, helping themselves to hors d'oeuvres served on silver platters by waiters in black trousers, white shirts, and long black aprons.

Through an archway was a smaller room, where the serious gamblers were playing blackjack and baccarat. In another room, a group of men was playing two-up. Horace led Ruby over to the edge of the circle. The 'well' in the centre of the floor was littered with notes and silver coins. Bets were taken, and the 'spinner' flipped two pennies in the air. 'Tails,' he called, which was greeted with despairing groans or exclamations of delight depending on which side of the coin the players had bet on.

'We can't forget our Australian roots,' remarked Horace.

'Aren't you afraid of being raided?' Ruby asked, her eyes wide as she took in her surroundings.

Striker smiled. 'We have a warning system of electric bells. They ring if the police are on the way.'

Ruby felt a surge of exhilaration and recklessness go through her, like a current of electricity. So, this is why Katherine came here, she thought.

Horace was studying her. 'You feel it, don't you?'

Ruby was silent, but she could feel the flush in her cheeks and the stirring of something within her. Something foreign. Something new.

'You're attracting attention. Men are watching you. Just like they did Kitty.'

She looked around, noticing that heads turned to watch her pass. It was a new experience, and it was intoxicating.

A waiter appeared at her elbow. 'Champagne, Miss Kitty?'

Horace took the glass from him and held it up to the light. 'Note the pale gold colour, Miss Kitty. The finest from France.' He held the glass close to his nose and inhaled gently. 'Aah. The scent of white flowers. A hint of orange peel and wild berries.'

He handed it to her. 'Taste it, my dear.'

'You're not having one?'

He fixed her with his piercing brown eyes. 'I don't drink. Clouds the judgment.'

Ruby attempted to mimic him, but her sense of smell failed her. She took a sip. Tightly knit bubbles exploded in her mouth. 'It's lovely,' she said. 'Delicious,' she added, taking another sip.

'Let's meet some people,' said Striker, leading her back into the main room. 'If you want to dance later, they'll be queuing up for you.' He appraised her. 'Steady on the champagne, Miss Kitty. You'll need your wits about you.'

Ruby took a deep breath and whispered, 'Quite right. Thank you.'

Thereafter came a stream of exquisitely dressed women, hovering in the general direction of Horace Striker, waiting for his eyes to rest on them, overtly eager to gain his attention. Instead of indulging himself, the gangster focused on Ruby, introducing her to judges and lawyers, politicians, businessmen and their wives, property speculators, artists and actors, all intent on paying homage to this man who knew how to give them a good, if illicit, time.

The occasional name was familiar, recalling someone about whom she had read in the papers or heard about in conversation, but so far none had appeared in Katherine's book of clients. Conversation offered no threat to Ruby's assumption of her sister's identity. No one questioned Miss Kitty's reappearance in Horace Striker's club. There was the odd expression of condolence regarding Stanley Duggan's unfortunate demise and concern for her well-being, given they had been 'so close,' but the presence of Striker discouraged anything deeper. There was a query about where she was now living, but Horace circumvented that line of questioning by saying that Kitty was his guest at the moment and would soon find a place of her own.

Ruby felt almost overwhelmed by this side of life, one which she had never experienced before. There were people here with impeccable reputations as pillars of society, and yet they were indulging in pleasures that could only be regarded as unlawful. Illegal gambling and alcohol in the company of fashionable women and men. Who would have thought? And they were perfectly at ease mixing in the company of a man of dubious means, Horace Striker.

And yet, she couldn't deny the ripple of excitement that passed through her as she put aside her conventional self and tasted life on the other side. It was so new to her to be admired for her looks, even though she knew that she was being frivolous. If any of those men who glanced her way saw her in her usual garb, they wouldn't give her a second look. She'd always prided herself on her intellect and her competency, both at school and in her job, rather than wearing fashionable clothes and looking pretty. But, on this night, she had to admit that there was something gratifying about being admired. Was she an intellectual snob for ignoring what she undoubtedly had, but never took advantage of? Why did she deny herself this pleasure?

Since her childhood, she had been locked into being the sensible one, one half of a pair, while the other twin could do what she liked and seemingly get away with it. If Katherine hadn't been there, perhaps she could have spread her wings socially, enjoying casual conversation and letting herself go, just a bit. But Katherine fulfilled that role, and Ruby couldn't compete with her, so she had given up trying.

Tonight, being Miss Kitty required great effort, and Ruby could not relax for a moment. She had to be wary of conversations that might trip her up, take her by surprise and expose her as a fraud. Even with Horace at her side, she was vigilant, avoiding any attempts from those who wanted to get her on her own. A couple of men tried to lure her onto the dance floor, but she was not confident of her abilities to play Katherine on her own as yet, and besides, her dancing skills in that area were still rusty, although Reggie had been encouraging.

Reggie. What would he think of her if he saw her now, she asked herself? Would he recognise her?

Her thoughts were interrupted by Horace. 'We should be getting you home.'

'I'm exhausted, Horace. I think it's time.'

'I'm having a select little event here next Saturday, an Egyptian party. I hope you can come. Unfortunately, I won't be able to take you. I have a business meeting so I'll be late. Ask Reggie to bring you. He knows who's who. And don't forget to wear a costume.'

As they were about to make their departure, a bald-headed, rotund little gentleman, carrying a gold-topped cane and wearing a monocle, made a late entry into the social club. He spied Ruby and made a beeline for her, while Horace Striker was preoccupied elsewhere saying his farewells.

'Miss Kitty. My dear young woman. My wife has been nagging me for weeks. She wants me to thank you for that delightful piece of jewellery that you were able to procure for her.' He looked around him, checking that they were out of earshot. 'In fact, we were wondering if you might—'

'I'd love to help you, I really would. But—'

She realised that someone was standing behind her. It was Hare, seemingly materialising out of thin air.

'Forgive me for interrupting you, Miss Kitty, but the car is ready. Sorry, Mayor Swithins. Mr Striker is very particular about leaving on time.'

'Of course. Of course.'

Ruby smiled sweetly as she recalled the entry in Katherine's notebook. 'I'm glad Mrs Swithins liked the bracelet. It was an excellent piece. I'll look out for something similar.'

Mayor Swithins flushed in appreciation. 'Thank you, Miss Kitty. So kind. I hope that I see you here next week. A gala Egyptian night. It should be fun.' He waved his cane in her direction and hurried off towards the baccarat room.

Ruby sighed with relief. She turned to Hare. 'Thank you so much. You saved me.'

'Pleasure, miss.'

He smiled and beckoned towards the door. 'If you come with me, we'll get you home. Well done, Miss Kitty.'

Chapter Twenty-Four

Reggie had listened intently when Ruby telephoned him at work about Horace's Egyptian party, the extravaganza to be held at The Stockade.

'Striker wants me to take you? Are you sure?'

'He suggested it.'

He ran his fingers through his immaculately coiffed hair and smiled, putting his feet up on his desk and admiring his highly polished, two-tone shoes. 'Do you know how hard it is to get an invitation to an event like that? The best people will be there.'

'You will come?'

'I'd be crazy not to. Would I have to stay with you all the time?' he asked, twisting his moustache.

'Just for a while,' she replied. 'I think I'll be fine. But if I'm not, I'll give you a signal. Is that alright?'

Reggie had replied in the affirmative, his mind moving on to the essentials. 'There's a costume shop around the corner from your office. What if we meet there late this afternoon, an hour before it closes? Could you get off work early? We can choose our outfits and then have supper afterwards. What do you think?'

'Supper?'

She had sounded uncertain. He reassured her. 'Just as friends. Nothing more.'

* * *

A few hours later, Reggie and Ruby spent an enjoyable hour trying on a fantasy of Egyptian attire: clothing, wigs, jewellery, decorative collars, and headpieces. That settled, they went on to a restaurant for a light dinner.

In a smart grey pin-striped suit, with red and blue tie and his collar nipped in by a silver pin, Reggie looked more suited to The Hotel Windsor, than to a casual eatery.

'How is Dusty?' Reggie enquired.

'His memory comes and goes. He is making progress. They say he'll be out of hospital soon.'

'I'll see if I can drop in tomorrow.'

'He'd like that. He admires you very much. Hopefully, he'll be well enough to go back to work soon.'

Reggie watched as the waiter uncorked the bottle of wine and poured a small amount into his glass to taste. He raised it up to the light, sniffed it, then took a sip.

'Very nice.'

The waiter refilled his glass and poured one for Ruby, then brought their meals.

She took a spoonful of chicken soup and smiled. 'Delicious.'

'Tell me about The Stockade. How was it?' asked Reggie, tucking into a Waldorf salad.

'Horace looked after me. He introduced me to people and made sure that I wasn't left to fend for myself. He was very nice.'

Reggie frowned. 'Don't take him too much on face value, Ruby. I've never heard of Striker being a fine upstanding citizen, looking out for women in danger. He's involved in all sorts of dirty dealings. A former detective with the Criminal Investigation Branch summed it up neatly. If Horace decides to have someone killed, he said, he has him thrown off a bridge, breaking both his legs first. Striker likes to send a message not to mess with him. If you are going to continue this relationship, be aware of that. And don't underestimate him. He's an intelligent man, very good at reading people.'

'I'll be careful.'

'I will be there this Saturday, but there may come a time when you're on your own. Don't drop your guard, whatever you do.'

'I appreciate your advice. And for helping me. All I want is to find Katherine's killer, then I'll leave that world behind.' She stirred the soup with her spoon, as if she were making up her mind.

'What is it, Ruby?'

She propped the spoon against the rim of the bowl. 'Can I tell you something strange?'

Reggie pushed aside his plate and leaned back, lighting a cigarette. 'Of course.'

'On Saturday night, I felt different.'

'What do you mean?'

'When my sister died, Dusty asked me what it was like to be a twin. It was hard to explain it to him. Two peas in a pod, my mother used to say. It was like looking at myself in the mirror when we stood facing each other. But, although we were indistinguishable in appearance, we were opposites when it came to character. Katherine was the wild one; I was the serious one. For every personality trait, we offered up opposites. She laughed easily; I didn't. She made friends; I didn't. She loved to go out; I didn't. She dressed to attract attention; I didn't.

'I know you're looking at me now, seeing only a secretary dressed in drab clothes. But that night at The Stockade, I felt different. I was dressed in Miss Kitty's clothes, pretending to be her, and it made me feel freer. Do you know what I mean?'

He shook his head. 'I don't think I do.'

Reggie appraised her. Her lustrous red hair was pulled back into a bun, a few errant strands brushing her ears. Her black dress, with its lace bodice, was presentable, but certainly not stylish, the colour tending to wash her out. But, in her favour, she had been gifted with high cheekbones and pale, flawless skin, despite a few errant freckles. And her eyes were quite beautiful, a lovely shade of green.

Unaware of being observed, she continued. 'You're a confident man. You've never been half of someone, like I have, as a twin. Like two halves of one personality. I had to grow up fast. Look after Dad when Mum died.

Look after Dusty when Dad died. Hold down a good job to bring in some money so that Dusty could finish school. Be the reliable one, not having any fun. You wouldn't know what that was like.'

Reggie blew a smoke ring and watched it dissipate. 'Actually, I do. My father was a gambler. A lady-killer. Spent money like it was water. I had to go to work at thirteen after he left with the maid. My mother was distraught. We were social outcasts, laughing stocks. But we had a friend in Captain Jack. He helped us when no one else would. Got us back on our feet. He found me work as an office boy at *The Argus*. I clawed my way up the ladder by dint of hard work and natural talent.'

He took another puff of his cigarette. 'My father came back two years ago. Claimed he was sick, but I knew better. He fooled Mother, but he couldn't fool me. Fortunately, he left again. And now Mother's met another parasite—'

He stared off into space. His cigarette burned down, and he butted it out. His eyes focused on her again.

'Sorry. I was side-tracked. What were we talking about again?'

'Katherine. Me being a twin.'

'Go on.'

She pushed the soup bowl aside and sipped her wine. 'No, I shouldn't. I'm boring you.'

Reggie shook his head. 'No, you're not. Tell me.'

Ruby frowned. 'Since I moved into Katherine's house, I've thought a lot about the past. How different we were. I suppose I've always seen myself as dull. Katherine did nothing to talk me out of that. She said I was boring.'

Reggie looked at her thoughtfully. 'How old was she when she left? Fifteen or sixteen?' Ruby nodded. 'Children that age can be cruel. Maybe what you're going through is nothing to do with Katherine. Maybe you're re-examining your life. What you want. What you believe. Who you really are. You're at a crossroads.'

'A crossroads. I never thought of it like that.'

'I'll tell you something too. I always wanted the security that money could buy. The nice things like good food and wine. And nice cars and clothes.

Those people who look down their noses at you have never been without money. They don't know what it's like to be poor.'

He leaned forward, his eyes on hers. 'But now I'd like something more than money alone. I still want that, but I'd like someone to share my life with. Maybe I'm getting older.

'I've met women with money, but they don't know me. The real me. The crime reporter who works hard. Who's ambitious. Who came from nothing. That's the essence of who I am.

'You might feel different, but you're still Ruby underneath and from what I've seen, that's a good thing. You seem to be a nice woman. Good company. But you need to enjoy yourself more.'

He laughed.

'What's so funny?' Ruby asked, frowning.

'Just think about it,' he said. 'You said that your life is boring. It's not dull or boring now.' He smiled, seeing her puzzled look. 'Consider. You've inherited a house. You're found out that your sister led a double life, smuggling Egyptian treasures. You're impersonating her. Your circle of friends now includes a gangster. You've met me, of course. Not dull.' He shook his head.

Ruby smiled. 'You have a way with words.'

'It's my job. Your problem is that you think too much. Don't agonise about who you are. Relax.'

'I'll try to take your advice.' She watched him as he refilled their glasses. 'There's something else, if you can take anymore.'

He chuckled. 'I'm listening.'

'Mr Messenger has threatened me. I have to give him the names of Katherine's clients, otherwise he'll blacken my sister's reputation and what's worse, ruin me and Dusty. I don't want to give him the notebook. I don't trust him. Really, Reggie, I don't know what to do.'

'Did you meet any of Katherine's clients at The Stockade?'

'I met Mayor Swithins. His wife was one of her customers.'

Reggie rubbed his chin. 'Maybe there's a way to deal with Messenger. Let me think about it. But, for the moment, Felix shouldn't have it all his own way. This is what I want you to tell him.'

* * *

Five minutes later, Reggie called for the bill and paid it. 'Time to go.'

'Thank you, Reggie. Hopefully, you won't recognise me on Saturday night.'

Reggie grinned. 'Cleopatra on my arm. I look forward to seeing this transformation of yours. I'll pick you up at eight o'clock.'

After dropping Ruby at home, Reggie drove back to his Swan Street house, parking his beloved Hupmobile in the back lane. As he put the key in the door, he chuckled at the prospect of the quiet little church mouse transforming herself into an exotic Egyptian queen.

'Not a chance.'

Chapter Twenty-Five

F elix Messenger sat at his desk in the Customs House, staring at a blank page. There was nothing to write up so far in Katherine Rhodes' slender file, apart from a few cryptic and scant notations on meetings with her sister. He was feeling compromised. It was his sworn duty to root out wrongdoing, prosecute and lock up criminals who contravened the laws of the land, and put fear into the hearts of those who refused to cooperate with him. But it seemed that he had met his match in Ruby Rhodes. Although she had contacted him and reluctantly agreed to carry out his instructions, she had persisted in voicing her expectation that he assist her in practical ways, rather than with pure lip service.

'What do you want?' he had asked her over the telephone.

'Egyptian jewellery,' she had answered.

'Why?'

'I would think that was obvious, Mr Messenger. What can I offer Katherine's clients if you don't give me something to sell? I don't have access to such things. Remember, I'm a secretary, not someone with criminal connections.'

His eyes narrowed. 'I'll have to think about that.'

'You have no choice,' she persisted, annoying him immensely. 'You need evidence if you're planning to raid Katherine's clients and prosecute them.'

He had to admit that she was right, but not to her face. Getting his hands on such treasures was not a problem, because there were seized items—physical evidence against those awaiting prosecution—stored away in the Customs House. No one would miss a pair of earrings or a necklace, he reasoned, given that it took a notoriously long time for cases to come to court.

'And if I do this?' he asked, his mouth a thin line.

'I'll give you the clients' names and addresses, and you can raid their homes and confiscate the goods.'

'What about the money they pay you?'

'I'll hand it over. What else would I do with it?'

Messenger was similarly frustrated when it came to extracting information about Horace Striker. Ruby refused to document who was at Striker's club, where it was located or what illegal activities were being pursued there.

'The police will raid them and shut them down. You lose, and so do I,' she argued. 'I won't find my sister's killer, and these so-called clients of Katherine's will disappear. Really, Mr Messenger, you don't think things through, do you?'

Again, she was right. There would be no prosecutions without her cooperation. There were international gangs out there in Singapore, India, Japan, and Australia that were defrauding Customs, using intermediaries such as Katherine Rhodes. He would never cut off the supply lines, but he could prosecute those who received the goods and, by doing so, deter others.

He had hung up the telephone, angry and frustrated. Four other files lay on his desk. Four other cases, going nowhere. What was happening to his career? He needed a big break if he were going to make his mark with the boss.

Messenger looked up as Jim Claxon strolled into the office. Inwardly, he groaned. The word was out that Claxon was on the cusp of being promoted by the Comptroller-General himself, thus stymying Felix's hopes for advancement.

'Still keeping your hands clean, Messenger? Antiquities? You're an old relic yourself. Right up your alley.'

'It's better than mixing with the dregs of society in an opium den.'

'That's where you're wrong. The Comptroller-General wants the illegal drug trade shut down, and he's prepared to reward those who try. People like me. You watch. I'll be on a train to New South Wales before you can say "Tutankhamun."'

128

Jim Claxon fanned a pile of photographs across Felix's desk. 'Mugshots of our latest arrests. Photographs of seizures. See this one? Opium to the value of one thousand pounds. Where's your seizures? A couple of cheap statuettes, a broken vase?'

Messenger scanned the photographs. 'You're missing one. I heard that one of your own was caught with opium in his possession. That says something about your lot. Ripe for corruption.'

Claxon rebuffed the barb. 'One bad egg. So what?'

'That's why I like to work alone.'

'More likely, no one wants to work with you, Messenger.' Claxon leaned over and rested his hands on the edge of the desk.

Felix stared at them with distaste. 'You're leaving finger marks. Is there something you want to say before you go?'

Claxon scooped up the mugshots then whispered, conspiratorially, 'There's talk about you being transferred to opium. I heard that Oakley is getting impatient with your lack of progress.'

'Comptroller-General Oakley to you.'

'Now, now. Don't be touchy. I'm just the messenger.' He chuckled, winking at Felix before he turned away.

Messenger wiped away the beads of perspiration that had formed on his brow. Any talk about him being transferred to drug raids made him nervous. He picked up Katherine Rhodes' file and stared at it.

'Ruby Rhodes is my ticket to Sydney,' he said through gritted teeth. 'If I'm not on that train next month, I'll make her pay.'

Chapter Twenty-Six

It was the night of the Egyptian party.

During her lunch break at Smith and Sons, Ruby had visited Dusty in hospital. He was making progress, according to the doctors, but there were still some signs of slight memory loss.

'Katherine,' he said, opening his eyes. 'It's nice to see you. It seems like years.'

'It's Ruby,' she replied. Remembering the advice of the doctor, she decided not to remind him of their sister's death. 'Katherine will be along shortly,' she added.

Dusty frowned. 'That's right.' He touched the bandages wrapped around his head. 'How did I get here?'

'Later, Dusty. We'll talk about it later.'

She watched as he drifted off to sleep. Then, unexpectedly, he opened his eyes and stared at her intently. 'I worry about you, Ruby. I hope you told Reggie what you're up to.'

Ruby blinked. She couldn't tell him about the Egyptian party or Felix Messenger's threats. Or that Reggie had been instrumental in introducing her to Horace Striker, thus arming her with the information and contacts that she needed to carry out her charade. In that moment, it occurred to her that the crime reporter had become her confidant and protector, and this was not something she could share with her brother, at least not for a while. Instead, she kissed Dusty and left.

Arriving home from work, with an hour to get herself ready, Ruby felt an unfamiliar frisson of excitement as she prepared herself for the Egyptian extravaganza. Reggie's enthusiasm had rubbed off on her. She had searched through Katherine's stock of books and magazines and found photographs of excavated tombs, whose walls were decorated with drawings of pharaohs and their consorts. With a bit of ingenuity and a reliance on her twin's cosmetics, Ruby hoped to reproduce the look of the Egyptian queens.

With her hair tied up in a bun on the top of her head, she slipped into a bath sprinkled with rose water. She lay back, appreciating the unfamiliar luxury of the scent and the calming effect it had on her. Fifteen minutes later, she towelled herself dry, put on her dressing gown, and dabbed some of Katherine's Chanel No.5 on her inner wrists and the base of her throat.

Ruby's makeup was elaborate and dramatic, using one of the photographs of Queen Nefertiti as a guide. After concealing her freckles beneath a liberal application of foundation and face powder, she carefully framed her eyes with a heavy line of kohl, from the corner of the tear ducts to the sides of her face, reminiscent of a cat's eye. On her eyelids she applied a thick layer of metallic, green eye shadow. Then she darkened and elongated her eyebrows so that they met the outline from around her eyes. Her eye makeup completed, she turned her attention to the rest of her face. She looked pale, she thought. Among Katherine's cosmetics was a small jar of rouge. She applied it to the apples of her cheeks and rubbed it in. Finally, she selected a rich, red lipstick and shaped her lips into a ubiquitous cupid's bow, a concession to the times. She studied her face in the mirror and felt a strange sense of dislocation. Someone else was returning her gaze. Certainly, it was not Ruby Rhodes.

From Katherine's wardrobe, Ruby selected a simple white sheath dress, mid-calf and split to above the knee. It fitted well, if a little bit too revealing. On her bed lay the accessories that she had hired from the costume shop: collar, wig, headpiece, and jewellery. Around her neck, she fastened the large golden collar, which was adorned with blue and red gems. She brushed her hair, then tied it into a top knot and lowered the voluminous black wig over her head. It fell into a myriad of small plaits over her shoulders. From the array of jewellery on the bed, she chose ornate drop earrings, convincing fakes which mimicked the yellow gold, lapis lazuli, and turquoise of the genuine article. She slipped a selection of oversized rings, conspicuous and eye-catching, onto her fingers while her wrists were adorned with bracelets vividly decorated with colourful hieroglyphs. On her feet she wore a pair of decorative sandals.

The final touch was an elaborate headpiece: a broad band of gold decorated with an array of lotus flowers and a royal cobra in the centre front, jaws open, ready to strike. She lowered it over her wig, adjusting it till it sat comfortably. Taking a deep breath, she stood in front of the mirror.

Ruby was nowhere to be seen. In her place was an extraordinarily beautiful, alluring creature from another time and place.

* * *

If Ruby's reaction to her transformation had been pronounced, Reggie's was priceless. When she opened the door, he looked her up and down, and shook his head in wonder.

'You look like an Egyptian goddess, Ruby. I admit, you take my breath away.'

Ruby had blushed at the compliment, so unexpected from a man of the world like Reggie. She couldn't bring herself to comment, given that she was likewise overcome by his transformation.

'What do you think?' he asked chuckling, gesturing at his costume. 'All I need is a chariot, rather than the Hupmobile.'

'You look very nice,' replied Ruby, trying not to gawk.

Reggie was wearing a sleeveless gold shirt with a white pleated tunic which came to his knees, complemented by a wide metallic waistband. The be-jewelled belt, from which fell a gold sash, was emblazoned with snakes, a sphinx, and pyramids. His headpiece was in black and gold stripes, held in place by a headband. On his wrists, he wore gold and black cuffs, whilst a large black ankh hung from a chain around his neck. Rather disconcertingly, Reggie's dark eyes were outlined in black kohl pencil, and he smelled of fragrant oils.

Ruby was in danger of being mesmerised by this vision of manhood. He was no longer Reggie da Costa, senior crime reporter, wearer of immaculate three-piece suits and two-toned shoes, but a very attractive member of the opposite sex.

As she took his arm and they walked down the front path, she sneaked a look in his direction, hoping that he wouldn't notice.

There was no doubt about it: this evening would be a test for her, in more ways than one.

Chapter Twenty-Seven

The Stockade had been transformed for the party, although the outside gave no clue as to what lay within. Ruby entered on Reggie's arm and was greeted by two burly men dressed as Egyptian guards. They were bare-chested, wearing red and white striped headdresses, wraparound kilts in white linen, and ornate collars around their necks. Holding golden spears, they stood guard beside the double doors, which were painted to resemble stone, inscribed with the words 'Tut's Tomb.'

But that was nothing compared to what awaited her inside. The doors were ceremoniously swung wide to reveal a mass of people, laughing, drinking, smoking, and dancing, attired in imaginative variations of Ancient Egyptian dress. There were bare-breasted women dressed in risqué white sheaths, pharaohs, and queens in elaborate outfits and eye-popping headdresses, dripping in golden and beaded jewellery, wearing heavy makeup and leather sandals. Mummies, swathed in thick linen bandages, with only their eyes, noses, and mouths visible, lounged against fake columns or strutted around the room, arms outstretched, evoking screams of delighted horror.

Waiters and waitresses were dressed accordingly, handing out cocktails with Egyptian-themed names and hors d'oeuvres that resembled miniature mummies and pyramids. Musicians, dressed as slaves, were seated incongruously on Egyptian thrones, playing popular songs, while the female singer was wearing little more than gold paint and a bulky black wig.

Enormous effort had gone into the decorations. In the corners of the room were statues of gods and goddesses, interspersed with fake palm trees, while on tables, canopic jars doubled as ashtrays. The walls were adorned with scenes from the tombs: paintings of pharaohs and their queens, sailing ships ferrying nobles to the afterlife, hieroglyphs and cartouches, jackals with pointy ears, falcons in flight and dogs with lithe bodies, all presided over by an enormous depiction of the Boy King, Tutankhamun, himself.

'I've never seen anything like this,' Ruby said, her face glowing.

'I've heard about it,' Reggie replied, his eyes wide.

One look at his face convinced Ruby that he was as enamoured as she.

'Do you know anyone?' she asked.

'How can you tell? They're in costume.' He turned to face her and took her hand. 'Let's dance. The band is magnificent.'

Swept away by the atmosphere, Ruby surrendered herself to the music. She remembered what a good dancer Reggie was, from the Wattle Path birthday party, as he led her through a selection of dances, from the quick-step to the Charleston.

It was fortunate, she thought, that Katherine's possessions included a good-quality HMV gramophone. In a cabinet, there was a pile of records, including James P. Johnson's 'Charleston.' Ruby had cranked up the gramophone and practised her steps until they came naturally. Now she had a chance to show off her skills.

The next hour would live in Ruby's memory as one of the most enjoyable times she had ever spent. She slung off the old Ruby and danced and smiled and laughed with Reggie, sometimes pulling herself up short that she had forgotten why she was there—to track down a killer—rather than having fun.

At one stage, she found Reggie's eyes on her and blushed beneath the thick makeup. 'Who are you?' he asked.

'I wish I knew.'

'I like the new Ruby.'

Disconcerted, she felt the need for a breathing space. 'Go on. Have some fun without me. You deserve a break.'

He looked longingly towards the gambling rooms. 'Are you sure?'

She nodded. 'I'll be fine. As you say, no one can recognise me under all this makeup.'

'If you insist.'

She watched as he crossed the floor to the two-up room and merged into the circle of those betting on the fall of the pennies: heads or tails.

Ruby found an empty table not far from the entrance. As she did, she heard a buzz spread through the room. Heads turned. It was Horace Striker, making his entrance. Wearing a black tuxedo, he stood out from the crowd. She watched him as he made his way inside. Guests clustered around him, like moths to the flame, basking in his company, wallowing in the attention he gave them.

After a few minutes, she noticed Striker signal to Hare. Shortly after, the gangster had disengaged himself from his admirers and was following his bodyguard through the crush towards her.

'Miss Kitty,' he said, kissing her hand and taking the seat opposite her. 'You look beautiful. Like an Egyptian princess.'

He waved away some of his acolytes who were hovering nearby and took a glass of champagne from a waiter.

'Drink?' he said, offering her the glass.

'Thank you, Horace,' she said, accepting it. 'To tell you the truth, I feel quite strange dressed like this. I'm not one for this kind of thing ordinarily. But I admit I'm surprised to see you in a tuxedo.'

'I'll share something with you, too,' he whispered, leaning in. 'I don't like costume parties. They make me feel uncomfortable.'

She looked at him appraisingly. 'Perhaps you like to maintain your distance?'

He chuckled. 'You are perceptive.' He looked around the room, his eyes narrowed. 'Where's Reggie? I thought he was supposed to be looking after you.'

'He's been most attentive. I let him have some time to himself.' Ruby paused. A bevy of females were lingering close by, waiting for a sign that they could approach the gangster. 'Look at all these women, Horace. I don't mean to pry, but is there a Mrs Striker?'

'It wouldn't be good for business.'

'I don't understand.'

'In my line of work, a personal life can be a hindrance. Attachments can be used against you. Emotions can cloud your judgment. Enemies are all around. They see your weaknesses and go in for the kill.'

'You've never loved anyone?'

'I didn't say that. But I keep liaisons at arm's length. It's better for me and for the object of my affections. I made a mistake in taking Stanley under my wing, grooming him for the future. I resent the fact that it hurt me so badly when he died. I wanted revenge, and I still do.'

'You hold a grudge?'

'Unfortunately, I do.'

'And if I got in the way of your business interests?'

Horace faced her, his eyes boring into her. 'Better not to know.'

Ruby went silent. After a short period, Horace spoke. 'I like you, Ruby. That's rare for me. I will protect you. However, I suggest you think carefully before you take any action that works against me.'

The thinly veiled threat hung in the air until he smiled. 'Don't worry, my dear. I'm harmless.'

Despite his words, she doubted that he was. Striker was a strange one. He rarely laughed, was sparing in his speech, and was unflappable, masking his true feelings behind a veneer of affability. In company, he didn't smoke, drink, womanise, or swear. But although his expression looked relaxed, his eyes were ever vigilant, ever watchful. Horace Striker was a study in control. Reggie was right; she shouldn't let her guard down.

'Look who's arrived? Mayor Swithins. You remember him.'

'Horace, my friend,' gushed the little man, running forward and grabbing his hand. 'What a wonderful event.'

Striker's face was a mask. 'Good evening, Mayor. And I see you've brought your lovely wife, Salacia, and your nephew, Nico. I believe you've met my friend, Miss Kitty?'

Nico was younger than Ruby, dressed in a black and gold kilt, a matching headdress, and a large golden ankh hanging from a chain on his bare tanned chest. Tall and handsome, with dark eyes and a ready smile, the young man was drawing admiring looks from the women who were standing near them.

But his eyes never shifted from Ruby. He reached out and kissed her hand. 'Miss Kitty, it's good to see you again. Nico McArdle, in case you've forgotten. But you can call me Nick. When my uncle told me that you were here last week, I had to come on the chance that you'd be back again. And here you are.'

His gaze made her uncomfortable. When and where had they met? She glanced at Striker, but his attention was elsewhere.

Mayor Swithins nodded. 'He's been at me all week. Miss Kitty, this. Miss Kitty, that.'

Nick smiled, his eyes still on Ruby. 'You must meet my sister. She's here somewhere. Probably dancing with one more besotted beau.'

Mrs Swithins broke in. 'I, too, wanted to meet you again, Miss Kitty. That piece of jewellery that you got for me is absolutely beautiful. See?' She held out her hand, her wrist encased in a rigid hinged golden bracelet featuring a falcon with outstretched wings, inlaid with semi-precious stones.

'If there's a chance that you could get me a matching necklace or earrings, I'd be very grateful.'

'Let's not talk business,' said Horace. 'This night is for pleasure alone.'

The Mayor's wife went red with embarrassment. 'Of course. I couldn't agree more.'

Ruby rallied and touched her arm. 'Another time.'

Salacia smiled, her gratitude obvious. 'Thank you, my dear. I'll ask the Mayor to set up a meeting.'

Nick stepped forward. 'Come, Miss Kitty. Let me see you do the Charleston again.'

'Again?'

'Like we did at Squizzy's place. When I first met you.'

'That's right. When was that?'

His eyes narrowed. 'The first of October. Surely you remember?'

'Of course. How could I forget?'

'Remember New Year's Eve? At Squizzy's club? That was some party. Classy, not the usual affair. I saw you from a distance. You were drinking at the bar. When I was finally free, you'd gone. I was very disappointed.'

'Why were you disappointed?' she asked.

He laughed at her question. 'As if you don't know. You were the most beautiful girl in the room. You still are, except that it's hard to see what you really look like under all that makeup. Hopefully, I'll find out.'

Ruby raised her eyebrows. Nick didn't lack confidence.

'I went back to Squizzy's,' he continued, 'but it was as if you'd vanished off the face of the earth. No one seemed to know where you'd got to. One fellow said that you were dead.'

'How awful,' said Mrs Swithins, in dismay.

Ruby leaned forward. 'Dead? How ridiculous. Who told you that?'

'Couldn't tell you. Some big ugly bloke. Someone said that he was down from Sydney.'

Mrs Swithins broke in. 'I told you to stay away from The Narrows, Nico. It's dangerous.'

The young man pooh-poohed. 'I can handle myself.' He held out his hand as the band struck up again. 'It's the Charleston. Dance, Miss Kitty?'

Ruby looked back at Horace Striker, but he was occupied with Mayor Swithins. She took a moment to compose herself, then answered, 'I'd love to.'

Nick led her out to the dance floor. She faced him, feeling nervous. Could she replicate her sister's performance from last October?

Uncertain at first, she started slowly, stepping backwards and forwards in time with Nick, then increasing her pace as they swivelled, kicked, and tapped their toes. As they danced, her confidence grew. Nick was athletic and light on his feet, leading her well, and soon she was relaxing, letting the music wash over her. A smile spread across her face as the band let loose.

Nick let go of her and positioned himself alongside her. She realised in dismay that he wanted them to do solos. This would be a test for her. She concentrated on mimicking his steps, for although they were dancing separately, they were still in time with each other. Arms swaying back and forth, hopping in between steps, toes in, heels out. As she looked briefly to the side, she was stunned to see that some of the dancers had stepped back to encircle them, whooping and cat-calling as Ruby and Nick mirrored each other's moves. Her mind back on the dance, she found herself enjoying the attention, becoming Miss Kitty, if only for a few minutes. As the music came to an end, there was a burst of spontaneous applause.

Nick escorted her from the dance floor, his hand in hers. 'You were good then, and you're good now.'

Ruby laughed, her eyes shining. 'That was wonderful.'

Horace was waiting at the bar. Ruby looked up at him and smiled. He nodded at her and handed her a glass of champagne. He leaned down and whispered, 'Very nice. You danced well. But watch yourself, my dear. Remember why you're here.'

She felt the flush on her face. He was right. She was there for a reason.

'Nick,' she said, 'I have to go to the powder room.'

'Don't be long,' he said, his eyes fixed on her.

* * *

Ruby was standing at the mirror, fixing her makeup, when a young woman walked in.

'I don't know how these Ancient Egyptians wore wigs in the heat,' she said. 'I'm so hot.' She pulled her wig off and dabbed at the perspiration with a towel.

'That's better.'

Her face now exposed, she turned and looked squarely at Ruby. 'I saw you dancing with my brother, Nico.'

Ruby struggled to control herself. It was Toula, from Dusty's birthday party, the girl that her brother had wanted her to meet. The one he so obviously admired.

'I'm Mayor Swithins' niece, Toula.'

Ruby's smile was forced. 'I'm Miss Kitty. Lovely to meet you, too.'

'I've heard about you but never had the pleasure. I live in Sydney ordinarily.' She dusted her face with powder, then fixed her lipstick.

'Are you staying long?' asked Ruby.

CHAPTER TWENTY-SEVEN

'No. I had what you might call a job. But it's finished.'

'A job?'

'A favour for my uncle. Nothing special.' She shrugged her shoulders.

Ruby nodded, then put her lipstick away and made a hasty exit. Back in the main room, she saw Horace Striker still chatting to the Swithins.

He looked her way, watching her intently.

Horace's bodyguard appeared at her elbow. 'Something I can do for you, Miss?'

'There's someone I know here. Someone whom I've met as Ruby. I need to leave. Could you ask Reggie da Costa if he could take me home? He's playing two-up. It's urgent.'

Hare nodded and strode off. Soon, he returned with Reggie in tow. The crime reporter looked rather put out, but he signalled to her that he would meet her outside. Nick hurried over towards her.

'You're not going?'

'I have to. Something has come up. I'm so sorry. It was enjoyable meeting you again, Nick.'

'Who's that?' He indicated the departing figure of Reggie.

'Just a friend. He drove me here.'

He took her hand. 'I can take you home.'

'I couldn't possibly put you to that trouble,' she said, pulling away from him. 'Anyway, my friend lives close by.'

'I've waited four months for this,' he said sharply. 'Where do you live? How can I contact you? I insist on seeing you again.'

She smiled, but the pressure was getting to her. 'Speak to Horace. He knows where I live. I must go.'

Nick was not to be deterred. 'You'll see me again, I promise you.'

As she climbed into the Hupmobile, Ruby breathed a sigh of relief. She was relieved to get away from Nick, but she was also consumed by what she had learned. As they drove home, Ruby told Reggie what Nick McArdle had said: that he'd seen Miss Kitty at the New Year's Eve party at Squizzy Taylor's club in The Narrows. And that, days later, a big and ugly man from

Sydney had told Nick that Miss Kitty was dead.

'It looks like it's time that I visited The Narrows,' she added.

Chapter Twenty-Eight

Ruby had never been so glad to see a Sunday arrive. So much had happened, and there was still so much to consider and analyse from the previous night. She badly needed a rest, but a visit to the hospital was non-negotiable. She had a bath, removing the last traces of makeup, then slipped on a dressing gown and ate a light breakfast. As she walked past the spare room, she paused in the doorway, undecided.

'Why not?' she asked herself.

Surrendering to temptation, she opened the door to Katherine's wardrobe and selected one of her 'day' dresses to wear.

* * *

Dusty was asleep when Ruby arrived. She took his hand and watched him, her heart swelling for love of him. There was so much she wanted to ask him, but it would have to wait until he had recovered.

Thoughts had been flying through her mind all morning: questions that couldn't be answered, confusion about whether she was doing the right thing. Sometimes, she wished that she could go back in time. Before Katherine died. Living a quiet life with Dusty. Working at Smith and Sons with nothing but work on her mind.

Life had become so complicated since she had inherited the house. The prowler in the alley. The assault on Dusty. The money under the floor. The discovery of Egyptian treasures in the jewellery box. Her 'friendship' with a gangster. Her new life seemed an eternity away from her old existence.

In one sense, the costume party had been the stuff of fantasies, so much escapist fun, but conversely it had accentuated her feelings of confusion, the sense that taking on Miss Kitty's identity was making the old Ruby slip away.

She should have taken Dusty's advice and let sleeping dogs lie. She should have accepted the police report that Katherine's death was accidental, and not gone out of her way to invite trouble. But it was too late now.

With the mystery of her sister's death central to her thoughts, there was no choice but to continue down the road she had taken. The die was cast. The discovery of the notebook had given her a starting point and, with Reggie's help, she might find out if Katherine's secret life was the reason for her death.

Deep in thought, Ruby didn't notice Reggie da Costa enter the room. He cleared his throat, and she looked up startled, then smiled. He had dressed with care, as always, selecting a single-breasted brown herringbone patterned suit, which coordinated with his bold striped tie and matching pocket square. He removed his fedora and stroked his moustache.

'You look different from last night, Ruby. That's probably a good thing for me.'

'I can't look like an Egyptian queen all the time.'

He chuckled. 'Just as well. You look very nice. New dress?'

She blushed, but didn't comment.

He nodded at the sleeping body in the bed. 'Thought I'd check on Dusty. How is he?'

Ruby's smile evaporated. 'Confused when he's awake. They say it will take time. Please, have a seat.'

Reggie pulled up a chair next to her. 'I've been thinking about what we discussed on the way home last night. I should have told you that I was there that night at Squizzy's New Year's Eve party.'

'You saw her? My sister, Katherine?'

'I was playing two-up. I didn't notice anyone.' He lit a cigarette. 'Now, what are we going to do about The Narrows?'

'I don't have any choice, do I? I have to find this man. The one who told

Nick that Miss Kitty was dead.'

Reggie took a long, slow draw of his cigarette. 'I've heard rumours that there's a gangster here from interstate, staying incognito, trying to break into the cocaine trade. I don't have a name yet.'

'You think that he might be involved in Katherine's murder?'

'Perhaps. Perhaps not. If you go to The Narrows, I'll come too, but we have to go separately. There's no Egyptian costume to hide behind this time. Squizzy knows me, and he'll be suspicious if we're together.'

Dusty stirred, then settled again.

'I forgot to tell you,' Ruby said, watching her brother. 'Do you remember Toula? The girl Dusty danced with at his birthday party?'

'Young? Pretty? Black hair?'

'That's right. She's Mayor Swithins' niece. Nick McArdle is her brother.'

Reggie whistled softly. 'That's unexpected.'

'I met her last night. She didn't recognise me because of my costume. Just as well, because she'd be wondering why Ruby Rhodes, Dusty's sister, was pretending to be Miss Kitty.'

'That was lucky.' He nodded slowly. 'I see where you're going with this. Does Toula know that Dusty's sister *is* Miss Kitty?'

'I doubt it.'

'Or that Miss Kitty had an identical twin?'

'According to Horace, no one knew that. Katherine kept her lives separate: Miss Kitty in the clubs; Katherine in the museum. And if Dusty did tell Toula that his sister had drowned, there's still nothing to connect Katherine to Miss Kitty.'

'I've another question for you. An important one. Does Dusty know that Toula is the Mayor's niece?'

'That I don't know. He never said.'

'When I interviewed Dusty, he told me that he was working on a story about corruption in politics.'

'He mentioned it, but I don't know the details.'

'I wonder—' He paused, considering. 'Toby Swithins was Mayor of Collingwood. He was what they called a "mover and shaker" in his day, trying to exert influence over the pre-selection of candidates. Then he cleaned up his act. That was a few years ago.'

'You're wondering whether Mayor Swithins is doing it again? And given that Dusty's been researching political corruption, you think—'

'That Toula might have been planted to find out what Dusty knows? It's possible.'

'That's highly likely, seeing that she told me that she was doing a favour for her uncle.' Ruby shook her head. 'That's terrible, if it's true.' She looked down at her brother. 'Dusty liked her. Really liked her. I hope you're wrong.'

'So do I. But what a coincidence. Are you going to tell him?'

'I can't. Not yet. The doctor said that he's to be kept calm. Anyway, he's not in a position to follow up his story for a while, so it can wait.'

'You have to be careful, Ruby. If Toula meets you as Miss Kitty, your charade will be exposed. She'll recognise you from the Wattle Path. She'll know that Dusty's sisters are identical twins, Ruby and Miss Kitty. Your plan will go up in smoke. She'll tell her uncle, and that will be the end of it.'

'That's true. The trouble is that Mayor Swithins wants to buy some more Egyptian jewellery for his wife. If I go to his place, I'll have to make sure that only he and his wife are there, not Nick and Toula.'

Reggie butted out his cigarette on a saucer. 'You danced with Nick last night.'

'I did.'

'He's a bit of a lady-killer from all accounts.' Reggie studied her. 'How did you find him?'

'Very persistent. He wants to see me again.' She laughed softly.

'Does he?'

'Miss Kitty, not me.'

Reggie stood abruptly. 'He's a bit young for you, isn't he?'

Her smile faded. 'What do you mean?'

'Nothing. But be careful.' He put on his hat.

'Are you going now? Don't you want to wait till Dusty wakes up?'

'I would ordinarily, but there's a report that I have to file for tomorrow's paper.'

CHAPTER TWENTY-EIGHT

He walked out into the corridor.

Ruby followed him. 'Reggie,' she called to his retreating figure, 'I don't understand. What's wrong?'

He turned around and came back towards her. 'I can only help you so much.'

'I'm not scared. Horace is protecting me, and I've had a bit of practice now being Miss Kitty. I think that I can convince people that I really am her.'

'You're putting yourself in danger. The fact is that you don't know these people. A slip of the tongue is all it takes.' He shook his head. 'I watched you last night. You relaxed too much. Mixing with the likes of Striker and Nick McArdle is not good for you. You might grow to like it.'

'Don't be ridiculous, Reggie. I'm amazed that you could come out with something like that. It can be fun, enjoying a night out at The Stockade, dressing up, putting on an act. But I am Ruby Rhodes, not my sister, and not some silly, empty-headed woman either.'

'I don't think you're stupid,' he protested. 'But I'm acting for your brother, being your protector, so take some notice of what I say.'

'Nick is just a friendly young man who likes a good time.'

Reggie shook his head. 'Nico McArdle is definitely not a friendly young man. He's unpredictable, ambitious, and hot-headed.'

'I think you're exaggerating. And I don't understand why you're so angry.'

Reggie sighed. 'I'm not sure if this was such a good idea after all. Pretending to be your sister. Mixing with the likes of McArdle and Striker. You need to keep your wits about you, Ruby.'

'Please come to The Narrows with me, Reggie. I need your help.'

'Of course, I'll come. But be aware that The Narrows is nothing like The Stockade. Squizzy's club holds the dregs of society.'

Ruby looked back towards her brother's room. 'I have to go. Dusty might wake up. But I will be careful, and I do appreciate your advice.'

Reggie touched his hat, then headed down the stairs.

Ruby made her way slowly back to Dusty's room. She was annoyed with Reggie. He had no right to dictate the way she should act. And if she wanted to dance with Nick, was it any business of his?

A groan came from the direction of the bed. She reached over and squeezed Dusty's hand. His eyes opened.

'Ruby.' His voice was weak and reedy.

'Yes, it's me.'

'I thought I heard voices.'

She looked towards the doorway. 'Reggie was here. He'll be back.'

'He's looking after you, isn't he?'

'Of course, he is. Perhaps a bit too much.'

Chapter Twenty-Nine

Reggie had his hands full, what with his new assistant, Dusty Rhodes, out of action, and crime stories piling up thick and fast. His concerns about his mother and her new beau, Valentine Peebles, as well as assisting Ruby Rhodes with the investigation into her sister's death, only added to his load.

He slept badly that night, a recurring nightmare visiting him every time he dozed off. Someone was stealing his beloved Hupmobile from its parking spot outside the grocer's shop. In the dream, Reggie ran down the stairs and out into the street. The driver turned around. His thick black hair, moustache, and toothy grin were instantly recognisable: Valentine Peebles. And, worse still, Peebles was wearing Reggie's best suit: the grey check one with the shiny silver lapels, that he had purchased from an exclusive men's tailor in Melbourne. Reggie watched in horror as Peebles waved at him, then revved the engine and took off in a cloud of exhaust, the Hupmobile and its driver quickly disappearing from view. Dread filled him as he climbed the stairs and stood before his expansive wardrobe. He took a deep breath and flung the doors open, only to recoil at the sight that met him. All his exquisitely tailored suits were gone, while a rack of empty clothes hangers rocked back and forth, back and forth, back and forth.

The sound of the rocking hangers merged with the ticking clock in the next room, as Reggie awoke. It was no good; there would be no more sleep tonight. He slipped his crimson velvet smoking jacket over his pyjamas and went out onto the landing, where his wall of wardrobes was situated. He threw open the doors and breathed a sigh of relief when he saw that his suit collection was intact.

Dawn was breaking through the windows of the sitting room, thin beams of light crisscrossing the imitation Persian rug. Reggie poured himself a Scotch, switched on the lamp, and settled himself on the couch. The file on the chemist shop robberies was open on the table, the resolution of the case evading him. Keen to tie up the loose ends of a story that had come thick and fast over the last few months, Reggie had interviewed the unfortunate victims and come away dissatisfied. Usually, targets of theft were only too willing to offer any information that might assist with the apprehension of the guilty party, but Reggie was unable to extract anything more than minimal information. Not only had the victims failed to report sightings of suspicious people loitering in the vicinity in the days before the robbery, but they showed little concern with the fact that they had been robbed at all.

Over the preceding days, Reggie had walked the length and breadth of Melbourne, interviewing the owners of affected businesses, possible witnesses who lived or worked close by, even those who had discovered the break-ins, but there was little to report on and even less in the way of clues.

Reggie shut the file and headed to the kitchen, where he fixed himself a hearty breakfast. As he drank his tea and devoured his sausages and eggs, he wondered if his meeting that day with Detective Sergeant Clary Blain would be fruitful. Clary had been Reggie's primary source of information on police matters for close to nine years now, apart from a brief period when he'd been demoted for drinking on duty. Despite the setback to his career, Clary's thirst for good Scotch had never slackened. And it was an unspoken agreement between the two men that fine whisky was the price that Reggie would pay in return for insider intelligence.

* * *

After a few hours spent in the offices of *The Argus*, filing reports and telephoning contacts, Reggie headed out to meet the detective. Clary's usual watering hole was the Duke of Wellington Hotel, on the corner of Flinders and Russell Streets. Although it was only three o'clock in the afternoon, the drinkers were crammed four deep at the bar. The pubs would be closed the following day, being Good Friday, and the workers were downing their beers like squirrels collecting nuts for the winter.

'The Duke,' as it was known locally, was a working men's pub. In all the years that Reggie had frequented it, nothing had changed: the noise, the thick haze of cigarette smoke hugging the ceiling, the well-worn furniture, cigarette butts littering the floor, the familiar smell of grog ingrained into the bare boards, and the slight odour of urine emanating from the gents' toilets.

Nothing had changed significantly about Detective Sergeant Clary Blain either, who was sitting at a table with an empty glass in front of him. The belt of his trousers was no longer visible beneath an ever-expanding belly. A few errant hairs still sprouted from his skull, and his bulbous nose and blotchy face were covered in spidery red veins, giving Clary the appearance of an over-indulged but affable, distant uncle.

Reggie nodded at Clary, then joined the scrum at the bar. 'Scotch and a beer!' he shouted to the bartender, handing over a ten-shilling note.

Drinks in hand, Reggie joined Clary at their usual table distant from the bar, where they could talk privately.

'Now, my friend, what news?'

Clary took a mouthful of Scotch and smacked his lips together. 'I tell you, Reggie, I'm at my wit's end. We got Squizzy for driving an unregistered vehicle. The beak fined him two pounds. And then, his ex-wife tried to get alimony out of him. What a laugh. He hasn't paid maintenance for ages, and he tells some sob story that he has no spare money. The judge adjourns the case, saying Squizzy should be given the chance to go straight. Straight?' Clary's face was flushed, making it almost glow in the dim light. 'Squizzy couldn't go straight even if they tied him to a rack and turned the wheel. He's as slippery as an eel, the little bugger. Makes a man turn to drink.' He picked up the glass and finished it.

Reggie nodded. 'He has juries in his pocket, that one. But he'll get his, in the end. You watch.'

Clary turned bloodshot eyes towards the reporter. 'What do you need?'

'The chemist shop robberies. What can you tell me?'

The detective lifted his glass, then realised it was empty. Reggie sighed and took it over to the bartender for a refill, then came back and sat down.

'The chemist shop robberies?' he reiterated, as Clary took a mouthful of whisky.

'It's a hard nut to crack, Reggie. We know that there are chemists selling cocaine directly to the gangs. To prostitutes and addicts too. We know that the chemists make little from the sales, compared to what can be made on the streets. The gangs manipulate and control the trade, inflating the price. But so far we have no one in the frame for any of the robberies. It's frustrating.'

'Does the top brass think there's a connection between the robberies?'

Clary raised an eyebrow. 'What are you saying? You reckon someone's organising this?'

'I don't have any firm evidence yet, but I think there's someone behind it. An outsider most probably. Let's face it, Clary, Melbourne gangs have never been renowned for their methodical approach to the commission of crime.'

Clary scratched his chin. 'It's an interesting proposition.'

Reggie nodded. 'Remember when Squizzy committed an armed robbery and didn't have a getaway car? He had to catch a taxi.'

Clary chuckled. He raised his glass and studied the amber liquid. 'I had a good laugh about that one. And even then, he got off. It reminds me of that recent robbery in Prahran. No one's been charged with that either. The thieves made off with nine ounces of cocaine. But they also grabbed headache tablets, cash, postage stamps, and twenty-three dozen toothbrushes.'

Reggie laughed. 'That headline in *The Truth* was a beauty. "Can Coppers Catch Cocaine Crooks with Clean Canines?"' He lit a cigarette and blew a smoke ring towards the ceiling. 'I heard something interesting that might be linked to the chemist shop robberies. There's some criminal type down from Sydney. He was seen at Squizzy's club around New Year. An ugly brute, according to my source.'

'That description could fit most of them. But it does tally with a rumour that some bloke is trying to muscle in on the cocaine trade.'

'No name?'

'Not yet. Sydney, hey? Could be connected. I'll have a chat to some of my informants.' Clary finished off his drink and wiped his mouth with the back of his hand. 'I better be off. I'm leading a raid on a bootlegger's parlour tonight.'

'Don't drink the proceeds, Clary.'

The detective chuckled. 'I like my Scotch.'

'You mean *my* Scotch.' Reggie leaned forward. 'Before you go, could you do me a favour? It's personal.'

'What is it, mate?'

'Can you check out the background of a Valentine Peebles? Criminal record? Anything dodgy about him, that sort of thing?'

'Sure thing.' Clary jotted the name down in his notebook, then touched the brim of his hat and pushed himself off from the table, weaving his way past the bar and out the door.

Reggie sat on, his mouth a grim line. He had only seen his mother a couple of times since her new beau had come into her life, and he didn't like the idea that someone should monopolise his mother. He also sensed that Peebles' motives were anything but pure. Experience had taught Reggie one thing: that his mother was easily charmed by suave, slick, and smooth-tongued men.

Even now, years after her philandering and irresponsible husband had left her, she viewed the absent Mario through the lens of rose-coloured glasses.

'Mario was so handsome,' she would often tell Reggie. 'Smouldering eyes, coal black hair, and white teeth. He could make that violin sing. He swept me off my feet, you know.'

With her tendency to excuse bad behaviour and her inability to see these men for what they were, Reggie would need good hard evidence that Peebles was after his mother's money, before he could get him out of her life.

Chapter Thirty

Ruby was walking down Swanston Street to Flinders Street station, having visited the hairdresser. She had taken the final step in her 'Miss Kitty' transformation by having her hair cut into a bob, realising that she couldn't hide it under a turban or a wig for much longer. Miss Kitty had short hair, after all. Ruby had stared at herself in the mirror, amazed at the change it made to her appearance. Without the weight of her long hair, she felt somehow freer. She wondered as she walked what Dusty would make of it, given that he had already remarked on the way she looked now, compared to a few months back.

It was five weeks since the assault, and her brother was now staying with her, after being discharged from hospital. It would assist with his recuperation, she insisted, before he took the big step back to work. While he was at Tanner Street, Ruby felt that it would be a nice gesture to invite John Gascoigne to dinner, as a way of thanking him for what he'd done for Dusty. Her brother had been less than enthusiastic, but had reluctantly agreed. To that end, she had dropped in at the museum on the way home the previous day, and invited Gascoigne to dine with them.

She glanced at the shop windows, not thinking about anything in particular, when a stone lodged in her shoe. She stopped abruptly to remove it, and caught a glimpse of a boy out of the side of her eye, about ten feet behind her. What struck her was that he had stopped too, and seemed overly concerned with checking his pockets. He was about thirteen years old, short, nondescript, wearing a knitted vest over a white shirt and tie. His baggy brown trousers were tucked into long black socks and he wore a checked newsboy cap.

As Ruby strolled down Swanston Street, she found excuses to stop and look behind her: checking in her handbag, doing up a button on her coat, looking at the time on her watch. The boy was obviously not skilled at shadowing people, and his attempts at subterfuge were almost laughable. At one stage, he dodged into a shop and, at another, he slipped into a laneway, then reappeared moments later. At first, she was amused by his lame efforts but, as time went on, she grew more concerned. Who was he? Why was he tailing her? Was it something to do with Katherine?

At the intersection facing Flinders Street station, Ruby waited for the lights. The boy was about two yards behind her now. She crossed the road, noting from the clocks above the entrance that there was a train to Richmond in four minutes. She mounted the steps and stood at the ticket box in the queue. Glancing back, she thought that the youngster had gone and breathed a sigh of relief. She passed through the turnstile, then was distracted by a commotion behind her. The station attendant was trying to stop the boy from jumping the barrier and had him by the arm. The lad was trying to slip through his grip and was staring at her departing figure with a panicked expression on his face.

Taking advantage of the situation, Ruby found the platform to Richmond and ran down the ramp as a train was pulling into the station. A door swung open, and an elderly lady stepped down, leaving the door open. Ruby looked up and saw the boy hurtling down the ramp, as the station master blew his whistle and waved his flag. She pulled the door shut and sat down quickly.

As the train gathered pace, she lowered the window and was relieved to see the young chap still standing on the platform, staring mournfully at the sight of the departing train.

Ruby sat back and shook her head. Where once she might have found her life too quiet and uneventful, she was certainly getting a taste of the other side, and she wasn't sure that she liked it.

Arriving home, she found Dusty relaxing in front of an open fire. She greeted him, then went into the kitchen to prepare dinner. She had decided as she rode the train that she wouldn't mention the boy to Dusty, because the last thing she wanted was to get him agitated. He was doing well, the doctors had said, with no apparent signs of trauma. His youth and physical fitness had contributed to his return to good health, but the less he worried about her, the better.

After dinner, Ruby stood and stoked the fire, while Dusty relaxed in an armchair, a blanket draped across his shoulders. She came and sat opposite him.

He looked up from the newspaper. 'You've cut your hair.'

'You don't like it?' She touched her hair self-consciously.

Dusty shook his head. 'Of course, I do. You look more … modern.'

'Thanks.'

'Why did you have it cut? I thought you liked it long.'

She stood and put another log on the fire, keeping her back to him, afraid that her face would give her away. 'It takes a long time to wash and dry. It's more convenient, that's all.'

'You're dressing differently, too.'

Ruby sat down. 'I want to look nice.'

'You always look nice.'

'Do I?' Her face reddened. 'I have a confession, Dusty.'

Her brother's expression changed. He looked very tired again. 'You've already told me that you're impersonating Katherine. And that you're mixing with the likes of Horace Striker. How much worse can it get? At least Reggie is keeping an eye on you.'

Ruby was in a hurry to reassure him. 'It's not that. I feel guilty because I've spent a bit of the money from under the floor on myself. About two hundred pounds.'

'Thank goodness that's all it is. Why shouldn't you?' Dusty shrugged his shoulders. 'Regard it as part of your inheritance.'

Ruby shook her head. 'I don't know. It doesn't seem right. I don't know where the money comes from. Perhaps I should give it away to charity.'

'Don't feel guilty, Ruby. You've done nothing wrong.'

'But Katherine might have. Eight thousand pounds is a lot of money. Perhaps I should put it in the bank, but won't the bank manager wonder what I've been up to?'

Dusty frowned. 'Leave it where it is for the moment. When I'm feeling more like my old self again, we'll explore the possibilities. Your birthday is in June. We could celebrate it in style. Like I did.'

'That reminds me,' Ruby began tentatively. 'Have you seen Toula lately?'

'Her? I broke it off. She lives in Sydney. She was only going to be in Melbourne for a few months.'

'You ended it? I thought you liked her.'

'I did. But she started to get on my nerves. Too many questions about my work. It was flattering at first. Made me feel important. She'd ask me about the stories I was working on. Who was I researching? Was I going to do a big exposé; that sort of thing? Then it became tedious.

'Reggie gave me some great advice on my first day at *The Argus*. He told me to keep that sort of stuff to myself. Keep my mouth shut. According to Reggie, a colleague of his had been working on a big story. Unfortunately, he confided in a "friend" before it was ready to hit the presses. The story got out, stolen by another newspaper, and he was left regretting his mistake. That resonated with me. It made me think twice about sharing what I was working on. So no, I don't see her anymore. She wasn't too happy about it. But she's back in Sydney now.'

'You made the right decision.'

Dusty leaned forward, watching her closely. 'I know you. What's going on?'

'Don't make me tell you.'

'Come on, Ruby. I'll nag you till you give in.'

'All right. If you must. Toula McArdle is Mayor Swithins' niece.'

Dusty whistled. 'So that's what this is about. How did you find out who she was?'

'I went to a party at The Stockade nearly two weeks ago. She was there. So was the Mayor.'

'You were at The Stockade?' He frowned. 'Didn't she recognise you?'

'I was dressed in Egyptian costume.' She paused. 'Think carefully, Dusty. This is important. Did you ever talk about Katherine? Does Toula know that Miss Kitty was your sister?'

'My memory isn't what it was, but I'm sure that I never referred to Miss Kitty. That's too private to share. I mean, that side of Katherine was involved in criminal stuff. I didn't want my friends to know about it. I might have mentioned to Toula that I had two sisters. I might have said that Katherine was dead, but I don't think I went into detail about it. It sounds selfish, but I didn't want to *talk* a lot to Toula. She was so much fun and so beautiful. I do sound hopeless, don't I?'

'You never told her that Katherine had an identical twin?'

Dusty shook his head. 'No, I didn't. I'm sure of that.' His expression changed. 'I can see where you're going with this, and it's another reason I don't like it. You're imitating Miss Kitty, and you're relying on two things. Firstly, that they don't know that Miss Kitty is dead, and secondly, that she had a twin who resembles her in almost every way. If either of these facts comes to light, your cover is blown, and you put yourself in danger. Not to mention that you're visiting some rough and tough neighbourhoods in your obsessive search for Katherine's murderer. Even with Reggie going with you, I still am worried that something might go wrong.'

Ruby bit her lip. 'When you put it like that, I can see how you feel. The trouble is that I can't let go of this. I've dipped my toe in the water, and I need to know what happened to her. If she did drown accidentally, at least I'll know, but while the doubt is there, I'll go on.'

'This isn't like you. You've always been so conservative and careful.'

'That's true. But I have to admit that I'm enjoying the excitement of being someone else for a change. I don't agree with what Katherine did with her life, the criminal side, but I'd like to experience something more than what I have. Doing this has made me see a whole different side to life. When I finally put this away, and stop being Miss Kitty, I hope that I have become somewhat more adventurous. I'm sick of being predictable. I'm sick of being reliable.'

'I don't mind you being more confident; that's a good thing,' said Dusty, 'but what you're doing is dangerous.'

'How can you preach to me when you're playing a dangerous game too?

158

What about your investigation into political corruption?'

Dusty rearranged the cushions behind his head and sank back against the couch. 'You have a point, I admit. It looks like Toula was planted to try and find out what I know. In the past, it was rumoured that Mayor Swithins was the central figure behind corruption in the Victorian Labor Party.'

'What sort of corruption?'

'Trying to influence the selection of candidates, rigging ballots, nepotism.'

'I never would have guessed. He seems like a nice man.'

'Very ambitious; only nice when it suits him. You're no threat to him, remember. I've heard that he spread rumours about one of his opponents being a communist. That put the bloke out of the running for his job.'

'And you think he's still doing that?'

'I'm not sure. They say he was warned off a few years ago. They say that a couple of the elder statesmen in the Labor Party told him to stop undermining the Party. But if Toula was planted to spy on me, you have to wonder whether he's decided to try his hand at it again.'

'Are there any signs that he's involved in corruption now?'

'It can't be proven, but there's supposed to be some shadowy figure who wants a stooge installed as a candidate for the next election.'

'Why don't they stand themselves?'

'It could be that they think they won't be elected. Someone with dubious connections or a criminal record, perhaps. Maybe they have other interests and would prefer to dictate policy from the sidelines.'

'How will you find out who it is?'

'I have a source in one of the political factions who's weighing up whether he'll give me information. Me being out of action has brought a halt to that. Except that I've thought up a headline for it.'

Ruby laughed and shook her head. 'The old Dusty is coming back.'

He smirked. 'If I were still with *The Truth*, it would be "Peddling in Politicians: Sleazy Spoils for Corrupt Candidates."'

'That's a good one,' said Ruby, then the smile left her face. 'It's crossed my mind that the person who attacked you might be involved in this business.'

'I hadn't thought of that, but it's possible.'

'Maybe they were looking for your notes, rather than Katherine's note-book.'

'Maybe they were.'

'Or maybe they wanted to stop you. When you broke up with Toula, they had to find a way to warn you off.'

The sound of a motorcycle brought Ruby to the window. The dying light of the day made it almost impossible to see more than the outline of a man dressed in black, astride his machine, as he paused outside her house. She pulled back the curtain to take a better look and, as she did, the rider took off at speed. She let the material drop back into place and returned to the couch, experiencing that now familiar feeling of uneasiness that had haunted her since she took on her quest to find Katherine's killer. Today, the boy following her, now this. Was she getting close?

'Who was that?' asked Dusty.

'No one. No one we know.'

Chapter Thirty-One

John Gascoigne arrived punctually at six o'clock. He was dressed in his usual shiny black suit with white shirt and cravat, his grey hair slicked back with Brilliantine. Clutching a black felt fedora, he was shown into the sitting room, where he stood with his back to the fireplace, warming himself.

He looked down at Dusty. 'How are you, Mr Rhodes? I hope that you've made a good recovery.'

'Thanks to you. Ruby told me that without you, I might have been in a bad way. I'm very grateful. And please, first names are fine.'

Gascoigne looked around him. 'The last time I was here, the place was a fine mess. Someone was intent on finding something. Did you ever discover what they were after?'

'No,' replied Ruby. 'As you say, if they were after something, they didn't find it.'

Gascoigne raised an eyebrow. 'Does that mean that you found it, or that they didn't?'

'Come now, John, let's forget that unpleasantness,' Ruby insisted. 'You're here so that we can thank you in a practical way. Have a seat, and Dusty will get you a drink.'

* * *

John Gascoigne thanked Ruby as she took away his plate. 'That was delicious. I haven't had a good English beef stew for a while.'

161

'You live on your own?' asked Ruby.

'I was engaged to a lady back in England, but my fiancée didn't want to travel to Australia.'

'Why was that?'

'I wanted a fresh start, whereas she was attached to her family. We agreed to dissolve the engagement. It was mutual.'

'Where do you live in Melbourne?'

'I bought a house in Albert Park, not far from the beach.'

Dusty lit a cigarette. 'What did you do in England?'

'I was too old to serve in the War, obviously. I worked at the British Museum, under Sir Jeffrey Smythe, Keeper of Egyptian and Assyrian Antiquities. A great man.'

'And then you took up a position at the Melbourne Museum.'

'That's right. In 1923. The work was similar, but obviously on a much smaller scale here. Australia doesn't have the same dedication to cultural pursuits that you find in the Mother Country. However, I have the opportunity to build a very good Ancient Egyptian collection on the basis of the knowledge I acquired in London. It's in the early stages at the moment; a few select pieces from the tombs, a mummy, and an impressive sarcophagus from the time of the New Kingdom.'

'Surely there would have been greater opportunities for advancement in London?'

'As I said, I wanted a fresh start. A new country away from war-ravaged Europe.'

Dusty leaned in closer. 'You interest me, John. You seem so English, so middle-class. It's obvious that you've had a good education. Why would you choose the *colonies*?'

Gascoigne glowered at Dusty. 'That's my business. You ask a lot of questions. I suppose I could ask you why you chose to work for a scandal rag rather than a reputable newspaper.'

Ruby was watching the interplay with deepening concern. 'What about some homemade apple pie? Come out to the kitchen and help me, Dusty.'

Her brother stood reluctantly and followed her out the back. She shut the kitchen door and faced him.

'What's all that about? You're spoiling for a fight. He nearly saved your life, and yet you talk to him like that. It's embarrassing.'

Dusty snorted. 'I don't like him. He's a stuck-up English prig. The man belongs in a museum.'

'He was a friend to Katherine when she needed one. He was kindness itself looking after you. Can you imagine what might have happened if he hadn't called an ambulance? And this is how you repay him? You disappoint me.'

Dusty was shame-faced. 'I do tend to overreact. I'm sorry. But he is a snob.'

'Make an effort. For my sake.'

The rest of the evening was restrained but polite, Dusty held in check by the occasional glare from his sister, while Gascoigne made an effort to be civil. Ruby, meanwhile, endeavoured to learn more about the sister she had not seen for ten years. In response to her question about Katherine's choice to go into hiding, Gascoigne admitted that he didn't want her to leave but felt that it was her choice.

'If it meant that she could take up her life, sometime in the future, free of fear, how could I argue with that? I did know that the museum would be a poorer place without her.'

'Have you appointed someone since?'

'We have. The administrative assistant that Katherine replaced agreed to return. But the truth is that your sister can never be replaced. I wish that she'd told me how she was feeling before she—'

'If she did—'

'It's plain that you still don't accept that she committed suicide.' Gascoigne stood, running his finger around the brim of his hat. 'It's late. I should go. Thank you for your kind hospitality, Ruby.' He glanced at Dusty and nodded. 'I'm glad you've made a good recovery.'

Ruby showed him out the door and watched him disappear into the darkness beyond the front gate. She heard his motorcar start up, then went back into the house.

'Well,' said Ruby, frowning at her brother. 'Are you satisfied now? You've insulted him, and we'll probably never see him again.'

'Why would we want to? Don't you find it a bit curious that he came here the day I was bashed?'

Ruby frowned. 'Surely you don't think—'

'What if I do? He's an odd one. The way he asked if you'd found anything missing? What if he came here, broke in, then bashed me?'

'And then he rang for an ambulance? Really, Dusty. That's ridiculous.'

'Perhaps you're right, but I feel that he's involved somehow.'

* * *

After Gascoigne had left, Dusty was getting ready for bed when he heard Ruby boiling the kettle. He put on his dressing gown and went into the kitchen. The opportunities to speak his mind were reducing by the hour, given that he was going home the next day.

He was convinced that she was keeping something from him. Every time he asked her why she was so intent on tracking down Katherine's killer, she hedged her answers and avoided facing the implications directly. Putting herself in danger. Stirring up trouble with Melbourne's underworld. Consorting with Squizzy and Striker. Why was she doing this when it could end so badly? But tonight, he was determined to get some sort of explanation out of her.

She was sitting at the kitchen table, sipping a cup of tea. She looked up. 'Cuppa?'

'Thanks,' he said, watching her as she got up and poured another from a white porcelain teapot. She added milk and sugar and put it down in front of him.

'Thanks, sis,' he said, taking a seat. 'We need to talk.'

'What about?' she asked.

'I'm going back to Port Melbourne tomorrow. Before I do, I need you to be honest with me.'

Ruby rubbed her eyes. 'I'm tired.'

'Answer my question. Why are you doing this?'

'Doing what?'

'You know what I'm talking about. It doesn't make sense. You never liked Katherine that much.'

'I don't believe it was an accident.'

'That wasn't my question. It's not about whether she died accidentally or was killed. I want to know why you are prepared to put yourself in danger?'

Ruby reached out and put her hand over his. 'I've denied my part in this for such a long time. Don't make me tell you.'

'Just say it. You're obviously upset about something.'

She sighed heavily. 'I'm not sure you'll like me once I tell you.'

Dusty was exasperated. 'I've known you for twenty-one years. You're my sister. The one who helped raise me. I know you have faults, but so does everyone.' He ran his fingers through his thick shock of fair hair. 'Tell me, Ruby.'

'I sound so petty. But if you insist.' She took a deep breath. 'When Katherine and I were sixteen, I was interested in this boy at school. He liked me too. Of course, Katherine couldn't let that happen. She stole him off me, then broke up with him a month later. She was always that way, wanting to have the things that other people had, including mine.

'Well, I was jealous and angry. I'm not proud of myself for what I did. One day, after school, she went down to the park. There were boys who used to congregate there. Meanwhile, I headed home, as usual. But, on the way, I stopped and let my hair out and put on some lipstick that I'd taken from Katherine's drawer. I visited Mrs Pinkerton. She was a widow, in her seventies. I acted all chatty, friendly like Katherine. I talked about boys and how I hated school. In effect, I pretended to be Katherine.

'Mrs Pinkerton was a nice old thing, but sharp as a tack. She went out into the kitchen to make us a cup of tea. While she was gone, I looked around and saw that she'd left her engagement ring on the mantelpiece. Gold and diamonds. Very valuable. I stuck it in my pocket. When I finished the tea, I said a quick goodbye and left the house.

'I knew she'd miss the ring. I knew that she'd put two and two together, and she did. She came down to our place while we were eating dinner and kicked up a fuss. Accused Katherine, not me, of stealing. I'll never forget the look on Katherine's face. Shocked and indignant. It was priceless. The trouble was that Mum and Dad had seen her do that act too many times, but this time I knew it was for real. Katherine was many things, but she was never a thief.

'Mrs Pinkerton stood there spitting fire and brimstone and demanded that Katherine's room be searched. Mum couldn't refuse. Of course, she found the ring in the top drawer. Mum was mortified. Katherine sat there dead silent. Not a word. Then she looked at me, a funny expression on her face. She knew. And I didn't say a thing, something that I'll never forgive myself for.'

'What happened then?'

'Katherine stayed calm. She admitted that she'd done it and apologised to the old lady. Dad was worried that the police would be involved, but Mrs Pinkerton said no, as long as he disciplined her. She was sent to her room and warned that there would be repercussions.

'The next morning, she'd gone. Packed a bag and let herself out of the house. The last anyone saw of her was on the station platform, boarding a train for Melbourne.'

'Was that it?'

'Mum and Dad were terribly upset, afraid that she'd come to harm. Dad spent days combing the streets of Melbourne, asking at hostels and guest houses if they'd seen her. Nothing. She'd vanished into the city. Then a couple of weeks later, a letter arrived. Katherine told them that she'd got a job and a room. They were not to worry about her. She was making a fresh start and thought it was the right time. But there was no return address. No workplace. Nothing. The envelope was postmarked: Melbourne General Post Office.'

'What did Mum and Dad do?'

'They were devastated. Nothing like that had ever happened in the family before. I wanted to tell them, but I didn't have the courage. Mum was dead three years' later. They said it was Spanish Flu, but I think she died of a broken heart.'

'You blame yourself?'

'Who else is there to blame?'

'But Katherine made life hard for you. She stole your boyfriend.'

'That doesn't excuse what I did. It was my own fault that I reacted that way. I had this sense of inferiority when it came to her, and I was jealous. Things came naturally for Katherine: doing well at school, having lots of friends, a good personality. She had everything that I wanted. I didn't fit in, and it ate away at me. When you are living side by side with someone who resembles you so closely, the differences occur in sharp relief.'

'And now?'

'I've learned to accept what I am, but there's been a change in me. When I put on her clothes, I feel a bit of Katherine in me, and I like it. It's as if I'm making up for her loss.'

'You shouldn't feel inferior, Ruby. You have qualities that she never had.'

'And vice versa. I understand that, Dusty. But I have to face the truth that I'm responsible for Katherine leaving home. And the consequences from that. It's been easy to blame her for everything, but it's come at a cost for me too. I act like an old woman when I'm only twenty-five. Serious, diligent, conscientious, dedicated to my job. But her death has made me realise that I want more. I want some fun. I want a man to like me, and I want to dance and have a good time. I'm lonely. I have few friends, and I've hidden myself away because of my guilt.'

Dusty took Ruby's hand. 'The past is the past. We can't change that.'

'What I did put her on a path to destruction. She fell in with the wrong crowd, and she lost her moral sense. And it's all because I didn't have the courage to admit what I did to her. I should have stood up and told the truth, but I let her take the blame. Alone in the city, without support or a family, she made bad choices in her life and put herself in danger.

'So, you see, I owe this to Katherine. I need to find out who killed her and bring them to justice. This is how I'll make reparation, even if it's coming ten years too late.'

Chapter Thirty-Two

Now that Dusty had gone home to his rented house in Port Melbourne, Ruby decided it was time to brave The Narrows. She was feeling nervous, after Reggie had reiterated that this area of Melbourne was home to illegal liquor, prostitution, gambling, and drug deals.

It was nearing seven o'clock when Reggie and Ruby set off for Squizzy Taylor's gambling den in Little Napier Street, Fitzroy, the last place that Katherine had been seen before her death. Without the crime reporter accompanying her, Ruby would never have found it. The entrance to the building was nondescript, situated in a cobblestone laneway, lined with corrugated iron fences and dilapidated factories and houses, an unpleasant odour emanating from the open drain a few yards away.

Ruby stole a glance at her companion. Reggie had dressed down for the occasion, wearing a subdued navy three-piece suit with a half belt across the back. His striped shirt was in the American style, set off by a blue and gold striped tie, rolled gold collar pin, and Fedora hat. Compared to his usual outfits, Reggie looked positively funereal.

The crime reporter seemed oblivious to the aura of neglect which had settled over the place like a threadbare blanket. He had, however, made a concession to the neighbourhood, parking his Hupmobile under the strong light of a street lamp in adjacent Gertrude Street.

'You go first,' he said as they approached the entrance. 'Knock twice. I'll wait five minutes, and then I'll come in too. Pretend you don't know me.'

He melted back into the shadows.

Ruby stepped up and rapped on the door. There was the grate of metal as the shutter of a peephole was raised. She could hear the breathing of someone inspecting her on the other side of the door. She calmed herself as the seconds passed. The bolt was drawn back, and the door swung open. She was blinded by the light from the interior. Squizzy's men, two enormous thuggish individuals, gave her the once-over and let her pass. As her eyes grew accustomed to the light, she learned the truth of Reggie's statement that Squizzy's club was a very different world from that of Horace Striker's Stockade.

From the moment that Ruby walked through the door, she was assaulted by a fog of thick cigarette smoke that hung from the low ceiling, along with the confronting odour of sweaty bodies and strong beer. There was no cloakroom, no waiters dressed in black trousers and white shirts carrying trays laden with hors d'oeuvres. Sawdust was strewn across the floor to catch spilled beer, cigarette butts, and worse. The patrons were undoubtedly working-class: hard-faced, rough men who were trying to add to their meagre wages by taking their chances with the roll of the dice, the flip of a playing card, or the fall of the pennies, heads or tails.

She felt totally out of place. Fortunately, she had dressed down, expecting that furs and silk dresses would not be acceptable in the seedy backstreets of Fitzroy. She had worn one of her new work outfits, in black and white, and teamed it with a cloche hat in black, which hid her new fashionable haircut. But, even then, she had miscalculated. She was still over-dressed compared to the standards employed by the few females who were in attendance. These women, to all appearances 'ladies of the night,' were nothing like the immaculately attired and exquisitely groomed women who frequented The Stockade. They giggled and drank and laughed and chattered, eyeing off those whom they thought might have the cash to spend on them. There was no band to dance to, only a piano player tickling the ivories and generally being ignored.

The gambling den was predominantly a male enclave. Labourers, clerks, and railwaymen, straight from work, were lined up at the long bar, drinking and placing bets as they watched the odds for the next race change on the blackboard. In one corner was a circle of men, playing two-up, whilst, in another, a group of card players argued with the dealer.

It dawned on Ruby that finding Katherine's killer in this place was unlikely. If her sister had visited The Narrows, she would have been in the company of friends, because a woman alone would never fit in.

A few men glanced her way, eyeing her up and down, but generally, she was ignored. She found a table near the bar and tried to make herself inconspicuous. One of the barmen noticed her and came over.

'Miss Kitty. This is unexpected. Can I get you a drink?'

'Champagne, thanks.'

She sat and watched as the hubbub grew around the two-up game. Someone was winning. Bets were taken before the pennies were flipped into the air again. The coins hit the ground. 'Heads!' the spinner called amid excited shouts. From the corner of her eye, she saw Reggie stroll past, nonchalant, finding a spot amongst the onlookers. The barman put a drink in front of her. She took out her purse to pay, but he shook his head and indicated a man not far away.

'It's on Mr Taylor.'

She looked over and saw a little man sitting at a table close to the entrance. It was Squizzy, if the photographs in the newspapers were any indication. He looked her way and nodded. She raised her glass and smiled.

Ruby felt the panic rising. She was stupid thinking that she could pull this off. Someone would see through her charade and, worse still, Reggie was nowhere to be seen, having disappeared into the crowd playing two-up. She needed to leave.

Finishing her drink hastily, she rose from her seat and started towards the main entrance. A pudgy man, wearing a three-piece suit and a bowler hat, pushed past her, coming from the direction of the card tables. She followed him with her eyes, and saw him shake hands with the little gangster, then take up the empty seat at his table.

She hurried past but heard someone call out, 'Miss Kitty!' It was Squizzy. A jolt of fear passed through her, but there was no way that she could ignore his summons. Ruby took a deep breath, then strolled confidently to his table, making her best effort to appear relaxed.

'Leslie,' she said, with a broad smile, calling Squizzy by his proper name. 'How nice to see you again.'

The little man raised his glass of beer to her, his concession to good manners.

'Miss Kitty,' he drawled, 'it's been a long time. New Year's Eve, I reckon. This here's Mr Kelly. I think you've met before?'

Mr Kelly nodded and stared at her, his face blank. Ruby smiled briefly, not trusting herself to answer, given that she had no idea who he was or where they'd met. His was not a name that Horace Striker had mentioned when he was 'educating' her about the gangs. She was desperate to get away, but Squizzy insisted on chatting with her.

'Didn't think this would be your cup of tea. A bit rough for you. How come you're here?' he continued, oblivious to the chilly atmosphere emanating from his companion with the bowler hat.

Ruby found her voice again. 'I missed the place. I've been away. How is Ida?'

'She's by the bar.'

He indicated a woman sitting on a bar stool; sipping a champagne; looking bored. Ida was around twenty years old, with crimped brown hair cut in a bob. She was of medium build, and had shapely legs, which she was intent on showing. According to Horace, Ida 'Babe' Pender, a former jazz dancer, was soon to be the third Mrs Taylor.

Up close, Squizzy was unimpressive, a mere five-foot-two inches in height, with a droopy left eyelid and an unattractive coarse face. She felt repelled by him and wondered how her sister could have sought out his company. His wealth, however, was evident, judging by the diamond rings on his fingers, his garish silk shirt and diamond tie-pin, and the silver-topped walking stick which was resting against the table. Next to him, Mr Kelly made no attempt to make conversation, his scarred, bulldog face appraising her without any attempt at good manners.

From the other side of the room, someone bellowed, and another howled in pain. A bottle smashed. Squizzy turned his head towards the fight, losing interest in her. Ruby took her opportunity and made her escape as Squizzy's henchmen came running, leaving their posts at the door, to pull the warring men apart.

She turned back and searched for Reggie amongst the throng, but he couldn't be seen. However, there was someone on the edge of the two-up ring, his face partially obscured, whom she recognised, one of many watching the brawl with interest. Ruby moved forward to get a better look. Distracted as she was, she had no chance to avoid a rough-looking man in a worn overcoat who bumped into her.

'You,' he growled. He grabbed her by the arm and propelled her out the door and into the alley, now devoid of Squizzy's goons. He shoved her up against the wall. 'I thought you was dead.'

Ruby began to shake. 'Who are you?'

'Short memory, Miss Kitty. Took me for an idiot, did you? Bloody shyster. That ring you sold me. Egyptian thing. For my wife.'

'What about it?' she managed to say.

His nose was inches away from hers, the beer on his breath almost making her gag. 'It was one of King Tut's, wasn't it?' He shook his fist in her face. 'It's brought us bad luck. The Mummy's Curse, they call it. I nearly lost my job. My wife wants to leave me. One of the kids is real sick. And I haven't won at the gallops since November. I want my money back.'

'What's your name?' she asked, her face ashen.

'Forgotten me, eh? That figures. It's Tom O'Toole.'

Ruby recalled the entry in the notebook: 'O'Toole. Silver ring with turquoise. Egyptian. November 1924. Ten pounds.'

'I'll give you back your ten quid, Mr O'Toole. I'll bring it next time I come here.'

'You must take me for a halfwit.'

'Never, Mr O'Toole.'

He grabbed her handbag and emptied the contents on the ground. He picked up the purse and opened it. Small change and a two-pound note. He scooped it up and put it in his pocket, then shoved the handbag back against her chest.

'We're taking a little trip, Miss Kitty. To your place, where you'll give me the rest, with interest.'

A voice came from behind him. 'I don't think so, Tom.'

O'Toole turned around. Leaning up against the wall was Reggie da Costa, smoking a cigarette.

'Stay out of this, mate.'

'Not likely. Let the lady go, and I won't tell Squizzy. You know how much he likes Miss Kitty. And he'll wonder where you got the money from to buy jewellery. I think keeping my mouth shut is worth ten quid, don't you?'

The man went white. 'You wouldn't. Look, Reggie, let's forget this. The sheila can go. We'll let bygones be bygones. If she lets me have the two quid.'

Reggie shook his head. 'I don't think so. You've given the lady a bad fright. Now give the cash back and pick up her stuff.'

O'Toole took the money from his pocket and pressed it into her hands, then went down on his hands and knees, gathering up the contents of the handbag.

'Sorry, miss. Mistake. Keep this between you and me?'

Reggie threw his cigarette down and ground it into the cobblestones. He grabbed the man by the shirtfront and shoved him up against the wall. 'If I hear that you make trouble for this little lady again, you can be sure that our mutual friend inside hears about it. Understood?'

The man nodded and backed off. He went inside without a second look.

Ruby was breathing hard. 'Thank goodness you came.' She kissed him on the cheek. 'Thank you, Reggie. I don't know what he would have done if you hadn't been here.'

The crime reporter touched his face where she had kissed him. 'Was that Miss Kitty or Ruby?'

'I'm not sure.'

He dusted off his navy suit, then offered her his arm. 'Let's go.'

'Why did O'Toole back off?' Ruby asked as they walked towards Gertrude Street.

'O'Toole is one of Squizzy's standover men. Likes to take a bribe from those who are scared of his boss, promising that he'll lay off them as long as they pay up. He couldn't take a chance that I'd tell Squizzy what he's been up to. Squizzy would be asking how he could afford to buy Egyptian jewellery on his wages.'

Ruby nodded. 'Now I understand. I doubt if there's anyone back there who's responsible for Katherine's murder, not even Mr O'Toole,' Ruby said. 'It's a working-class club, not the sort of place that my sister would have visited much, as far as I can tell. New Year's Eve was a classy affair, according to Nick McArdle. Not like tonight. Squizzy was surprised to see me. That is, me as Miss Kitty. I won't come back here again, that's for sure.'

Reggie smiled. 'That's good. They're a rough crowd. I meant to ask. Did you notice a man? About five feet six, on the heavy side, scarred face? Bowler hat?'

'He was talking to Squizzy. Mr Kelly.'

'Mr Kelly? Interesting.'

'You know him?'

'Know of him. "Black Jack" Kelly. He's from Sydney. Brawler turned boxer. Now retired. Found a new calling as a standover man with the gangs up in Darlinghurst. A rap sheet as long as your arm. Violent assault, robbery. Strange that he should be down in Melbourne, talking to Squizzy. Word on the street was that they loathed each other. That doesn't bode well for the coppers.'

'Squizzy seemed to think that I'd met Mr Kelly. Rather, that Miss Kitty had.'

'Stay away from Kelly,' advised Reggie. 'He's dangerous.'

'I could tell. He gave me such a look.'

Reggie surveyed the street as they reached the Hupmobile. 'We should get out of here.'

'What a good idea,' she agreed.

The clientele of the neighbourhood at that time of night was anything but friendly. Vagrants wandered past, looking for food or drink in the piled-up rubbish on the street. Drunks sat in the gutters, hugging their bottles. Gangs of youths slunk by, eyeing the low-slung, flamboyant Hupmobile Series R Special Roadster.

As they drove away, Ruby recalled the familiar face on the edge of the two-up ring. In the ruckus with O'Toole, she had forgotten about him. She couldn't be sure, but if she were right, it begged the question: what was John Gascoigne doing in one of Squizzy Taylor's clubs?

Chapter Thirty-Three

The Spanish Mission home of Mayor and Mrs Swithins was impressive. Situated in the fashionable suburb of East Melbourne, the two-storey house was roughly rendered in rose-coloured stucco, and was surrounded by walled gardens and courtyards. With its romantic iron balconies and shuttered windows, along with spiral columns supporting the multiple arches of its porch, it stood out from the grand Victorian mansions of the 1880s that surrounded it.

The Swithins had extended an invitation to Ruby, through Horace Striker, to view their extensive Egyptian collection and to discuss future acquisitions. She had acquiesced, but only on condition that no one be present except the Mayor and his wife. The last thing that she wanted was the distraction of Nick McArdle or his sister, Toula, visiting unexpectedly from Sydney. And there was the added complication that Toula might recognise her from Dusty's birthday party. The Swithins had agreed, believing that Miss Kitty was very particular about protecting her reputation and avoiding scrutiny.

Ruby lifted the large metal knocker and rapped on the Spanish-style carved door. She took a deep breath and stepped back.

'Welcome to the Casa di Swithins,' said the Mayor's wife, opening the door wide to admit her.

Ruby stepped inside. 'What a beautiful house you have.'

'We visited California a couple of years ago. Spanish Mission is all the rage. I had to have one.'

'It's lovely, Mrs Swithins.'

'Please, Miss Kitty. Call me Salacia.'

'What an unusual name.'

'She was the Roman goddess of salt water.'

Ruby raised an eyebrow. 'Interesting.'

The Mayor's wife was dressed to impress, in an expensive, but fussy suit in ivory georgette with a frilly collar. Her plump little face, with turned-up nose and watery blue eyes, was framed by painstakingly crimped hair.

'Here's the Mayor,' she said in hushed tones.

The man himself entered the room, his monocle reflecting the light from the heavy Spanish-style chandelier, whilst the waistcoat of his three-piece suit was straining to contain his burgeoning stomach.

Ruby was greeted effusively and offered afternoon tea. As they drank and ate, it was obvious that Mrs Swithins was eager to move on to the reason for Ruby's visit: arranging the purchase of another item of jewellery from the Pharaoh's treasure trove.

'I can't guarantee that I can match what you have,' admitted Ruby. 'My choices are defined by what my suppliers can offer me. I will do my best.' She was, in fact, wondering what Felix's offerings would be.

'I wouldn't have it any other way,' Salacia gushed. 'Your taste is excellent, Miss Kitty. If you can give me a few moments, I will get the pieces that I've bought over the last few years. Perhaps my dear husband might show you his special collection?'

The Mayor beamed. 'An excellent idea, my dear.' He raised his monocle and looked Ruby in the eye. 'Come with me, Miss Kitty.'

They passed through rooms decorated in the Spanish style, with dark polished boards and soaring vaulted ceilings, set off by wooden beams and wrought iron light fittings. The rooms were plain stucco, painted in rich reds or greens, with Persian rugs and stone fireplaces, an entertainer's delight. Heavy Spanish furniture filled the spaces.

At one end of the Mayor's study was an impressive set of double oak doors, which featured a decorative brass lock. The Mayor produced a large key from his coat pocket.

'Prepare to be amazed, Miss Kitty.'

He turned the key and pushed the door open. The room was dark; the blinds were drawn across the windows. He switched on the lights and looked at her in anticipation.

Ruby let out a gasp. In front of her was a shrine to the Egyptian pharaohs.

She followed Mayor Swithins through the vast space, gazing in wonder at the splendours that were on display. Two statues of falcons, each ten-foot-tall, carved from stone and wearing ornamental crowns, guarded the entrance to the room, one on each side of the double doors. Further in was a magnificent golden chariot on a dais, lit strategically so that it drew the eye.

An alabaster box on a waist-high platform contained four glazed pottery canopic jars.

'They contain the mummy's organs,' the Mayor explained. 'Each jar is sealed with a lid representing the four sons of the god, Horus. The human head represents Imsety, who guards the liver. Hapy, the one with the head of an ape, guards the lungs. The lid shaped like a jackal is Dwamutef. He guards the stomach. Then there is Qebhsenuef, the falcon, who guards the intestines.'

'You know so much,' commented Ruby.

The Mayor looked pleased and took her arm, leading her on to the next exhibit. Housed in a large glass cabinet was a treasure trove of rings, necklaces, bracelets, and hair decorations, made of gold, turquoise, and lapis lazuli.

'You like them?' he said, watching for her reaction. 'But then you'd know how valuable they are.'

Ruby was mesmerised. 'Of course. Remarkable workmanship.'

Next to the glass cabinet, on a raised platform, were a dozen figurines arrayed like soldiers.

'What are these for?' she asked, pointing at them.

The Mayor smiled. 'Slaves to cater to the pharaoh's needs in his journey to the afterlife. Fascinating, isn't it?' He indicated shelves full of miniature furniture, pots, stone vessels, and other household goods. 'The pharaoh would use those too.'

He pointed at one of the colourful murals that adorned the walls. 'See that picture? It shows a scene from the *Book of the Dead*, with the deceased travelling in a ship to his destination.'

Ruby shook her head in wonder, overcome by the splendours around her. No museum that she had ever visited had held treasures like these.

Next was an elaborately painted chest, its lid thrown back to reveal papyrus scrolls. 'These exhibits of yours. Is everything real?'

'A few are imitations, good ones, but most are from the tombs. Come, look at my most treasured possession.'

He led her over to a stone sarcophagus, the lid decorated with a stylised depiction of its occupant. The Mayor ran his hands over the carving, his expression a study in reverence. 'Inside is a real Egyptian mummy from the time of the New Kingdom. It's over three thousand years old.'

'Can I see it?'

'I only open it once a year, on my birthday. It must stay in its coffin, so that it doesn't deteriorate.'

'You love these things, don't you?'

'Indeed, I do, Miss Kitty.' He touched the sarcophagus one last time as if he were reluctant to leave it. 'Now, we must get back to Salacia. She'll be anxious to talk to you.'

As they walked back towards the living room, they heard raised voices.

'I told you not to come here!'

'I want to see her.'

'She won't like it. She specifically asked that we be on our own.'

Ruby and the Mayor entered the room, only to find Salacia red-faced and angry, while Nick McArdle lolled in an armchair, apparently unconcerned with being reprimanded by his aunt.

When he saw Ruby, he jumped up and strode towards her, taking her hands in his. Even without the accoutrements of Egyptian dress and makeup, he was just as striking. He had a handsome face, with lively brown eyes and long eyelashes, black hair, and a sensuous full mouth. His three-piece brown and cream checked tweed suit was in the latest fashion, his trousers tucked into long brown leather boots.

'Miss Kitty. Please forgive me, but I had to see you.'

Before she had a chance to reply, Mayor Swithins turned on his nephew. 'You were told to stay away today. Get out now or I'll send you back to Sydney. Now, go!'

Nick's dark eyes glistened. He uttered an obscenity and stalked out the door.

'Don't mind him, Miss Kitty,' said the Mayor. 'My brother was the same. Hot-headed and impulsive. Never listened to anyone.'

Mrs Swithins stepped forward, her face red with embarrassment. 'Please don't let Nico put you off, you know, in regard to the—'

'Don't worry, I don't blame you for this,' Ruby assured them. 'I have to be so careful, as you can understand.'

'Of course, of course,' said the Mayor, taking her arm. 'Nico is incorrigible. Determined to have his own way.' He shook his head in disgust. 'Now, let's get down to business.'

Salacia was leaning over the table, her eyes bright as she fawned over her Egyptian treasures. There was a range of exotic jewellery, including a ring of coiled gold with a snake's head, another with intricate carvings of hieroglyphs, an elaborate necklace of turquoise and lapis lazuli beads, and the hinged golden bracelet, decorated with a falcon that she had worn to the Egyptian party.

Ruby stepped up and imitated Silas Bacon's approach, examining each piece with what appeared to be an expert eye, making little comments of appreciation.

After a few moments, she addressed them. 'I think I may have just the thing. A recent shipment from the Middle East from one of my premier suppliers.'

Salacia Swithins' face lit up, her eyes sparkling.

'Can you tell me more, my dear Miss Kitty?'

'I might not do justice to the pieces if I did. Do you require more than one?'

'Two would be more than satisfactory. Earrings and a necklace.' She turned to her husband, her expression deferential. 'Unless you think I'm being a little bit selfish? My birthday and our wedding anniversary, Toby dear?'

'Of course, of course. But it does depend on the price.'

Ruby smiled and said her farewells, promising that she would contact them again once she had a chance to examine the contents of the latest shipment. The Mayor and his wife showed her to the door with an excess of attentiveness and gratitude.

Outside, Nick McArdle was waiting, as she expected. He was astride a motorcycle, complete with sidecar.

'Let me give you a lift home.'

'I'll take the tram.'

He shook his head, his dark eyes searching her face. 'How could I let you do that?' His tone was confident, self-assured, cocky. 'I need to know you better.'

She stood, uncertain, feeling flustered. It was hard to read him and it was complicated by the fact that she found him attractive, in a dangerous way. Inwardly, she asked herself what harm it would do to accept this one invitation.

'As far as the city then. I have an appointment in an hour.'

He smiled. 'Your carriage awaits.' His hand lingered in hers as he helped her into the sidecar. 'To the city then. Just for now. But you have to promise me that I'll see you again. I *need* to see you again.'

Chapter Thirty-Four

As Reggie caught the tram down Swanston Street, it crossed his mind what a magnificent city Melbourne was, with its wide streets, cinemas and theatres, department stores, and ornate office buildings, dominated by the town hall with its magnificent portico and clock tower. The footpaths on each side of the road were full of shoppers laden with bags, mothers with children, businessmen hurrying to meetings, and spruikers shouting out at the tops of their voices, trying to lure people into shops. The tooting of motorcars, as they dodged pedestrians, cyclists, and horse-drawn buggies, was almost drowned out by the rumble of trams. It was what he loved about Melbourne: the feeling of energy, the hustle and bustle, combined with the capacity for chaos.

Turning his mind to work, Reggie felt that the resolution of the chemist shop robberies was close at hand, if he could secure the witness statement that would confirm his suspicions. He knew now that 'Black Jack' Kelly was in Melbourne and had been for months. There was talk on the streets that Kelly was expanding his business into the Melbourne cocaine market, along with offering protection as a side racket. He'd been keeping a low profile in the Victorian capital since the previous September, being sighted very rarely, but had recently emerged from the shadows to be seen in the company of Squizzy Taylor, as witnessed by none other than Ruby Rhodes herself.

Reggie dismounted from the tram and crossed at the intersection of Bourke and Swanston Streets. He stopped to look in the window of a gentlemen's outfitter, which was displaying a suit made popular by the Prince of Wales in grey flannel with white chalk stripes. The cut, with its narrow waist and hips, emphasised the shoulders, making the wearer look more athletic. Reggie looked down at his thickening waistline and sighed.

Two doors down was French's Apothecary and Chemist. The bell on the door tinkled as he entered. Displayed on the shelves of a Baltic pine cabinet, which occupied an entire wall, were bottles in clear, blue, and amber glass, containing beef extract, cod liver oil and liniments, as well as patent medicines to cure headaches, dislodge bile, prevent disease, facilitate sleep, and improve memory. A large wooden counter dominated the room. On it was a book for recording prescriptions, an elaborate set of scales, and a mortar and pestle. Glass-fronted cupboards faced out towards the customers, housing packaged boxes of commercially produced pills and remedies.

The man behind the counter was unfamiliar to Reggie. He had a shiny bald head, bristly eyebrows, and prominent ears.

'Can I help you, sir?'

'My name is Reggie da Costa. I was looking for Bert.'

'That bastard,' the pharmacist snarled. 'He sold up. Left the business, worst luck.'

Reggie's eyebrows shot up. 'What are you talking about?'

The chemist looked at him belligerently. 'Two weeks after I moved in, we got robbed. How would you feel?'

Reggie took out his notepad and pen. 'I'm senior crime reporter with *The Argus*. Can you give me any information about the break-in?'

The man's expression changed in an instant. He looked wary, anxious. 'I've got nothing to say to you. We were robbed. Like I told the coppers.'

'Any indications that you were likely to be a target? Suspicious bloke lurking around? Maybe a visit from someone asking questions, demanding money, or offering protection?'

'You better leave, mister.' He took out a handkerchief and mopped the beads of sweat that were popping out on his forehead. 'I have enough trouble and don't want no more. Bad decision, buying this place. Wish I hadn't. That's all you'll get from me, so off you go.'

Reggie shrugged his shoulders. 'Here's my card if you think of anything.'

The chemist scowled and threw it in the bin.

Reggie stood outside, looking thoughtful. He checked his watch. There was a meeting of the editorial committee in two hours, and he'd been asked to give a summary of the stories he'd be working on for the next month. He had enough time to take the tram to Bert's place and back, if he went now.

* * *

Over three years had passed since he had visited Bert French's brick terrace house in Brunswick. Back in 1922, the chemist had been his major source in breaking the news that cocaine was being sold illegally. It appeared that some of his fellow pharmacists did not hold themselves to the same standards that Bert did, and were catering to the 'snow habit' of drug addicts as well as ex-soldiers back from the war. Bert did not want to see the reputation of his profession sullied by unethical colleagues and hoped to bring it to the attention of the authorities by speaking off the record to the press.

Now Bert had retired, according to the person who had bought his business, but Reggie wondered whether there might be more to that than a desire to grow roses.

He knocked on the door and heard footsteps coming down the hallway.

Bert peered around the door, then opened it wide, a welcoming grin on his face. He was approaching fifty, stout with short legs. 'Reggie. What brings you back to Brunswick?'

'Part work and part pleasure. It's good to see you again, Bert. I was wondering if you still lived here.'

'As you can see. You're still making headlines. Good work you did, breaking the Cornelius Stout case. Come on in.'

In the kitchen, Bert sat back and studied the reporter. 'What brings you here, my friend?'

Reggie took an envelope from his bag and spread some newspaper clippings across the table. He tapped them, one by one.

'Chemist shop robberies. Prahran. Richmond. Carlton. Melbourne. And now your shop's been robbed. I went around to see you and heard you'd sold up. Must admit, I was surprised. That business was a good one. Great position; plenty of passing traffic. You've been there for years.'

Bert shrugged. 'Time for a change.'

Reggie detected a shift in the atmosphere, not unlike what he had experienced with the new owner. Bert had become less friendly, more reserved.

'What are you doing now?' Reggie asked.

'Nothing much, mate. Taking some time off. Doing some gardening.'

Reggie had noticed the weeds out in the front yard. 'Really?'

Bert shifted in his chair. 'Very busy, mate. Getting my affairs in order.'

'Is that right? Look, I'll be straight with you, Bert. You put me on the right track back in '22, and I'll always be grateful for that. Remember that I never named you. I protect my sources.'

'What do you want to know?' Bert asked, grudgingly.

'I've been investigating these chemist shop robberies. I have a theory and I thought you might like to confirm it, given you're not in the business anymore.'

'What's this theory?'

Reggie pointed at one of the newspaper clippings. 'The safe was left open.' He pointed at another. 'The back door was unlocked.' Then the third. 'The drugs were on the fourth floor, and the thief knew to go up there. Looks fishy to me. It makes me suspicious. It seems too easy.'

'And you're saying what—?'

'That pressure was applied on the shopkeepers to cooperate before the robbery. So, I'm thinking. A bloke shy of fifty, making good money, with no plans to go into another business, sells up out of the blue, and two weeks later his shop gets robbed. Seems a bit odd. Anything you want to tell me?'

'Are you going to quote me?'

'I told you I wouldn't. Any information you give me is in the strictest confidence.'

Bert looked doubtful. 'I don't know.'

'You can trust me, Bert.'

He sighed, an inward struggle apparent. Then he blurted out, 'It makes me bloody angry what's happened! Bugger them.'

He stood up and opened a couple of beers, put one in front of Reggie, then took a swig of his own.

'This bloke turns up. About four months ago. Pudgy character wearing a bowler hat. Face like he's run into a brick wall. Puts the hard word on me to pay up, or I might have some "accidental" damage to my property. Protection money, that's what he wants. He picks up a couple of bottles and smashes them on the floor. I get the message. "How much?" I ask. He says, "Five quid a week." I agree. I mean, what choice did I have?

'For the first couple of months, one of his men turns up as regular as clockwork and takes the money. Then the bloke comes back. Wants more. I say no. Then he puts this proposition to me. Let him rob my shop, just the once, and he'll leave me alone. I tell him he's crazy. He tells me that he'll burn the place down if I don't agree. I ask him what he wants me to do. Make it easy for him, he says. Leave the safe open or tell him where I stash the cocaine. I figure that it isn't going to stop at one robbery, like he says. I reckon he'll come visiting regularly.'

'What did you do?'

'I was a lucky bastard. There's this bloke who's wanted to take the shop off my hands for ages now. I ring him up, and we come to an arrangement. I move out; he moves in. Two weeks later, he's robbed. Not so lucky for him.'

'You think this bloke threatened him too?'

'Without a doubt. It's a good business. Lucrative, in fact. Just ripe for the picking.'

'You didn't warn the buyer?'

'How could I, Reggie? He'd pull out of the deal. Look, I feel bad about it, but it's survival of the fittest. I had no choice.'

'What about the police?'

'What would they do? I had no idea who he was. And I didn't doubt that he'd bash me up if I reported it to the coppers.'

'Anything you can tell me about him?'

'One of his thugs called him BJ.'

Reggie nodded slowly. 'Just as I thought.' He stood up. 'Thanks, mate.

Enjoy your retirement. By the way, those weeds out front need a bit of attention.'

Bert French followed him outside. 'Not a word, Reggie.'

The reporter put his finger to his lips. 'Not a word, my friend.'

Chapter Thirty-Five

Felix Messenger shook his head at the latest missive from the Comptroller-General of Customs, Robert McKeeman Oakley. It was the worst possible news. Within two weeks, the Customs Department would be re-organised so that priority would be given to breaking the drug trade in Sydney and Melbourne. The plan was that staff would be re-assigned from their present duties and combine with the police to close down the opium dens of 'Little Lon' and The Narrows, as well as the international trade in morphine and cocaine coming through the ports.

This was Messenger's worst nightmare. Searching cargo ships and interrogating foreign seamen, raiding offensive smelling and filthy opium dens, investigating and arresting 'drug fiends' (the scum of society, in his view), was the dreadful scenario that now awaited him. It was a dirty job, and he didn't want any part of it. He'd participated in a raid back in 1920 of a house in North Melbourne and found a couple in bed, their two daughters huddled close by, one with whooping cough, both filthy and neglected. Cocaine, morphine, and a used syringe lay on the floor. But it was the smell that he could never forget, loathsome in its stench of urine, excrement, and vomit. That memory had stayed with him.

He wasn't suited to that sort of work. He wasn't suited to tracking down addicts and stopping their source of supply. He was suited to the sort of work that he was now pursuing: the noble cause of closing down the black market in antiquities. If only he could secure the conviction of one private collector, a significant one at that, he could prove to the Comptroller-General that his role in Customs was a valuable one and escape being swallowed up in an assault on the drug trade.

The memorandum spurred him on. If he were to have Ruby Rhodes' cooperation, then he must procure some Egyptian jewellery, matching the buyer's requirements, from the vault at the Customs House.

* * *

On Friday morning, Felix Messenger strolled up Flinders Street and stood before the imposing façade of the Customs House, the treasure trove of government income, given how much customs duties contributed to its revenue. It was an impressive structure, its architecture based on an Italian Renaissance palace. The building, Felix believed, reflected the importance and status of Customs investigators, such as himself.

After passing the guard on duty, he took the staircase up to the Long Room. Its elegant proportions made Felix's chest swell with pride; this was where he belonged, not in some evil-smelling ship's hold. It was busy that day, full of merchants and their agents waiting for their forms to be processed, or paying duty on imported goods.

He left the Long Room and headed for the Bond Store on the ground floor. It was here that seized goods were held in bond until customs duty had been paid: opium and whisky smuggled into Melbourne by ship, illegal distilling equipment confiscated in raids and, of course, Ancient Egyptian jewellery and treasures which had not escaped the sharp eyes of Customs inspectors.

After showing his credentials to the security guards, he entered the bluestone vaults of the Bond Store. It was cold inside, and he shivered as he turned up the collar of his coat. Only recently, Customs had been tipped off about the arrival of a package from the Middle East, purporting to contain copies of some of the treasures from the tombs of the pharaohs. The shipment had initially attracted a paltry amount in import duties, but further examination revealed that it contained authentic pieces, concealed beneath the fakes. As a result, the goods had been seized. It would take time for the perpetrators to come to court, given that they had absconded and could not be found. No one would miss a necklace or bracelet or a pair of earrings and, after Miss Kitty's clients were raided, Felix would return the goods to the vaults of the Bond Store.

He spent half an hour looking through the shipment until he found two items that fitted Ruby's requirements. A dramatic pair of golden earrings and an elaborate necklace inlaid with carnelian, turquoise, and lapis lazuli, were his choices. Each had been tagged, with a description of the item, their approximate value, and the details of the seizure. He removed the identifiers and put them in his pocket, to be re-attached later. Felix returned the jewellery to their boxes, then concealed them in the inside pockets of his coat.

As he passed the security guard and signed himself out of the vault, he smiled to himself. Tomorrow, he would visit Miss Rhodes and hand over the jewels. And once the raid was over, he would be on a train to Sydney, where he belonged.

Chapter Thirty-Six

It was three o'clock on a Saturday afternoon. Reggie was sitting at his desk at *The Argus*, reflecting on his visit to Brunswick. His Remington typewriter was sitting in front of him, a blank sheet of paper in the roller, waiting for him to start typing his exposé on the theft of cocaine from pharmacies.

His conversation with Bert French had confirmed his theory about the chemist shop robberies. The mastermind behind them had been identified as BJ. From his correspondence with his Sydney counterpart, Reggie knew that 'Black Jack' Kelly was commonly referred to by his initials. The gangster had left behind his little empire in the state of New South Wales to establish a lucrative protection racket in Victoria. It was hard to know whether he intended to put down roots in the southern state or install a deputy to oversee his new domain after he returned home. It was clear from Bert's description that Kelly was putting his personal touch on 'persuading' the chemists to cooperate with him.

Was he now in cahoots with Squizzy Taylor, given that Ruby had seen them together? Was Kelly the brains behind the operation, while Taylor provided the muscle? It was an interesting proposition. Certainly, Squizzy didn't have the mental wherewithal to come up with the idea of forcing the chemists to cooperate in their own robberies, and the coppers would not have considered it likely either. In lots of ways, it was brilliant. Instead of risking being interrupted in the middle of a break-in, the thieves would have the way open for them to get in and out quickly, with a minimum of fuss and no need for a safe-cracker.

After he had left Bert French, Reggie had visited one of his old haunts in The Narrows, looking for his snitch, one of Henry Stokes' boys. It hadn't taken him long to find Bluey, his red hair visible amongst the drinkers inside the Rob Roy Hotel in Gertrude Street. A couple of beers and five shillings were enough to persuade Bluey to 'spill the beans' on Black Jack Kelly's new venture.

'Squizzy and BJ are new best mates,' he shared. 'Wouldn't trust either of them. They won't last. The boss reckons Squizzy will want a bigger cut than he's getting for his part in the operation. He reckons that there'll be trouble and BJ will be back in Sydney *toot sweet*.'

Reggie now had his story, one that would make headlines in *The Argus* and force the police to take action, hopefully sending BJ back to Sydney with his tail between his legs.

The initials, BJ, had prodded his memory. He had seen them somewhere before, and it took a couple more beers for it to come to him. He smiled to himself when he realised that it would give him a valid excuse to visit Ruby again.

Ruby Rhodes. From the moment he had seen her dressed as an Egyptian queen, he couldn't get her out of his mind. Perhaps it was the shock of seeing the little church mouse transformed into a beauty. He found her intriguing too, and he admired her courage in infiltrating the gangs of Melbourne.

However, he had reservations about her determination to find Katherine's killer. The world of gambling dens, and consorting with the scum of Melbourne society, such as Tom O'Toole, Squizzy Taylor, and Horace Striker, was his domain rather than a place for a respectable woman like Ruby, and the sooner she was out of it, the better. For the first time in his thirty-eight years, Reggie was experiencing the unfamiliar desire to protect someone apart from his mother.

Chapter Thirty-Seven

Dusty was at Ruby's house in Tanner Street, working on his report about corruption in the Labor Party. It was too noisy at his place. The new boarder was proving to be very sociable, and most of the time, that was fine, except for when Dusty wanted to concentrate on writing a report or was facing a deadline. Having the house to himself, with Ruby out somewhere, was perfect.

The rumours circulating around Mayor Swithins were growing, that he was improperly increasing membership of a local branch to benefit his cronies. In exchange, these new members would support the preselection of a particular candidate who, once he was endorsed by the Party, would contest the next election. The operation would be paid for by the person who wanted a puppet in parliament that he could control. No matter which way you looked at it, the practice was corrupting the democratic process, with the electorate's interests running a poor second.

Within the Party, such practices were referred to as 'irregular' and were often not taken seriously, but there were moves afoot by concerned Party stalwarts that shady deals in the selection of candidates should be wiped out. In New South Wales, some fifteen years earlier, Labor Party officials had disqualified over fifty members from voting, for fear that the candidate they supported would unduly favour those who were behind his pre-selection, at the expense of the constituency.

Dusty was hopeful that his report would expose the practice to the public, not only in the interests of democratic process, but because he had heard that a particular gang leader was involved and was interested in influencing the direction of the government. The identity of the gang leader was a closely guarded secret, and Dusty's regular informants were disinclined to reveal the name for fear of reprisal.

Even though he felt like he was closing in on the Mayor, Dusty lacked the final piece of evidence to give his story credence.

He looked up when he heard Ruby's key in the lock. She came into the sitting room, carrying four large shopping bags.

'Home at last,' he said. 'Where have you been?'

'At Smith and Sons, working.' She unpacked the bags and smiled at him. 'I bought this on Friday. Isn't it lovely?' She held up a smart suit in navy blue check. 'I've decided to brighten up my work clothes.'

'Very nice. It looks like you've spent a bit,' he said, nodding at the rest of them.

'The money under the floor. We still haven't talked about what we should do with it.'

'Spend the rest of it. Forget about where it came from.'

'I might spend a bit, but certainly not all of it. You can have some too.'

'Me? What would I do with money?'

'Buy some new clothes, for one thing. I mean, how old is that coat?' She pointed at his tweed jacket with the patched elbows. 'And your trousers?'

Dusty inspected himself and shrugged his shoulders. 'You know I have no real interest in that sort of thing. I like to think of myself as a working man. Not middle-class. As Chaucer said, "the salt of the earth."'

'If you're quoting Chaucer, then you're definitely not working-class. You're university educated, and you're in a white-collar job.'

'But my sentiments are with the working man.'

'You'll take the money, though?'

He frowned. 'I suppose I could do with it. Reggie keeps going on about the importance of making a good impression, and he's usually right. It would make for a nice change to wear clothes that aren't worn out.' He nodded. 'You've talked me into it.'

'Good.'

'Talking about the working man, fancy Mr Smith making you work on a

Sunday.'

Ruby took off her coat and hung it over the back of a chair. 'I didn't mind. A pile of orders came in late yesterday, and I offered to put in a couple of hours this morning. They've been very considerate over the last few months, and I think I owe them.' She noticed the folder in his hand. 'Working hard too? On a Sunday?'

Dusty grinned. 'I need confirmation for my story. I'm dealing with influential people, and they'll sue me if I'm wrong. Now if I were still with *The Truth*, I could print all the rumours and innuendo I like, but *The Argus* is a different world.'

'You sound like Reggie and his chemist shop story. He's waiting for confirmation too. He told me that a gang member from interstate is involved. He hasn't got a name yet.'

'He will. Reggie's a marvel. He knows everyone.'

'You like working for him?'

'I do. He's teaching me so much about being a newspaperman. Having contacts. Checking sources. He's very patient.'

'Reggie isn't what I thought he was,' said Ruby slowly. 'Initially, I thought him vain. More concerned with his appearance than anything else. But there's more to him than that. He had a hard time growing up. His father deserted them.'

'I didn't know that.'

'Don't tell him I told you.'

'Of course not.' He studied her. 'Do you like him? I mean, really like him?'

'He's helped me with this Miss Kitty business.'

'That's not what I meant.'

'He's interesting. I feel like I can talk to him. I like being with him.'

Dusty looked up, distracted, as the sound of an engine disturbed the quiet. 'Is that a car?' He stood and looked out the window. A young man wearing goggles, a flat cap, and a brown-checked suit, was sitting on a motorcycle, the engine revving. 'Bloody hell. It's Nick McArdle.'

'What's he doing here?' asked Ruby, frowning. 'How did he find out where I live?' She stared at Dusty as the repercussions of Nick's visit dawned on her. 'What are we going to do? He doesn't know about you and me being brother and sister.'

'This isn't good. I'm sure that he knows that I've been scratching around trying to get evidence against his uncle.'

Dusty cast his eye around the sitting room. A new photograph of himself with Ruby was on the sideboard. He quickly shoved it into the drawer, his sister watching on with concern.

'Quick, Dusty. Go out the back.'

'I can't. My motorcar's out front, and he will have recognised it.'

They watched as Nick edged the motorcycle forward so that it was beside the Australian Six.

Dusty turned to her, a glimmer of a smile on his face. 'I have an idea. Now's your chance to show me what a good actress you really are.'

Chapter Thirty-Eight

Nick was sitting astride his motorcycle, his goggles around his neck, staring in through the side window of the tan Australian Six automobile parked outside Miss Kitty's house. He was still staring at Dusty Rhodes' car when the man himself exploded from the front door, his hat in his hand, a folder under his arm, his face red with anger. He was looking backwards and shouting at someone inside the house.

'Stupid woman! You'll be sorry that you didn't cooperate with me. I promise, I'll smear your name all over the papers.'

Dusty noticed Nick and scowled. He yelled over his shoulder, 'Your boyfriend is here!'

By this stage, Miss Kitty was standing in the doorway, looking at the reporter with disgust. She shook her fist at him. 'Get out. Don't ever come back here again or I'll get the police onto you.'

Dusty threw his files onto the front seat of the automobile and got in. He stepped hard on the starter button and the car sprang into life. His hands gripping the steering wheel, *The Argus*'s reporter took off fast, leaving a cloud of dust in his wake.

Nick parked the motorcycle next to the curb then dismounted. Miss Kitty was hovering in the doorway, smiling uncertainly.

'Come in, Nick,' she called. 'You're welcome, even if he isn't.'

Holding his cap in his hands, Nick walked up the path and stepped up onto the porch.

'What was that all about?' he said, studying her intently.

'He's a reporter. He wanted information. I said I didn't have any.'

'Can I come in?'

'Of course.'

Nick followed her through into the sitting room, glancing around him.

'Nice place, Miss Kitty.'

'I like it.' She looked flustered.

'What's bothering you?'

'How would you feel if a reporter forced his way in and interrogated you? I need a drink.'

'Let me do that for you.' He poured two glasses of sherry from the crystal decanter on the sideboard, then offered her one.

She took a sip and smiled at him. 'I hope you're not here to give me a hard time.'

Nick raised her chin and gave her a peck on the cheek. 'Pure pleasure.'

He picked up the photograph of Katherine and Stanley Duggan. 'Your fiancé? I heard he was killed.'

'In September last year,' she replied softly.

'He's been gone, what, eight months? Time for you to start again.'

'Start?'

'Start living.' He sat down. 'Did Rhodes say what he was working on?'

'Not really. Something about political corruption. When I said that I didn't know anything, he became abusive.'

'How did he know where you lived?'

'I could ask you the same thing.'

Nick chuckled. 'I oiled the tongue of someone who knows you.' The smile left his face. 'Did Rhodes ask about me?'

'Why would he?'

'No reason. After all, I'm only Mayor Swithins' nephew down from Sydney enjoying Melbourne's nightlife. And, of course, meeting beautiful women.'

He stood and took her hand. 'I'm taking you out on my motorcycle.'

Miss Kitty shook her head. 'It might rain.'

Nick wasn't taking no for an answer. 'Come for a little ride. The weather's fine. There's a motion picture that I want to see. Now off you go and get ready.'

She hesitated at first, then nodded, returning shortly after, wearing a light coat and a close-fitting hat.

'That's better,' he said, looking her up and down.

Outside, the black BSA motorcycle, with its green and cream petrol tank and matching sidecar, gleamed in the thin rays of the afternoon sun. Nick escorted Miss Kitty around to the sidecar, opened the door, and helped her in.

After mounting the bike, he kick-started the engine, then put his flat cap on backwards, adjusted his goggles, and produced a pair of leather gloves from the pocket of his jacket. He leaned down towards his passenger. 'Hold on, Miss Kitty. I'm going to give you a ride you'll never forget.' He patted the handlebars. 'Top speed of fifty-five miles per hour.'

She looked up at him, her eyes wide.

'Let's go!' he cried above the roar of the engine.

He gunned the machine, and they took off fast down Tanner Street, heading towards the city.

* * *

Surprisingly, Ruby enjoyed the ride; the briskly chill wind of May blowing hard against her face; the exhilaration as Nick changed lanes effortlessly, weaving in and out of traffic on the way to the city. Never had she felt less in control, and yet, she was almost sorry when it ended.

A Thief in Paradise was showing at the Paramount Theatre in Bourke Street. As they strolled into the cinema, Ruby was aware of the effect that Nick was having on her. That reckless, devil-may-care attitude, that air of confidence that could not be curbed, the way he walked, almost strutting, was both seductive and unsettling, making her feel that she was out of her depth. She was no Miss Kitty, and she knew deep down that he would find her wanting.

The lights went down, the curtains opened, and the music swelled, compliments of Signor Kost's orchestral accompaniment. Ruby was acutely aware of Nick's presence, as he leaned in towards her and made the occasional comment about the film as it progressed. Then he reached for her hand and held it tight.

Up on screen was Ronald Colman, the bearer of a thin black moustache which hovered above his top lip. When she had first met Reggie, Ruby had noticed that his moustache was like that of a film star, but the name had eluded her until now. She glanced at Nick, and the thought crossed her mind that she would prefer to have Reggie sitting next to her.

She turned her attention to the movie again and felt a growing sense of uneasiness as the story progressed. Set on a Samoan island, it told of a beachcomber called Maurice, who dived for pearls with Philip, the disinherited son of a millionaire. When Philip died, after a shark attack, Maurice returned to the United States and assumed the dead man's identity, with the intention of deceiving Philip's father.

Ruby stole a glance at Nick. Was it possible that he was sending her a message through his choice of film: that he had been involved in Katherine's death and intended to expose her as a fake? And yet, Nick appeared oblivious, showing no sign that he suspected her at all. Perhaps it was a coincidence after all?

As they left the theatre, Nick remarked, 'I'm not convinced that Maurice would get away with impersonating Phillip. Someone would guess, wouldn't they?'

'I agree with you,' she replied, trying to hide the tremor in her voice. 'Particularly if they looked nothing alike.'

'But what if he were a brother or a twin?'

Ruby could only shrug her shoulders, given that she couldn't trust herself to speak.

He took her hand again, and they strolled back to the motorcycle, where he helped her into the sidecar.

Nick put on his goggles and riding gloves. 'Now, Miss Kitty. How about dinner?'

'I'd love to, but I have to get home. Perhaps another time.'

Nick stared down at her. 'You're refusing me?'

She met his gaze. 'I'm sorry, but not tonight.'

His face darkened. He revved the engine, and the motorcycle responded, then he pulled out into the traffic, the machine accelerating through the gears. They thundered down St Kilda Road, leaving everything in their wake.

Nick rode hard, his eyes fixed on the road ahead. He cut in front of automobiles, ignoring the blast of car horns and the raised fists of outraged drivers. He raced down the side of stationary trams with little concern for those who were dismounting. His hand on the throttle, he tore past wide-eyed pedestrians who scuttled to get out of his path. His body was like a coiled spring; his shoulders were tensed, anger emanating from him. No one was safe, no inch was given, as Nick gunned the machine with a total disregard for Ruby's safety as well as for those who inadvertently got in his way. The ride into the city, two hours earlier, seemed absurdly tame compared to this. All Ruby could do was to hang on, but her anger was mounting.

By the time that they reached Tanner Street, Ruby was incensed. Reggie was right: Nico McArdle was hot-headed; in fact, he was downright unstable.

She got out of the sidecar and stood on the footpath, her hands on her hips, while Nick sat astride his bike, goggles up, looking straight ahead. His expression was stony, aloof.

'Goodbye, Nick,' she said, forcing him to acknowledge her.

'I won't come in. I have better things to do,' he replied.

'I don't remember asking you,' she said.

His eyes flashed. 'Any woman would have jumped at the chance to have dinner with me.'

'I'm not any woman. And why would I want to have dinner with someone as self-centered as you? You nearly killed us on the way home, just because I refused you.'

He sneered at her. 'You're not what I remember or expected. I'd also say that you're not what you pretend to be. Goodbye, *Miss Kitty.*'

Chapter Thirty-Nine

It was advertised as a gala event at the Wattle Path Palais de Danse, and Reggie was determined to attend. He had secured tickets from one of his many contacts and was in the unfortunate position of not having a partner to accompany him. Two nights previously, he had spent the evening with a lovely young lady at Leggett's Ballroom, showing off his skills at the tango. Later, as they relaxed in the comfort of a room in one of the better hotels, he found that her beauty and youth were not enough to quell his rising sense of boredom. She listened, but she didn't understand. She made the occasional comment that offered nothing to the conversation. She obviously admired him, but he found that it didn't compensate for her vacuousness. Reggie realised, in horror, that he was maturing.

A phone call enquiring about the progress of Ruby's search for her sister's killer was excuse enough to invite his new friend to the extravaganza. Ruby had accepted, which both surprised and pleased him. She was a reasonable dancer, he thought, although she lacked confidence. But he could remedy that, by means of skilful instruction and by example.

* * *

On Saturday evening, Reggie drove Ruby to the Wattle Path Palais de Danse. They parked on the Lower Esplanade and walked up the road to the venue, arm in arm. The theme of the gala event was the North Pole, so Eskimos, Norwegians, and Icelanders, swathed in fur and clutching their snowshoes, were lined up at the entrance, ready to present their tickets.

Others had pleased themselves as to their choice of clothing, either wearing conventional dress or fancy costumes. Cowboys and Indians, pirates, Elizabethan lords and ladies, fairies, Japanese maidens, and even two people dressed as peacocks waited in the queue.

Ruby had tried on numerous dresses from Katherine's wardrobe, finally choosing a shimmering ice-blue silk cocktail dress that suited her colouring. It was rather risqué, she thought, with its dropped waist and low-cut V-shaped back. She slipped it on and paired it with several strands of pearls, set off by a feather boa in varying shades of blue. She'd crimped her hair and decorated it with a silver hairband in the shape of a coronet, inlaid with fake sapphires.

Reggie looked the part, in his grey check evening suit with silver lapels, white waistcoat, and white bow tie. His thin moustache was neatly trimmed, his thick hair flat and slicked with Brilliantine.

Wattle Path had been transformed for the event, in shades of blue and white, as became the arctic theme. Scenes of snow and icebergs, and Arctic birds and animals, decorated the walls, given a realistic touch by means of lighting effects. Dazzling crystal balls reflected a kaleidoscope of colours as they twirled above the dance floor. On the stage, Harry Yerkes's Flotilla Dance Band was playing 'Everybody Loves My Baby, but My Baby Don't Love Nobody but Me' to an enthusiastic audience. Reggie took Ruby's hand and led her onto the dance floor.

Over the next hour Ruby lost track of time, as she danced the slow waltz, the fox-trot, one-step, and quick-step. In Reggie's arms, sometimes held close, she let go of her natural reticence and relaxed, succumbing to the music. She was surprised that he hardly seemed to notice some of the younger, prettier girls who glided past.

Taking a well-earned break, Reggie and Ruby found a table on the edge of the dance floor. As they sipped champagne, a singer did a moving rendition of 'It Had to Be You,' backed by the Flotilla Dance Band.

The dance floor emptied out. To the amusement of the audience, two professional dancers, dressed as penguins, waddled into the middle of the floor to enthusiastic applause. The band leader raised his baton, and the orchestra launched into the opening bars of the tango.

The male penguin stepped forward, his head held high and his spine as straight as his costume would allow, while the female tilted backwards onto his flippers. They snapped their heads around to gaze at each other, sending the audience into gales of laughter as their beaks clashed.

The music gained in volume and intensity; the passion of the dance at odds with the high farce on display. The penguin couple moved into the *corte*, with both ungainly bodies tilting into a lunge. Suddenly the female penguin wrapped her webbed foot around the male's hip and leaned back into a dip, supported by his flippers. After holding the position momentarily, she righted herself and produced a fish from a hidden pocket. She sniffed it, then slapped her partner's face with it, back and forth, back and forth, in time to the music. The audience roared with laughter. When the music ended, the penguins bowed deeply to spontaneous applause, then waddled off the dance floor.

'I've never seen anything as funny as that,' cried Ruby, tears of laughter running down her face.

'One day, I'll teach you how to dance the tango,' said Reggie, chuckling. 'What they did took great skill.' He took his wallet from his pocket. 'I'll get us another drink.'

Ruby watched as Reggie walked away. She looked around her at the sea of happy and excited faces and, for the first time, felt like she belonged. She was in the company of an interesting and worldly man who had transformed her life since she had met him. He was handsome too, and he made her feel at ease. No man had ever had that effect on her before.

But she wondered whether their friendship could withstand her taking him fully into her confidence.

* * *

The evening drew to a close, and the patrons flooded towards the main entrance. Outside, a gentle breeze wafted off Port Phillip Bay, bringing a welcome chill after the warmth of the dance hall.

CHAPTER THIRTY-NINE

'I really enjoyed myself, Reggie,' said Ruby.

'Me too.'

They walked in silence towards the Lower Esplanade. Ruby stopped beneath a street lamp.

'I wish—'

'What, Ruby?'

'That I knew what the future would bring. Everything seems so uncertain.'

'Doesn't that make it more exciting?'

'In some ways, I wish I could go back to what I was before.'

'Is that right? The old Ruby?'

She considered his question. 'No. I think she's gone. But I'd like some certainty about what is going to happen.'

'In what regard?'

She walked on, avoiding his gaze. She looked out to where a crescent moon sent shimmers of light across the waters of Port Phillip Bay. 'I'm scared, Reggie. I didn't want to ruin tonight by telling you.'

They had reached the Hupmobile. He leaned up against the door. 'What's happened?'

'Felix Messenger came around this afternoon. He brought the jewellery. I don't have an excuse anymore. I have to do what he says.'

'I told you I'd come up with something. You have to trust me.'

'I do, but there's also the problem of Nick McArdle.'

Reggie's eyes narrowed. 'What's he done now?'

'He arrived, unannounced, at my place last Sunday.'

'Dusty told me about the film you saw. He wasn't happy about that.'

'It does seem like too much of a coincidence, taking me to the theatre to see *that*. Do you think—'

'That Nick had something to do with Katherine's murder? I wondered about that too. Are you seeing him again?'

'That's very unlikely, given how we parted. He actually told me that I wasn't what he expected. That I'm not what I pretend to be. He'd met Miss Kitty before. Do you think he realises that I'm an impostor?'

'I doubt it. There's the possibility that you're reading too much into his opinion of you.'

'He's too wild for me. I wanted to get away from him as soon as I could.'

'I thought you liked him?'

'Not anymore.'

'I'm relieved.' He touched her arm. 'I think McArdle is a reckless young man. Not your type at all. Steer clear of him.'

Ruby nodded. 'Now, what do I do about Felix Messenger?'

Reggie's expression changed. He stroked his moustache. 'Have you looked at the jewellery?'

'He told me not to.'

'Ignore that. Let's take it to Silas Bacon. What if I pick you up tomorrow, and we head to Fitzroy?'

'Why would you want to see Silas again?'

'Because I don't trust Messenger to play fair with you. He might double-cross you, even when you give him what he wants.'

Chapter Forty

It was Sunday, early afternoon, an hour before he was due at Ruby's house. Reggie wiped some dirt off the front white-wall tyre of his Hupmobile, then looked over at his mother's house across the street. A 1923 Summit Roadster was parked outside. It was Valentine Peebles' motorcar. Reggie frowned and strode across the road. Using his own key, he let himself in and hung his hat on the stand in the hallway.

'Mother!' he called.

There was a flurry of activity further down in the kitchen. Valentine Peebles emerged first, doing up his jacket; his sleek, black hair gleaming in the light. Behind him came Mavis, her face bright red with embarrassment, smoothing the front of her dress. To his consternation, Reggie noticed that one of the buttons on her bodice was undone.

'Reggie. You should have let me know you were coming,' she said.

'Surely I don't need to make an appointment to see my own mother?' he countered. 'What's *he* doing here?'

Valentine piped up in a thin, reedy voice, 'This is your mother's house, let me remind you. She has the right to invite whomsoever she chooses.'

Reggie ignored him. 'We need to talk, Mother.' He stared at her, his face tight.

Mavis touched her beau on the arm. 'Perhaps you should go, Val. I'll see you tonight.'

Valentine Peebles looked from one to the other, his dark eyes showing little concern. He shrugged his shoulders. 'As you wish, my dear.' He kissed her on the cheek and, ignoring Reggie, gathered as much dignity as he could muster and left the house.

'Sit down, Mother.'

Mavis turned her big, blue, innocent eyes on him. 'What can you possibly have to say? You've embarrassed me in front of Val.'

'Who is he? What do you know about him?'

'If you must know, Val has had a very hard life. His mother died after he was born. He was raised by an uncle and aunt who treated him very badly.'

'And his father?'

'He committed suicide in the 1890s Depression.'

'How unfortunate.'

Mavis glared at him. 'You disappoint me. What have you become?'

'Your protector, if you must know.'

'Protecting me from whom?'

'Yourself, mainly. You have so little, Mother, and yet you're ready to throw it away on types like Peebles.'

Mavis drew herself up. 'Actually, Val is offering me a wonderful opportunity. He's in finance, you know. He's heard of an investment that will double my money, and he's prepared to let me buy in.'

Reggie spluttered in disbelief. 'You have no spare money.'

Mavis sat back, preening herself. 'But I will, if I sell the house.'

Reggie closed his eyes and offered up a small prayer. 'He's years younger than you, and he's after your money.'

Mavis's mouth became a thin line. 'I'm entitled to some happiness. Val treats me well. He makes me feel young. He looks after me. And he loves me.'

Reggie choked back an exclamation of scorn. 'I saw him at Wattle Path two months ago. He was with a woman, a much younger woman than you.'

Mavis's expression was stony. 'I think you should go, Reggie.'

* * *

By the time he parked outside Ruby's house, Reggie had shifted through various moods: from anger and disgust to dismay and on to despondency.

What was he going to do to stop Valentine Peebles bankrupting his mother?

Not even his new lightweight cream-checked suit could lift his mood.

He rapped on the front door and stepped past Ruby into the sitting room, forgetting his usual good manners. He sat on the Chesterfield staring absent-mindedly at a picture on the wall.

She followed him into the room and stood with her hands on her hips. 'What's wrong, Reggie?'

He slowly looked up at her, and a wave of recognition passed over his face. 'I'm so sorry. I wasn't thinking.' He looked away again.

'What is it? Tell me.'

He stole a glance at her. 'Are you sure you want to hear?'

'Of course. You've listened to enough of my worries.'

His mother's sorry history came out in a rush of emotion: of her tendency to fall in love with the wrong sort. First, his father, then Valentine Peebles, amongst others.

'She's a hopeless romantic,' he explained, throwing up his hands in exasperation. 'She never sees the worst in people, always the best.'

'Is that so wrong?'

'It is if the man in question wants to bleed her dry.'

'What are you going to do about him?'

'My contact in the police department is checking Peebles for form.'

'What's that mean?'

'Criminal history. Complaints against him. That sort of thing.'

'And if he finds something?'

'Then I have to think of a way to scare him off my mother.'

'She'll be heartbroken if you interfere. And she'll find it hard to forgive you. It would be better if *she* breaks off the relationship.'

Reggie nodded his head and glanced at her. 'That's a good idea. The question is, how?'

'I don't know, but I'm sure you'll think of something.'

He smiled slowly. 'You have faith in me.'

'Of course, I do.'

Reggie studied her, taking in the changes that the last few weeks had wrought. She looked different in her bright, strawberry-coloured dress, which complemented her flame-red hair, now cut into a stylish crimped bob. She looked very smart, he thought, and wouldn't be out of place in a Parisian salon.

'Are we going to Dr Bacon's house now?' she asked tentatively.

'Not yet. There's been a development in your sister's case that I need to discuss with you.'

'Go on.'

'It concerns the chemist shop robberies and, rather surprisingly, Katherine. Let me explain. I was chatting with one of my sources, a chemist who shall remain nameless. As you know, Black Jack Kelly is operating in Melbourne, although his territory is usually Sydney. My contact told me that Kelly offered protection for a price and then moved into the cocaine racket, with one unusual point of difference. He came up with rather a novel approach to securing supplies of the drug. My chemist friend had to agree to being "robbed." In return, they wouldn't burn down his shop.'

'I don't understand.'

'It is rather complicated, I admit. There's been a lot of chemist shop robberies over the last few months, and I'd noticed that some were rather peculiar. The back door ajar; the safe unlocked. That sort of thing. Most unusual, you'd agree. The thieves entered the chemist shop, found the cocaine, and made it out of there without a hitch. Not one of these business owners has offered a clue as to the identity of the thieves, and none of them seems willing to offer any information that might lead to their discovery.'

'Isn't that strange?'

'It certainly is.'

'I have to ask. What does this have to do with me or Katherine?'

'Black Jack is also known as BJ.'

Ruby looked at him quizzically.

Reggie smoothed his moustache. 'I'd seen "BJ" somewhere before.'

'Where?'

'In Katherine's notebook.'

A look of recognition came over Ruby's face. 'Of course. The last column in her book. I never would have thought of that.' She stood up. 'I'll go and get it.'

She returned, the notebook in her hand.

'Here,' he said, showing her. 'Katherine added a new column in October last year. See, up the top, "BJ," and then if you look down the column, she's written the amount next to the entries.' He started to read: '10th October. Joe Calypso. Statuette. £145. BJ £30; 30th October. Francis Whishaw. Turquoise ring. £160. BJ £40. There's a lot more, right up into December.'

Ruby shook her head. 'Protection money. He was taking a cut of whatever she made.'

'That's right, and this proves it. Kelly is a nasty piece of work. He's involved in protection rackets up in Sydney. Specialises in them. One of my snitches reckons BJ arrived in Melbourne in early September. Very hush-hush. He's been expanding his business into Victoria and cosying up to the likes of Squizzy Taylor. They're both involved in the chemist shop jobs, he says. Squizzy provides the muscle; BJ the brains. If Kelly did mix with Stanley Duggan, that would have brought Katherine into his circles, and he might have found out what she was doing. With Stanley gone, he targeted her and made some easy money.'

Ruby nodded. 'Horace told me that he didn't see Katherine after Stanley died. Otherwise, she might have asked him to protect her from Kelly. No wonder she was scared.' Ruby looked over at Katherine's photograph. 'Maybe she refused to pay him, and he killed her.'

'I'd doubt that.'

'But you should have seen the blank, cold look that BJ gave me when he saw me at Squizzy's. If he thought I was dead, he wouldn't be happy seeing me walking around, large as life. And don't forget that Nick said that a man told him that I was dead. An ugly man.'

'There's no guarantee that it's Kelly, but when you put it like that—' He tapped the notebook. 'If BJ had Katherine killed, and then sees that she's still alive, he might try again.' His voice softened. 'You'd be in danger.'

'Do you think he had Stanley Duggan killed too?'

Reggie shrugged his shoulders. 'I don't know, but I think we're getting closer to the answer.' He looked at his watch. 'Time to go. We're going to be a bit late. By the way, do you have the jewellery on you?'

Ruby patted her bag. 'I wonder what Dr Bacon will say.'

'I think I know.'

She looked at him. 'You're being cryptic. Are you going into the fortune-telling business?'

Reggie smirked. 'In this case, I don't need a crystal ball or a pack of tarot cards. Sometimes, you just know.'

Chapter Forty-One

S ilas was expecting them when they arrived. He hurried down the front path and opened the gate for Ruby.

'Miss Rhodes. So nice to see you again.' He shook her hand gently. 'Do come in. You too, Reggie.'

The little man was clad in a grey pair of trousers and a white dustcoat. He led them into the kitchen and beckoned for them to take a seat. The magnifying loupe and the set of scales were on the table.

'As you can see, I'm ready for you. I've been reading up on some of the features of the latest finds in Egyptian antiquities. Quite fascinating.'

'Before I show you the jewellery, could you explain something to me?' asked Ruby.

'If I can.'

'I met a man two weeks ago. He said that the ring Katherine sold him was unlucky. The Mummy's Curse, he called it. What did he mean?'

Silas chuckled. 'It concerns the excavation of Tutankhamun's tomb. People who entered the burial chamber died suddenly. It's nothing more than a myth, Miss Rhodes. An unfortunate coincidence. After Howard Carter discovered the tomb of the Boy King in November 1922, the man who financed the excavation, Lord Carnarvon, died the following April. There was speculation that this was the curse of the pharaohs striking down those who invaded a sealed tomb. The fact is that Carnarvon was bitten by a mosquito and died from blood poisoning. But people panicked. Suddenly the British Museum found itself in possession of mummies, statues, and even shrivelled hands and feet which had been taken from the tombs.'

'They were afraid that they'd be cursed? That's ridiculous.'

'Very true. There's another story about a rich American who bought the mummy of the high priestess, Amen-ra. He was on the *Titanic* when it hit the iceberg. People said it was the Mummy's Curse that killed him.'

'More likely he drowned,' observed Reggie drily.

'Exactly,' said Silas. 'Enough levity, Miss Rhodes. Let's see this jewellery of yours.'

'Hear, hear,' remarked Reggie, looking at his watch.

Ruby withdrew two small parcels from her bag, wrapped in brown paper and string, and handed them to Silas. Within, there were two boxes, both clad in expensive leather. Inside the first one was a pair of earrings with thin strands of blue and red beads hanging from a wide ring of engraved gold.

Silas placed the loupe against his eye socket, then examined one of the earrings closely with the magnifier, turning it over as he inspected it. He then placed the earring on the scales and adjusted the weights.

'Interesting,' he said.

The second box contained a pendant on a gold chain, an elaborate piece shaped like a falcon with outstretched wings, inlaid with carnelian, turquoise, and lapis lazuli. Silas went through the same process, looking at it from different angles, inspecting it closely with his magnifier then weighing it. He placed the jewellery back in their boxes, leaving the lids open.

'The earrings are fake. A good fake. They are not made of real gold, or electrum as it was, which was a mixture of gold and silver. If you feel the weight of these earrings, you will find that they are very light. Probably gold leaf, definitely not solid gold.'

'And the necklace?' asked Reggie.

'Again, a fake, but a poor one at that. The Ancient Egyptians used glass and gems. Although the stones in this necklace appear to be real, they are most probably paste. In this case, molten leaded glass has been poured into a mould, coloured with metallic oxide, and then cut and polished. The other sign that the necklace is fake is that the falcon is supposed to represent the god Horus. Unfortunately, his beak appears straight, not curved as it should be.'

Ruby was shocked. 'I'm giving fakes to Mayor Swithins? What was Mr Messenger thinking? Imagine if the Mayor showed these to a jeweller? Or he guessed for himself? I'd be in deep trouble.' She turned to Reggie. 'Do you think he made a mistake?'

The crime reporter shook his head, scowling. 'If Messenger got these from the Bond Store, he did it on purpose.'

'How do you know that?' she asked.

'I know someone in Customs. The procedure is standardised, according to him. They have experts who inspect and tag seized items so that the authorities can determine what legal action should proceed. These pieces would most probably have been part of a shipment which contained genuine jewellery. It works like this. Smugglers will claim that they're importing imitation antiquities. They put the fakes on top. On the declaration, they'd write something like: "Samples only, no commercial value." If Customs did a cursory inspection, they'd charge minimal duty, not realising that the real thing was concealed elsewhere, maybe sewn into clothing or in the false bottom of a suitcase or box. Once the goods are passed and released, the smuggler charges big money for the genuine items.'

'Mr Messenger knew what he was giving me.'

'He did,' agreed Reggie.

'That's disgraceful. Now what do I do? Do I give them back to him?'

'He'd claim he didn't know,' said Reggie. 'That wouldn't stop him from trying to use you again.'

'Go to the police, Miss Rhodes,' suggested Silas.

Ruby put the boxes in her handbag. 'What do I tell them? That I'm helping Customs stop the black market? That my sister was a criminal? As soon as I involve the police, that's the end of my investigation. I'll never find out who killed Katherine.'

Silas followed Reggie and Ruby to the door. 'I don't know what to suggest,' he said. 'It troubles me that the museum was being used. It would never have happened while I was in charge.'

'Thank you, Dr Bacon,' said Ruby, shaking his hand. 'You've saved me from making a terrible mistake. Reggie was right. I shouldn't trust Mr Messenger. His behaviour is despicable.'

They said their farewells and went out to the car.

As she got in, Ruby said, 'I would like to teach Mr Messenger a lesson, but I don't know how.'

Reggie smoothed his moustache and smiled. 'I told you I'd come up with a plan, and I have. It's perfect, if I do say so myself. I'll tell you about it on the way home.'

Chapter Forty-Two

The latest winter fashions in the shopfront windows, the autumn sun filtering through the plane trees as they shed their yellow-brown leaves, the chatter of workers heading home after a day at the office, all of this was lost on Ruby as she strolled down Swanston Street towards the station. Her life had changed significantly since she had become embroiled in finding Katherine's killer. No longer the meek little secretary, overlooked and lacking in confidence, she was now learning the benefits and disadvantages of taking on a new persona.

There was no doubt that her colleagues were reacting differently to her. Along with compliments about her appearance, unheard of once, she noticed that her workmates, and even her boss, were asking her opinion on a range of issues, whether it be about work, social matters, current events, or even politics. In the past, she would have kept her views private, but now she felt a growing confidence to express her opinions and was amazed to see people nodding their heads in agreement.

The change was undoubtedly welcome, but her new life was bringing its challenges too. A letter from Horace Striker had arrived prior to her visit to Dr Bacon. It had been brief, enquiring as to how her investigation into her sister's death was going and whether she required any further assistance. She had responded and was to meet him on the coming Sunday. At the time, when she had replied, she had not been aware of Felix Messenger's deception, which now added an extra layer to an already complicated situation. However, Reggie had come up with a plan which would extract her from the clutches of the duplicitous Customs officer and still keep her in the 'good books' of the intimidating Horace Striker. The only question was whether she had the courage to go through with it.

On the train ride home, she thought about Reggie. It was impossible to envisage how she would have carried out her impersonation of Miss Kitty without his assistance. He had been invaluable, and yet it went deeper than that. When she'd seen him dressed as an Egyptian pharaoh, her heart had skipped a beat. At the time, she had thought him beyond her reach, but lately, she'd noticed that he was more attentive and seemed to enjoy her company. How otherwise to explain his invitation to the Wattle Path dance? In truth, she'd never met anyone like him. He was ambitious, confident, intelligent, and very entertaining. He was preoccupied with his appearance, she had to admit, but she put that down to insecurity. It was understandable, given his early difficult life and his struggle to make something of himself. Everyone has their idiosyncrasies, she thought, including me, but as long as they did no harm then it wasn't a problem.

Reaching home, she saw her neighbour, Clarice, standing at the gate waiting for her.

'I've been keeping an eye out for you, Ruby. Baked you some scones. I was going to leave them next to the front door, but I thought one of the dogs in the street might eat them.'

Ruby smiled. 'That's sweet of you. Would you like to come in for a cuppa?'

'No thanks, love. I've got to get the dinner on.' She paused. 'Remember when your brother got bashed? I was thinking about it the other day. I realised that I forgot to tell you something.'

Ruby took a step towards her. 'What, Clarice?'

'I was outside bringing in the washing that afternoon. Around three o'clock. There's a gap in the fence next to the lane. I saw a car parked there. I thought it was funny because it's usually your brother's car or the neighbour's, but it wasn't either. I opened the back gate and went out and had a look. It was a black Model T Ford.'

'Did you notice the registration plate?'

'Can't say I did. But I do remember one thing.'

'What is it?'

'The Ford had a dent in the mudguard.'

Ruby took a deep breath. 'A dent. You're sure?'

Clarice nodded. 'I know it's not much, but I thought I should tell you.'

'Did you notice when the car left?'

'I heard a motor start up about half an hour later.' Clarice handed her the scones. 'Does that help you at all?'

'Yes, it does. Thank you for the scones and the information. I think you've solved an ethical dilemma for me.'

Clarice gave her an uncertain smile and waved as she made her way back home.

'No doubt about it,' Ruby said out loud, her face a study in grim determination. 'Felix Messenger has a lot to answer for. He's the only person I know with a black Ford and a dent in the mudguard. Horace said I was keeping something from him, and he's about to find out what it is.'

Chapter Forty-Three

Reggie had a lot on his mind. If it wasn't the chemist shop robberies and Ruby's revelation that her brother had been bashed by none other than Felix Messenger, it was the situation concerning his mother and Valentine Peebles.

His discovery of Black Jack Kelly's involvement in the robberies occasioned a visit to none other than Detective Sergeant Clary Blain. As usual, the detective was propping up the bar at the Duke of Wellington Hotel, staring mournfully at an empty glass.

Heads turned as Reggie walked in, dressed in a grey-striped suit with wide pants and a high waist. Sartorial elegance was relatively unknown in the working-class pub. Indeed, work boots, rough khaki trousers, and collarless shirts were the preferred mode of dress at The Duke.

'Clary, my friend, the well is dry,' Reggie observed.

'Not for long.' The detective leaned over the bar and beckoned to the bartender. 'Scotch. One of your best.'

'A beer for me.'

They sat down at their usual table, away from the rest of the drinkers, and shared some observations about the state of criminal activity in Melbourne.

'Any news on these chemist shop robberies, Clary?'

'The pressure is on. Some clown wrote to your paper claiming that criminal gangs from London are operating in Melbourne. I saw that letter, Reggie. I'm amazed that your editor could print such rubbish. "Melbourne's Reign of Terror." Really?'

'Grist for the mill, mate. It's how we sell newspapers.'

Clary finished his whisky. 'And we've had a deputation from tradesmen asking for protection from the gangs. They reckon that the police need to crack down on crime. As if we don't?' he added, pushing his empty glass around the table. He held it up to the bartender, who came over and refilled it.

'Cheer up, Clary. Here's something that might interest you. There's a Sydney gangster who's moved his business down to Melbourne.'

'Who, exactly?'

'Black Jack Kelly. I have it on good authority that he set up a protection racket late last September. Now he's branching out into a more lucrative field. He's the one behind the chemist shop robberies. He leans on the shopkeepers to cooperate. They agree to be robbed, and tell him where the cocaine and the cash will be. A door's left open, the safe too, which makes it easy. If they don't agree, they're in trouble. BJ is the brains behind the operation; Squizzy provides the thugs to carry it out.'

'Who is this source?'

Reggie tapped his nose. 'I can't divulge his name, but he's reliable.'

'Black Jack, eh?' said Clary, frowning. 'Down from Sydney? Makes sense. Nasty piece of work, from what I've heard.'

'Street brawler turned bare-knuckle boxer. He had a reputation for head-butting and kidney punches. One of my colleagues in Sydney filled me in. Black Jack left the sport fifteen years ago, presumably while he still had some brain power left to make good money. He went into protection at first. Leaned on brothel owners and bootleggers to hand over a percentage of their profits so they'd be left alone. It only took a couple of "accidental" fires or an unfortunate mishap resulting in two broken legs, and his reputation was established. Mention "Black Jack" and the money was paid.'

'And now he's here. That's not good.' He stared disconsolately at the last of his whisky and drained it. 'Is there any evidence against him?'

'The chemists won't talk, for obvious reasons.'

Clary rubbed his chin. 'I could bring him in.'

'And charge him with what?'

'Good question.' He raised his empty glass and signalled to the bartender.

Once it was full again, he held the amber liquid up to the light. 'Nectar of the gods,' he commented, then drank it down.

Reggie watched two men walk past and sit down at the next table. He leaned forward, his voice low. 'I'm telling you this, but you can't use it. A young woman died on New Year's Eve. Drowned. There's evidence to suggest that she was involved in smuggling Egyptian antiquities into the country and selling them to private collectors. I've seen her notebook. She paid out a percentage of the profits to BJ. Her sister thinks that Kelly might have had her killed because she refused to keep paying.'

'And what do you think?'

'I'm not sure. You're killing the goose that lays the golden egg.'

Clary nodded slowly. 'I see your point, but he has a temper.'

Reggie drained his glass, then shrugged his shoulders. 'It can't be proven anyway. My opinion, and it comes from long years of observing and reporting on scum like Squizzy Taylor and his cronies, is that the arrangement between Squizzy and BJ will self-destruct. People like that get greedy and want a bigger cut. If Squizzy thinks he's being cheated, he'll cancel the operation.'

'You reckon that it will go away eventually? I can hardly do nothing.'

'I agree, but I have a suggestion. Why don't you put a rumour out on the street? You have your contacts, your snitches. Say that Kelly isn't giving Taylor what he owes him. Say that Kelly is extracting cash from the chemists *before* the robbery in return for minimal damage to their premises. Squizzy is hot-headed. He'll believe anything. He's overly suspicious. He's also afraid of losing face. And you know how disorganised he is. There's no way that Squizzy will check whether it's true or not.'

Clary shook his head in wonder. 'What a mind you have, Reggie. Devious as the best of them. Please, don't go over to the other side. You'd be a criminal mastermind, and I'd never outwit you.'

Reggie cracked a smile. 'Thanks, mate. One more?'

Clary scratched his nose and nodded. 'Reckon so.'

He raised his hand to the bartender. Reggie waited as another whisky arrived.

CHAPTER FORTY-THREE

'Now, do you have anything for me regarding Valentine Peebles?'

Clary took a sip, then looked at Reggie intently. 'Peebles is a petty criminal, but he's evaded the long arm of the law, so far. He preys on a particular type of woman. Middle-class, widowed, in her fifties or sixties. Wines and dines them, wins them over with an excess of charm, then goes in for the kill. He's supposedly single, gives them a sad story about his miserable life then, once he's gained their trust, he departs with their money.'

'Have any of these women taken him to court?'

'Not so far. Basically, a couple of women made complaints, then withdrew them. I reckon it's embarrassment. They realise that their names will be in the newspaper. The social implications would be too great.'

Reggie sighed. 'He's escaped so far.'

Clary's face lit up in a smile. 'I'm pleased to say that Mr Valentine Peebles has met his match. His last conquest lost approximately ten thousand pounds. When she realised that she'd been duped, she contacted her brother. Unfortunately for Peebles, he's a top lawyer, a King's Counsel, in fact.'

Reggie shook his head in wonder, a broad smile on his face.

Clary continued. 'Mr Peebles doesn't know it yet, but he's going to face some serious charges. I think that once word gets out, there might be a few other ladies who will join the queue to see him in court.' He paused and looked Reggie in the eye. 'Who's the unlucky woman?'

'Just a friend. Would your lady be prepared to tell her the truth about Peebles?'

'It's Mavis, isn't it?'

Reggie raised an eyebrow. 'How did you guess?'

'I know you. I can't imagine you worrying about anyone else like that.'

'He's trying to get her to sell her house. She'll have nothing if he succeeds.'

'I know my lady will help you. She's a strong woman, and she's prepared to go public.'

'Will she get her money back?'

'I doubt if he still has it. Probably spent it by now.'

'More's the pity. If you can, could you organise for her to come to my house next Sunday afternoon? Around two o'clock? Telephone and let me know.'

'You're asking your mother along?'

'Indeed, I am. Hopefully, she can talk some sense into Mavis.' He looked at Clary's empty glass. 'Another?'

'No thanks, mate. I'm cutting down.'

Chapter Forty-Four

Horace Striker was sitting at his desk in his Shamrock Street abode when Hare put his head around the door.

'Miss Rhodes to see you, sir.'

'Bring her in, then leave us.'

Ruby was feeling understandably nervous, given that the news she was about to divulge might upset him. She had weighed up the consequences of cancelling their meeting, but knew that equated to cowardice. He had helped her, and she couldn't ignore that. Without his assistance, she would never have got so far in her enquiries.

She had dressed relatively conservatively, wearing one of her new work outfits, a smart midnight blue pin-tucked blouse with a matching skirt. Her cloche hat was trimmed with a cream silk ribbon. As usual, Horace was conservatively attired, in a sharply cut, double-breasted three-piece suit of fine charcoal-grey wool.

He stood when she walked in, then beckoned her to sit.

'It's been a while, Ruby.'

'Indeed, it has.'

He offered her tea, which she refused, wanting to get the visit over and done with.

'You seem nervous,' he observed. 'Tell me what's been happening.'

Ruby recounted her experience at Squizzy Taylor's club in Fitzroy, her altercation with Tom O'Toole, and Reggie's intervention.

'Good to see that Reggie's looking after you.'

Ruby blushed.

'You like *The Argus*'s crime reporter?' he asked.

'He's been very helpful,' Ruby countered.

'Time he was settling down.' He studied her. 'What else do you have for me? Any suspects?'

'When I was at Mr Taylor's, I met Black Jack Kelly.'

'That one.' Horace frowned. 'BJ gives the gangs a bad name. No integrity, just brute force. What have you learned about him?'

'Reggie thinks he's working with Squizzy Taylor. The chemist shop robberies.'

'I did wonder.'

'I believe that my sister was paying him off. There are entries in her notebook of payments made to a "BJ." Perhaps she refused to cooperate with him, and he killed her?'

He raised an eyebrow. 'Perhaps he wanted more than money.'

'Do you think he killed Stanley because of her?'

'And then, with her fiancé out of the way, he pressured her?' Horace picked up his nephew's photograph and stared at it, then put it down. 'To be honest, I don't think so, but it might explain why no one squealed on him. Down from Sydney, incognito. Out of plain sight.'

Ruby sat forward. 'I've also had a bit to do with Nick McArdle. He said that a big ugly bloke told him that Miss Kitty was dead. I think that it may be Black Jack Kelly that he's talking about. But there's also the chance that Nick is lying. What if he killed her, not Kelly? He was obsessed with her. Maybe she turned him down? Then there's the film he took me to. It was about someone impersonating a dead person. I ask myself if it were a coincidence, and I don't know. What do you think?'

Horace sat back in his chair. 'Nico's a young man on the way up. Very ambitious. And then again, rather impulsive. Too impulsive.' He frowned. 'There's been whispers about violence.'

Ruby sighed. 'This is so complicated.'

'That's true. However, I sense that there's something more you want to tell me.'

'You are perceptive. I have wanted to talk to you about something for a while now.'

'Go on.' Horace's eyes narrowed. 'I'm not going to like this, am I?'

'Probably not, but it has to be said.' She took a breath. 'When I first moved into Katherine's house, I was visited by Felix Messenger.'

'That little rat.'

'Indeed. It was a case of mistaken identity. He thought that I was my twin, as you can imagine. When he found out Katherine was dead, he suggested that I should impersonate her.'

'To what end?'

'So that he could catch her clients in possession of smuggled goods.'

'And what did you say?'

'I said no. But he came back a second and third time, threatening me. He said that he would blacken my reputation by exposing Katherine's criminal past.'

'I don't understand, Ruby. What's this got to do with me?'

'Mayor Swithins' wife, Salacia, is a client, as you know. I was to sell her some jewellery, provided by Mr Messenger, and then he'd raid their house.'

Striker nodded. 'The Mayor and his wife would either go to prison or face a hefty fine. And then, I suppose, Messenger said that he'd leave you alone. Is that right?' Ruby nodded. 'Did you believe him?'

'I didn't know what to believe, but I felt I had no choice.'

'Why are you telling me this? Is it a case of a guilty conscience?'

'Yes and no. Yes, because I never wanted to do this. The Swithins are friends of yours. And they haven't done anything to hurt me. I agree that they're breaking the law, but it isn't my job to bring them to justice. I also felt like I was double-crossing you when you've been so good to me. I am so sorry.'

'What's the "no" then?'

'Felix Messenger lied to me. He gave me fake jewellery to sell to Mrs Swithins. You can imagine what the Mayor would do if he found out. Good money for fakes. I'd be in big trouble.'

'Is that all of it?'

'Not quite. Mr Messenger was at my house the day that Dusty was bashed.

His car was parked in the back lane. My neighbour noticed it. I believe that he was ransacking my house for the notebook that listed Katherine's clients.'

'And you think that Dusty came home and interrupted him. Dusty didn't see his attacker, did he?'

'No, he didn't. But Mr Messenger drives a black Model T Ford with a dent in the rear mudguard. That was the car parked behind my house.'

'Do you think that Messenger might be behind your sister's death?'

'It's possible. Judging by the pressure he's been applying to me, I wouldn't be surprised if he did the same to Katherine. She said in her letter that she was in trouble. Maybe she was in trouble with Customs. Maybe Mr Messenger lost his temper. He's capable of violence, and he has no conscience. He put Dusty in hospital rather than be caught in the act.'

Horace pursed his lips, his eyes staring at some indeterminate object on the other side of the room.

'There's a problem with that reasoning. If he killed Katherine, why would he come around to your house?'

'Maybe he found out where she lived and wanted to get the notebook.'

'That may be true. One thing though: the raid on the Swithins can't happen.' He tapped the table impatiently. 'Felix Messenger,' he added. 'What are we going to do about you?'

Ruby leaned forward. 'Reggie had an idea.'

Horace's piercing brown eyes met hers. 'Yes?'

Chapter Forty-Five

Reggie watched as Mavis da Costa sat quietly on the couch, fiddling with her wedding ring. She was sitting opposite a well-dressed lady, who was wearing a fashionable dress in navy and cream floral. If her matching gloves and expensive broad-brimmed hat didn't indicate a woman of quality, the chauffeur in his bespoke grey suit, waiting outside on the street next to a highly polished Buick, confirmed it.

At first, his mother had been angry when she was told the reason for the invitation to join him for afternoon tea, but once Valentine Peebles' former lady friend climbed the stairs and shook hands with her, her indignation subsided. In front of her was a woman whom she could only describe as 'genteel', a woman from the moneyed classes who had also fallen for Peebles' charms.

Reggie served tea and, taking his cue from the silence that descended on the two women, decided that his absence could only encourage a more intimate conversation between the ladies.

He nodded at the visitor, then kissed his mother on the cheek. 'I'll leave you two to get acquainted. I'll be back in half an hour.' Mavis's face was a mask, her eyes fixed on him.

As Reggie descended the stairs, he heard the visitor say, 'I believe that you and I have something in common.'

His mother's voice was unusually high. 'Indeed?'

'A mutual acquaintance in Valentine Peebles.'

* * *

229

Outside on the street, some forty minutes later, the Buick was gone. Reggie climbed the stairs to find Mavis sitting quietly on the couch.

'Mother,' he said tentatively, 'how are you?'

She looked up at him, her face sad. For the first time, Reggie noticed the fine wrinkles which surrounded her big, blue eyes.

'I was angry with you,' she said, 'but now I can only thank you.' She patted the seat next to him.

He sat down and took her hands in his. 'I'm glad of that,' he said. 'I've been worried about you. Tell me what happened. Was she a nice lady?'

'Very much so.' She smiled for the first time. 'Did you know that she is friends with Mildred Bardsley Smith?'

'It's a small world, Mother.'

Mildred was one of Mavis's old friends from her school days, who had stood by her through the lean years when she was a deserted wife with a young child to raise.

'She asked me to call her Louisa. Imagine that?' said Mavis, wide-eyed. 'And I just met her. She's also invited me to a musical soirée next Friday night. I said that I would have to see if you can take me. She offered to send her chauffeur, but I thought that was too much to ask.'

'How kind. Of course, I'll take you there.'

'Such a nice, well-born, and genteel lady.' She looked away. 'It was criminal what Mr Peebles did to her.'

Reggie raised his eyebrows. Valentine Peebles had gone from the familiar 'Val' to a distant 'Mr Peebles' in the space of an afternoon.

'I won't go into details,' she said, the bitterness in her voice evident, 'but he treated her abominably. Took her money, then tried to extract more from her. Fortunately, her brother became involved and employed a private detective. It appears that Mr Peebles has a wife and three children. He lives comfortably in Elsternwick, obviously off the money he has stolen from ladies such as Louisa.'

Reggie was relieved that Mavis was indignant rather than upset.

'She told me that she met him at a concert recital at the Melbourne Town Hall. Poor Louisa had lost her husband only two years before, and she was lonely. It was one of her first outings without her beloved Charles. Fancy taking advantage of a widow. Outrageous!'

Reggie held his tongue while she talked, afraid to break her mood. He wanted her to be angry; he wanted her to be sympathetic to Louisa.

Finally, having recounted their conversation, Mavis made a request of her son that set him back on his heels.

'Would you drive me to Mr Peebles' place, Reggie? Now?'

'Is that wise?'

'Oh, yes. I have something I want to say to him.'

'You're not going to yell at him, Mother?'

Mavis tut-tutted. 'Of course, I won't. That would be most unladylike.'

He escorted her down the stairs and handed her into the Hupmobile. Reggie revved the engine and accelerated down Swan Street. The automobile responded well; its four-cylinder engine equal to the task. They headed down Punt Road and soon were en route to the home of the soon-to-be former beau of Mavis da Costa.

* * *

Valentine Peebles lived in a handsome, red brick Victorian house with leadlight, box-bay windows, and a pretty front garden.

'Do you want me to come with you?' asked Reggie.

'That would be very nice, dear,' she replied.

Mavis took his arm, and they went up onto the front porch. Responding to their knock was a well-dressed woman in her late thirties, possessing an attractive open face. She was holding a baby in one arm while two young children had a grip on each of her legs.

She looked at them questioningly. 'Can I help you?'

'You must be Mrs Peebles. My name is Mrs da Costa, and this is my son, Reggie. Would your husband be at home?'

Reggie noticed that the contemptible Valentine was cowering behind his wife in the shadows of the hallway, a look of unbridled fear on his face. His slicked black hair stood in vivid contrast to his blanched features. His wife turned to him and, with an edge to her voice, invited him to step forward and meet his visitors.

Mavis was unruffled as she stood face to face with the Lothario who had duped her. She eyed him up and down, her distaste clear, and then, in a calm and emotionless voice, said, 'Good afternoon, Mr Peebles. I wish to inform you that I am no longer interested in investing in your financial ventures. My house is being withdrawn from sale. Furthermore, our friendship is over, and I do not wish to see you again. Do I make myself clear?'

The man stood in the doorway, his mouth flapping like a fish out of water, but with no sound emanating from it. His wife stepped in front of him and shut the door.

Reggie offered Mavis his arm. 'You were wonderful, Mother,' he said.

From inside the house, they could hear raised voices.

Mavis ignored them. 'Come, Reggie, take me home.'

Chapter Forty-Six

Reggie da Costa was feeling very pleased with himself. His new protégé, Dusty Rhodes, now back in the thick of crime reporting, was coming along nicely. During a quick meeting earlier that morning, Dusty had shown him a progress report of his investigation into political corruption.

Reggie whistled. 'Well, I never. Tread carefully, my friend. You're dealing with some powerful people. You need to be sure that you're right about this.'

'I'm sure he's behind it. Everything points his way.'

'Get the evidence first, before you make accusations.' Reggie frowned and tapped his desk with a pencil. 'Your sister might inadvertently get involved in this. Remember, she's been mixing with those people. You don't want to get her into trouble.'

Dusty nodded. 'You're right. I should tread carefully.' An impish grin crossed his face. 'I have a headline now. "Corrupt Candidates Create Chaos. A Devious Dodge to Ditch Democracy." Or there's "Shifty Swithins Backs Bent Ballot."'

Reggie chuckled. 'Really? Remember that you're not with *The Truth* anymore. You've come up in the world. And, on that note, I can't help observing that your wardrobe has undergone some improvement too.'

Dusty laughed nervously. 'My sister's doing. She says that I have to look more professional. She's given me some of the money to buy new clothes.'

Reggie's ears pricked up. 'Some of the money?'

'Katherine's little cache of cash. Almost eight thousand pounds. Hasn't Ruby told you?'

Reggie was silent. He wondered why Ruby hadn't mentioned it.

* * *

Later that morning, Reggie received a telephone call from Detective Sergeant Clary Blain which confirmed that Black Jack Kelly and Squizzy Taylor's precarious partnership had fractured irrevocably, after spurious rumours had hit the streets claiming that the Sydney gangster was taking a greater slice of the pie than had been agreed on. Clary had laid the seed, as suggested by *The Argus*'s senior crime reporter. Sources had witnessed a 'dustup' between BJ and Squizzy over the division of profits from the chemist shop robberies. Fortunately for Taylor, he had been backed up by two of his henchmen, otherwise, the fisticuffs that followed might have been one-sided, but it was said that Black Jack more than held his own in the encounter. He was last seen boarding a train for the New South Wales border.

On an even brighter note, Valentine Peebles had been expunged from his mother's life, her house had been withdrawn from sale, and the Reggie-Mavis relationship had been restored to pre-Peebles status. It was a source of constant amazement to Reggie that his mother could not see from the start that Peebles was an exact duplicate of Mario, her disreputable husband. From his natty dress to his black Brilliantined hair, Valentine was uncannily reminiscent of Reggie's father. Indeed, his personality also mirrored that of Mario's, oozing charm whilst cultivating relationships that would benefit him financially. Reggie knew that others like Valentine Peebles would raise their smarmy and lecherous heads in the future, but hoped that memories of her conversation with the wronged Louisa would linger longer in Mavis's mind.

He removed his waistcoat and undid his collar stud. It was time to get to work. His typewriter was before him, a single sheet of blank paper in the roller. Taking his cue from the humorous and alliterative headlines of *The Truth* newspaper, he started to type: 'Snow-Sniffing Sydney-Sider Sells Up.'

Reggie chuckled as he screwed up the paper and threw it into the rubbish bin. He took a new sheet and wound it onto the roller. His fingers hit the keys: 'Black Jack Kelly Run Out of Town.'

'That's better,' he said.

Chapter Forty-Seven

With his report finished and at the typesetter, and with Valentine Peebles out of his mother's life, Reggie felt the need to celebrate. In his time at *The Argus*, he had appropriated a wardrobe in the staffroom for his sole use, fitted it with a mirror, and stored a spare pair of socks and a clean shirt on standby for when he needed to go straight from work to a social event. The suit he was wearing still looked sufficiently fresh, while a quick buff of his black shoes did the trick. From a toiletry bag, he took a bottle of hair lotion and worked a few drops through his thick black hair, then combed it carefully into place. A quick trim of his moustache with a pair of nail scissors was the final touch. He stood back and surveyed himself in the mirror. Those touches of grey around his hairline gave him a distinguished look. He smiled, the pearly whites of his teeth glinting in the mirror. He still had it, that indefinable something that made heads turn.

Arriving at the Café Denat, Reggie decided that a treat was in order. Not his usual choices from the à la carte menu but the specialities of the House: Huitres en Cocktail, Potage Savoia, Canard Roti aux Pommes, and Asperges Tourmaline, all for the princely sum of six shillings.

As he sipped from a glass of good Burgundy wine, he almost patted his stomach with satisfaction. The meal was a culinary triumph, he decided, compelling him to send his compliments to the chef.

His feeling of bonhomie surrounded him like a warm blanket. Perhaps he should invite Ruby to go to the cinema with him on Saturday night? He'd noticed that The Kinema at Albert Park was showing a double feature. The first was *Reckless Romance*, starring Sylvia Breamer, which would appeal to

Ruby, while the second was more to Reggie's liking: *Fires of Fate*, based on Arthur Conan Doyle's *The Tragedy of Korosko*. It was the story of a group of tourists who were attacked by a marauding band of Dervish warriors while they sailed down the Nile. Lots of action and *derring-do*. Then again, with Egyptian treasures being foremost in Ruby's mind, that film might be of interest to her as well.

He sat back in his chair and observed the other diners in the restaurant. There was a mix of couples, young and old, as well as businessmen doing deals. It occurred to him that it would have been pleasant having Ruby there. Not as Dusty's sister or someone needing advice on handling an investigation, but as a woman, a friend. Not for the first time, he noticed a shift in his attitude towards her.

Over the years, Reggie had created a vision of what his wife would be like. His first prerequisite was that she should be attractive, preferably beautiful. With her new wardrobe and the changes that she had made to her appearance, there was no doubt that Ruby Rhodes matched that description. The second requirement was that his wife should be well-connected and rich. Here was a sticking point. Ruby was certainly not the former, and the £8,000 stashed somewhere in her house would never be classified as riches, although it was a handy amount. He came to the last prerequisite for a wife: she should be submissive and defer to his opinions on all things. Ruby failed on that point too.

Thus, based on his three main requirements, Ruby fitted only one.

Reggie watched the couples as they left the restaurant, hand in hand. Why couldn't Ruby fit his fantasy? His fantasy? For the first time, it dawned on him that his dream wife was a fantasy. Such a woman probably did not exist, and it was debatable whether such a woman would even satisfy him. He'd had enough pretty, shallow lady friends in the past, who had become tiresome as the relationship reached its inevitable conclusion. And now, with his fortieth birthday looming, he acknowledged that such women did not offer him the companionship that he craved. But, when he thought of Ruby, he saw a person who had some depth, who was intelligent, and had a purpose in life. He enjoyed their conversations and was sure that she found him interesting too. And, yes, she was very agreeable to look at.

He finished his wine, wiped his mouth with the napkin, and called for the bill. With it came another heavy dose of reality. The wine had cost more than he had expected. He stood and placed a ten-shilling note on the plate.

As he walked out into the street, Reggie breathed in Melbourne's wintry night air. It was enough to clear his head, at least for a while, of an activity that was completely foreign to him, one that he had warned Ruby Rhodes against: self-analysis and introspection. Enough with self-analysis. Enough with introspection. This wasn't the normal state of mind for Melbourne's greatest crime reporter. There were murders to solve, robberies to investigate, witnesses to interview. His public was waiting.

Chapter Forty-Eight

On the other side of town, Dr Silas Bacon was wrestling with a dilemma. The post earlier that day had brought news from London, news that would require a response on his part. He re-read the letter, then laid it aside. It was from his former colleague, Basil Farquhar, who had moved to London in 1921 to take up a position at the British Museum. Silas stood and walked up and down the length of the hallway, contemplating what he should do.

It had been two months since Silas had written to his friend, enquiring about John Gascoigne, after he had heard that Katherine Rhodes had engaged in smuggling antiquities into the country, using the museum as a front. He had found it hard to believe that Gascoigne was unaware of this, although the man had flatly denied it. Silas had written to Farquhar because he wanted to know whether Gascoigne was as highly credentialled as his references implied.

Farquhar's letter was a revelation. It exposed more than Gascoigne's duplicity; it revealed the tactics of the man who had been Gascoigne's boss. It was known in museum circles that Sir Jeffrey Smythe, Keeper of the Egyptian and Assyrian Antiquities section, valued having the best collection in the world as a matter of national pride. And to achieve this, he had put aside any semblance of ethics. Farquhar wrote that Smythe had smuggled an Egyptian papyrus out of Egypt in a crate of oranges and had, apparently, encouraged British Museum officials and their local agents to smuggle antiquities into England, using a range of tactics. Treasures had been secreted in diplomatic pouches, and Customs officials had been bribed. Furthermore, favours had been asked of those in the Egyptian Service of Antiquities to turn a blind eye to the contents of cases containing treasures from the tombs. Apparently, Sir Jeffrey had justified his actions by saying that he had saved the British Museum the trouble and expense of conducting its own excavations.

These accusations shocked Silas to the core, but there was more to come. Although Farquhar found Sir Jeffrey's actions to be problematic, he was scathing when it came to John Gascoigne. It was common knowledge throughout the museum that the now curator of the Melbourne Museum had been quietly dismissed, although for what reason no one was prepared to say. The matter had been hushed up. However, Farquhar had unearthed the truth. It appeared that Gascoigne had also been involved in smuggling antiquities, not for the greater good of the British Museum's collection, but for his own benefit. It was suggested that Mr Gascoigne had a gambling habit, which consumed large sums of money.

Armed with this information, Silas was in a quandary. What should he do? Should he alert the Melbourne Museum's administration to the circumstances of Gascoigne's departure from the British Museum? Inform them that Gascoigne had been involved in smuggling and had lined his own pockets with the money that he made selling treasures on the black market? That he also had a gambling problem?

It seemed the right thing to do, but then he hesitated. The British Museum, Gascoigne's former employer, would likely deny the accusations; they would not want his illegal activities made public, because it would blacken their reputation. Furthermore, Silas would appear to be no more than a disgruntled ex-employee of the Melbourne Museum. He had no physical proof, only hearsay. No matter which way he looked at it, Gascoigne would keep his job.

Silas examined his own motives. It was undeniable that he had been blindsided when he had been retired forcefully. He had worked side by side with Gascoigne for a little over a month and had not been convinced that his successor was more qualified, knowledgeable, or experienced than he. Now, with Farquhar's letter in his hand, he felt vindicated, but there would be no resolution for him. It was a Pyrrhic victory. His job was gone, never to return.

The involvement of Katherine Rhodes was, however, another matter. There was positive proof that she had engaged in these activities and that she had profited from them. But who had started this illegal operation? Was it the administrative assistant herself, or was it John Gascoigne? Had he enticed Ruby Rhodes' sister to join him in the smuggling business, promising big profits, and then pretended it was all her doing when she died?

There was only one person who could uncover the truth, and that person was Reggie da Costa. Silas put on his coat.

Chapter Forty-Nine

Dusty Rhodes was sitting at his father's rolltop desk, in Ruby's house, typing up the final piece of his investigation into political corruption. His Port Melbourne home was, as usual, no haven for a reporter seeking peace and quiet. His house-mate was good company, but sometimes he made too much noise.

Arriving at his sister's home that Sunday morning, Dusty found that Ruby had gone out unexpectedly, but would return soon, according to the note that she had left him. She was meeting up with John Gascoigne at ten o'clock at the museum. Obviously, she was making further enquiries about Katherine. Perhaps as to whether Gascoigne knew about Black Jack Kelly?

Dusty looked at his watch. Reggie was due shortly, and would hopefully give the stamp of approval to his report on Labor Party politics, before it went to *The Argus*'s solicitors to check if there were grounds for legal prosecution.

As Dusty pulled the completed report from the typewriter, he heard a knock on the back door. It was Reggie.

'Did you park in the lane?' asked Dusty, grinning, as he opened the door to his colleague. 'You can't risk the Hupmobile being vandalised by the local larrikins?'

Reggie nodded. 'Exactly.' He looked around the kitchen. 'Ruby's not here?'

'She's out.'

Reggie's face fell ever so slightly. 'More's the pity. Will she be home soon?'

'I think so. She's gone into the city.'

'Now, where's this report of yours? Hope you're not stepping on too many

242

toes.'

'You can decide.' Dusty led the way up the hallway to the spare bedroom, where he'd set up two chairs in front of the desk.

Reggie picked up the report and flipped through the pages. 'Give it to me in a nutshell. What are your findings?' he asked.

'Mayor Swithins is up to his neck in Labor Party shenanigans.'

'In what way?'

'He's been recruiting new members for the electorate of Collingwood.'

Reggie smoothed his moustache. 'The Mayor, eh? It doesn't surprise me that he's back to his old tricks. He's ambitious and ruthless and driven.'

'It's different this time around. Swithins is not paying for the memberships himself. He won't be controlling the candidate who wins the seat.'

'So, who's the candidate and who's pulling the strings?'

'The candidate is someone you know: Nico McArdle. And the man who is paying for the memberships and who'll pull the puppet strings is Horace Striker. If Nico gets elected to parliament, it will be Striker dictating his policies and opinions and how he votes on issues.'

Reggie sighed. 'Imagine a gangster like Horace Striker having a say in the law-making process? There's enough corruption in government without adding a criminal to the mix. And McArdle will do whatever Horace tells him. He'd be afraid not to. Where did you get this information from?'

'The disgruntled politician who's going to lose the backing of the branch. He's angry. He's worked hard for the electorate, and he's going to be replaced at the next election. He wants to see the practice stamped out.'

'This is important, Dusty. Is he prepared to go on the record about this?'

'He is. And he has friends who'll testify, if it goes to court.'

'What a coup for you. I'm impressed.'

'I do have to warn Ruby. Striker isn't going to like it when I expose Nick and him being in cahoots.'

Reggie sat back and frowned. 'That's a real concern. We can talk to her when she gets home.' He glanced around the room, his gaze settling on the rolltop desk. 'My Grandpa Morgan had one of those. A beautiful piece of furniture it was. I think it was sold off when he went broke. I used to love sitting at it. It had a secret compartment.'

He leaned forward and pulled out one of the drawers.

'Bloody hell! I don't believe it. It's got a false back.' Behind the drawer was an empty space. But it wasn't empty at all. 'There's something there,' said Reggie, reaching in.

'What on earth?' exclaimed Dusty, as he watched Reggie extract a small book. 'It's a diary.'

On the cover of a leather-bound book were inscribed the initials 'KAR 1924' in gold lettering.

Dusty stared at it. 'Katherine Ann Rhodes. Who would have thought?'

He pulled his chair closer to Reggie's, and together they looked in wonder as Reggie thumbed through the pages.

Dusty shook his head. 'I don't believe it. Katherine's diary. And it's for 1924. Turn to September. That's when Stanley Duggan died. Let's see what she says.'

Reggie found the place. 'Here it is. September 4. She writes, "My darling is dead. He was stabbed in an alley off Little Lonsdale Street. Why, I don't know. I am heartbroken. Horace says he will find out who did it. God help his killer if Horace catches him."'

Reggie skimmed the pages, skipping a few entries. 'September 14. She writes, "I went to the funeral. It was awful. I cried and cried. I don't know what I will do without him."'

'Now, this is interesting. October 1. "I went to Squizzy's club. Dressed myself up for the first time since Stanley's death. I drank too much. Squizzy introduced me to some bloke called BJ. I didn't like the look of him. He looked me up and down like he was examining horse flesh."'

'October 20. "I've bought a house in Richmond. I'm wondering if I should lock myself away until the heat is off. Horace won't see me. BJ is putting pressure on me to pay up."'

He scanned the next few pages, then muttered an obscenity. 'December 3. "My last day at work. I can't cope with John. He actually got down on his knees and begged me to marry him. He's obsessed. I had to wonder if he had something to do with Stanley's death."'

CHAPTER FORTY-NINE

'Gascoigne. Bloody hell. You know what this means?'

'Read the last entry,' Dusty said, leaning forward, tense.

Reggie flipped through the pages until he reached the 31st of December.

'"My last night out tonight. Tomorrow I go into isolation. No parties. No clubs. No gambling. No drinking. I'll be like a nun. John continues to write to me. In the last one, he said that if he can't have me, no one will. He sounded so angry that I wonder if he meant it. I've been sending most of his letters back unopened. After all this time, he still doesn't understand that I don't want to be with him. He scares me. When and if I get through this, I promise that I'll start afresh and make it up with Dusty and Ruby. Perhaps 1925 might be the start of a new life for me? I can only hope.'"

Dusty looked at Reggie, his face pale. 'Ruby's gone to see John Gascoigne,' he whispered.

'What? Today? She might be with him now?' cried Reggie. 'What if he killed Katherine?'

'We need to get to the museum,' said Dusty. 'Ruby doesn't know who she's dealing with. Which car will we take?'

Reggie jumped to his feet. 'No question about it. The Hupmobile. I've been wanting to see what she can do.'

Parked out in the back lane, the low-slung, forest-green roadster resembled a hibernating beast about to be awoken from its sleep. Reggie pressed the starter, and the creature roared into life, disturbing the quiet of the morning. He threw it into second gear, and the car surged forward, careering wildly as it sped across the uneven cobblestones of the laneway. At the corner, Reggie swung the wheel left into King Street, the tyres screeching as they made contact with the concrete road surface. As Tanner Street loomed ahead, Reggie applied the brakes, then floored the accelerator after the turn. Now, with a stretch of straight road ahead, he expertly shifted gear, the engine responding as the car gathered pace.

But there was still Punt Road to navigate, it being the main thoroughfare to the city. Reggie hit the brakes, bringing the Hupmobile to a shuddering stop as they waited impatiently at the intersection for a break in the traffic. The car idled noisily, its growl reminiscent of a caged tiger. Reggie swore as a never-ending stream of motorcyclists, drays, horse-drawn buggies, assorted motorcars, and cyclists sauntered nonchalantly past, blissfully unaware of the impatient and reckless driver chafing at the bit to join them.

Meanwhile, Dusty was leaning forward, his hands flat against the dashboard, his head shifting from one side to the other, watching for an opportunity. 'Now's your chance, Reggie!' he cried as a slight break appeared in the traffic.

Reggie floored the throttle, the automobile bursting from the side street into the traffic. At the same time, a pedestrian stepped out onto the road in front of them.

'Bugger!' cried Reggie. 'Hold on!'

He braked hard, skidding to a halt, then accelerated around the man, who stood transfixed as a haze of forest-green flashed past him, missing him by inches.

Reggie's evasive tactics brought them onto the wrong side of the road, facing oncoming traffic. He gripped the wheel and turned it hard, his foot flat to the floor, the rear end of the Hupmobile flipping out as he swerved to miss a horse pulling a dray-load of beer barrels.

'Imagine if we'd hit that? Foaming beer all over the road!' yelled Dusty above the roar of the engine.

Reggie's cheeks flushed with excitement as he fought to get the steering under control. 'What a car. Come on, let's go!'

Now, in third gear, the four-cylinder engine of the Hupmobile Series R Special Roadster responded and the automobile surged forward, powering up the hill past the parkland adjoining the Melbourne Cricket Ground. The needle on the speedometer was creeping up, past its purported top speed of thirty-five miles per hour.

'Faster, faster!' Reggie cried. With the top down and the wintry wind in his face, Reggie felt a heady mix of agitation and exhilaration as the automobile thundered on towards the museum, leaving all in its wake. Heads turned, horns blasted, and pedestrians ran for cover in the face of a juggernaut driven by a madman.

As the speedometer ticked over forty-five miles per hour, Reggie gripped the wheel, unwilling to think about what awaited them when they finally stopped, if they could. Beside him, Dusty closed his eyes and, uncharacteristically, offered up a silent prayer.

Chapter Fifty

I
t was a chilly, bleak day in Melbourne, dark clouds obscuring the sun, autumn leaves swirling around the open spaces, like little whirlwinds in the desert. It was mid-morning when Ruby reached the museum. The interior was in darkness, the blinds drawn, a sign announcing that the building was closed stuck on the door. She shook her head. All this way to meet with John Gascoigne, and the place was shut. On a whim, she tried the door and found, to her surprise, that it was open. She entered the foyer and saw that a light was on in Gascoigne's office, on the other side of the main exhibition space.

It was deathly silent in the blackness of McCoy Hall; the temperature had dropped, and the air smelled musty and stale. Ruby experienced a sense of foreboding. Her imagination, usually well under control, was sparked by the other-worldliness of the place. It was as if she had stepped into a mausoleum which, in a sense, it was. She tried to shrug off the feeling, but it persisted. Then, as she was about to leave, she saw the outline of John Gascoigne, the light behind him, in the doorway of his office.

'Ruby, come in.'

She took a deep breath and threaded her way between the preserved bodies of wild animals, which loomed up on each side of her. Wily, lithe, yellow-eyed coyotes bared their fangs at her; the monstrous bulk of a gargantuan elephant seal, thick with blubber, cast its shadow across her; a lion, its jaws fastened around the throat of a wildebeest, eyed her menacingly; while, on the far side of McCoy Hall, a pair of Kodiak bears, smothered in thick, coarse fur, reared up onto their hind legs, poised for a fight to the death. Aided by the feeble light emanating from the skylights, outlandish shadows played across the walls and floor, cast by the skeleton of a pterodactyl suspended above her, its supporting wires invisible in the gloom. Ruby looked up and fancied momentarily that the winged reptile was about to swoop down and seize her in its beak.

Reaching the welcome light of the office, she shrugged off her sense of disquiet and shook John Gascoigne's outstretched hand, then took a seat opposite him.

Gascoigne's face was welcoming. 'What brings you here, Ruby? A social visit?'

She shook her head, her voice flat. 'Nothing so simple or pleasant, John. I've found a notebook. It was Katherine's. I think I know who killed my sister.'

The smile left his face. 'You do?'

She leaned forward. 'You see, I'll be honest with you. I find it hard to believe that you know nothing about what happened here.'

'I don't know what you mean.'

She stared at him, her face grim. 'I think you do.'

'What did she say in this diary of hers?'

Ruby stared at him. 'Diary?'

'Notebook, then.' He folded his arms across his chest.

Ruby ignored his question. 'I've given this a lot of thought,' she said. 'You're involved in this. She couldn't have done it without your knowledge. The names of suppliers, the delivery of the goods. It must have been done through the museum. It's all in the notebook.'

'I've told you that I knew nothing,' he said, his voice expressionless.

'She must have told you that she was trying to get out of the business?'

He shook his head. 'It's her own fault. She was mixing with the wrong crowd.'

'You haven't been truthful with me,' she insisted. 'It's all in the notebook. Everything.'

'Everything?' His voice raised a notch; his eyes narrowed.

'Yes, everything. You need to tell me. I need to understand,' she insisted.

Gascoigne looked away, his face working. Ruby was aware of the silence, the darkness of the museum, the fact that she was alone with him. The sense of foreboding returned.

Gascoigne turned on her, his voice harsh. 'She was greedy. She wanted too much. And then she wanted it to stop.'

'Katherine told you this? What did you say to her?'

'I told her I would protect her, but she wouldn't have it.' There was a sob in his voice. He paused, trying to calm himself, then thumped his chest, emotion getting the better of him. 'I was prepared to forgive her for what she did to me. Introducing me to those scum. Squizzy and his lot. I lost nearly everything. And she said that it was my fault. My fault?'

Ruby was stunned. So, it *was* Gascoigne whom she'd seen gambling at Squizzy's club. The old shiny suit. The frayed and dirty cuffs. Money troubles.

Gascoigne kept talking, gabbling, filling the room with his justifications. 'I did so much to free her from the mess she was in. Stanley Duggan was a thug. He dragged her into that world. She was going to *marry* him. I thought if he were gone, we could go back to what we were.'

Ruby could just hear him above the buzzing in her ears, as the implications of his words finally registered. She heard herself say, as if in a whisper, 'You killed Stanley?'

'The world's a better place without him. We had such a special relationship, you see. But she wouldn't have it. She wanted to leave. I begged her not to go.'

She sat, holding her breath, then she leaned forward. The words came in a rush.

'Did you kill Katherine?'

He looked at her, his face a mask, expressionless. 'I gave her one last chance, and she refused me.'

She stared at him, her eyes wide. '*You* killed Katherine.'

The accusation hung in the chilly air of the museum. Her sister's death was no accident, after all. All Ruby's theories, all her speculation, all wrong. Black Jack had nothing to do with Katherine's death. Not Nick, not the gangs, not the private collectors. There was only one person left. And that was the man who was sitting in front of her.

Ruby got to her feet, but Gascoigne was too quick. He blocked the doorway, looming over her, his voice low and menacing. 'I told you to leave it alone. I told you that you could end up dead. You wouldn't listen. You wouldn't let it go.'

Ruby looked past him, out into the main hall. No sounds from the bustling city infiltrated the thick stone walls. The museum was deathly silent; the only witnesses to Gascoigne's admission being the bulging, bloated, and distended shadows of carcasses as they played across the walls, caught by the glare of the office light.

'What happened on New Year's Eve?'

'I followed Katherine to Squizzy's club and waited in the alley until she came out. The bitch fought me, but I got her in the end.' He pulled up his sleeve to show a jagged scar. 'Look what she did to me. She struggled, but people thought she was drunk. I tied her up and drove her to my place in Albert Park. By then, she'd quietened down. I tried to talk to her, make her see sense. I told her that we could have a good life together.

'You know what she did? She laughed at me. *Me, John Gascoigne.* I was angry. I slapped her, and still, she laughed. I've never hit a woman before. It was Katherine's fault, not mine. Treating me like that. Laughing at me. I'd had enough. I untied her and told her we were going out.' He paused, breathing deeply. 'She tried to run for it. I grabbed the first thing I could: the poker from the fireplace. She was at the front door trying to get it open when I hit her across the back of the head. She fell. I looked at her then, lying on the floor, and I knew that she was no better than that fiancé of hers, both scum of the earth. I carried her out to the car, walked her down to the St Kilda pier, and threw her over the edge. Then I went home and made myself a cup of tea.'

She stared at him, unflinching. 'You were the man at the pier on New Year's Day. You let her drown.' Ruby drew herself up and faced him. 'What are you going to do to me?'

Gascoigne leaned up against the door jamb, his mood shifting, no

251

longer agitated, no longer angry, now cool and calm. He appraised her dispassionately, as if she were one of the specimens on display.

'Wouldn't it be fitting if you ended your life where this whole sorry saga began: at St Kilda pier? Poor Ruby, they'll say, when they find your body. She couldn't cope with the loss of her sister. She couldn't accept that Katherine died in a terrible accident. She tried to uncover a murder where none existed.

'In a few hours, you'll be reunited with Katherine.'

The sound of footsteps broke the silence. Reggie and Dusty emerged from out of the gloom.

'She'll be at home, Gascoigne,' said the crime reporter. 'You, however, will be hanging from the end of a rope once the Law gets through with you.'

At first, Gascoigne was startled by the appearance of the two men. He looked from one to the other, summing up his opponents. Then he bellowed loudly, his voice reverberating off the walls of the museum. He charged at them. Gascoigne was a bear of a man, with his wild mane of hair and large frame. He knocked Dusty off his feet, sending him flying.

He turned his attention to Reggie. He grabbed him by the arm, the two wrestling each other, cursing, grunting, and straining. They separated, breathing heavily. Reggie's eyes narrowed as he noticed that the sleeve of his expensive three-piece woollen suit was dangling from the armhole. This meant war!

Facing off, Gascoigne rushed at him again, but Reggie feinted a step to the left then dodged right, his aggressor wrong-footed. Gascoigne lost his balance and went sprawling, sliding across the floor towards the Kodiak bear exhibit. The Englishman regained his feet, breathing heavily. He glared defiantly at the crime reporter.

'You're not getting me!' he bellowed, his fists clenched.

Intent on Reggie, he had forgotten Dusty, who had edged his way along the side wall of the exhibition space, so that he was now behind Gascoigne.

Reggie, meanwhile, was bracing for the final showdown with a man who was inches taller and pounds heavier than he. He beckoned to his adversary. 'Come on, you coward!'

Gascoigne was red in the face, breathing hard. He took a deep breath and was about to hurl himself at Reggie when Dusty yelled at the top of his lungs, 'John!'

The big man swivelled around, bewildered, but saw nothing in the darkness. Too late, he spun back just in time to see Reggie's left hook connect with his jaw. His legs buckled under him. He staggered back, falling against the nearest platform and dislodging one of the bears. He stared upwards and watched, wide-eyed, as the mammoth beast, weighing several hundred pounds, rocked backwards and forwards. Then it toppled over, burying him beneath a thicket of coarse brown fur.

'Good work, Dusty,' Reggie said, surveying the carnage and wiping the dust from his suit. He grinned, then put his arm around Ruby's shoulders and drew her to him. 'You're a brave girl.'

She shook her head in dismay when she noticed the torn sleeve. 'He's ruined your suit, your beautiful suit.'

'Don't worry about it. That can be mended, whereas you're irreplaceable.'

'He was going to kill you, Ruby,' said Dusty, 'like he did Katherine.'

'He's not capable of hurting anyone now,' said Ruby, surveying the leg that was just visible beneath the bear.

Reggie nodded. 'At least we now know who killed Katherine and Stanley Duggan.'

A deep, sonorous voice came from behind Reggie. 'Who killed Stanley?'

Into the light stepped Horace Striker, accompanied by four of his bodyguards.

'Horace, it was Mr Gascoigne,' said Ruby. 'He wanted Katherine for himself, so he killed Stanley. Then, when she wanted nothing to do with him, he killed her. He would have killed me, too, if Dusty and Reggie hadn't shown up. Reggie knocked him out.'

Horace approached the bear and nudged it with his foot. Gascoigne's arm flopped out. 'Good job, Reggie,' he said dryly.

'Shouldn't we call the police?' said Ruby.

Horace turned to her. 'I told you once before, my girl, that I don't work that way. No police.'

He signalled to his men. Burke and Hare stepped forward, pushing the carcass off Gascoigne. The big man looked up at them, his eyes wide with fear.

Striker stepped forward. He rested his knee on Gascoigne's chest, brought his face up close to that of the Englishman, then whispered in his ear, 'You're going to regret the day you were born.'

Horace nodded at his bodyguards. Taking their cue, they grabbed a whimpering Gascoigne by the arms and legs and carried him out the door.

Outside the office, a young boy was hovering in the doorway. He was about thirteen years old, wearing a knitted vest, baggy brown trousers, and holding a checked newsboy cap.

'I know you,' said Ruby.

'I think you've met Marty,' said Horace. 'He's still learning the ropes about tailing people.'

'He works for you?'

'I thought you needed protection. I've had someone watching you most of the time.'

'The man on the motorcycle?'

'One of mine.'

'The man in the alley?'

'A random prowler, I'm afraid.'

Ruby smiled bleakly and ruffled the boy's hair. 'I'm sorry I made it so hard for you, Marty.'

The boy looked up at Striker and grinned. 'I'm getting better at it, sir. She never saw me today.'

Horace nodded. 'You did well, my boy.' He shifted his gaze to Reggie and Dusty. 'Now get this young lady home. If you think that Ruby has had a bad day, it's about to get a lot worse for Mr Gascoigne.'

Chapter Fifty-One

There was to be one final formal meeting between Horace Striker, Reggie, and Ruby. It took place a week after the revelation of Gascoigne's involvement in the murders of Katherine Rhodes and Stanley Duggan.

They were sitting in Striker's office in Shamrock Street. The atmosphere was much more relaxed compared to the first time when Ruby and Horace had met.

Horace nodded at her. 'You're looking well.' He cleared his throat. 'There were some aspects to this business that I thought you should know. Reggie has published his report in *The Argus*, and the police have re-opened their investigations. Hopefully, they will name Gascoigne as the main suspect in the murders of Kitty and Stanley and issue a warrant for his arrest.'

'Where is he, Horace?' asked Ruby.

'I don't think you want to know. Let's just say that his punishment was fitting given the circumstances. He won't be bothering you in the future.'

Reggie smirked. 'Very accurate.'

Horace ignored him, addressing Ruby. 'When you first came to see me, you made me reconsider my approach to finding my nephew's killer. You believed that someone had murdered your sister. I asked myself: what if Stanley's death wasn't about business? What if it were personal? Not the gangs, not the drugs, not the gambling, but someone who had a personal grudge against Stanley himself? What if Miss Kitty was involved?

'Then Black Jack Kelly became a suspect,' he continued. 'Reggie uncovered the fact that he was running a protection racket on Kitty. I had him checked out. He arrived in Melbourne shortly *after* Stanley died. So that took him out of the frame. I regret that I didn't stop his ill-treatment of Kitty, but I can't change the past.

'I knew also, through my association with Nico McArdle, that he had nothing to do with Stanley's or Kitty's deaths. I'm afraid his choice of film was an unfortunate coincidence, nothing more. I'll leave it at that.

'We looked closer. People Kitty mixed with. Her friends and then her work colleagues.

'Finally, we looked at Gascoigne. He was in deep trouble financially. His gambling was out of control. Horses. Two-up. Cards. A lot of money had been passing through his hands—not the modest wages of a museum curator—so we knew that he must be up to his neck in the antiquities business too. It wasn't only Kitty who was doing the dealing.'

Reggie nodded his head. 'My contact, Dr Bacon, found out more about Gascoigne. He was on the take in London and was asked to leave. The man had a gambling problem then, too.'

'That makes sense,' agreed Striker. He leaned forward. 'I sent Burke and Hare to look through his house while he was out. They found photographs of Kitty. It was obvious that he was obsessed with her. There was a photograph of Kitty and Stanley. His face had been scratched out. They found a couple of letters written in mid-December that she'd returned unopened to him. They were nasty. He was threatening her.'

He addressed Ruby. 'We thought we better get you in and update you, but things moved fast. Marty was following you when he saw you go into the museum. He contacted me immediately. I got in the Daimler with Burke and Hare and the boys and headed there, but we might have been too late if it hadn't been for Reggie and your brother.'

'I'm so grateful, Horace. To you and Reggie.' She sneaked a glance at the crime reporter and then focused her attention back on Striker. 'You never had to do all this for me. You didn't owe me anything.'

Striker nodded his head. 'That's true. The fact is that I was doing it for me and for Stanley. But you interested me, Ruby, because you were prepared to take on a task that most people wouldn't have. I admired you for that. Like everyone else, I accepted that Kitty's death was accidental, but you showed me that I was wrong. Without you, I'd still be sitting here, wondering who killed Stanley. At least, now I know, and I can be happy in the knowledge—'

'Yes?'

'That the ledger is in balance.'

Reggie sat back. 'I heard that Felix Messenger's raid hit a snag.'

Horace grunted. 'Indeed, it did.'

'What happened?' asked Ruby, looking from one to the other.

'It seems that Mayor Swithins has two collections,' Reggie explained. 'A set of real Egyptian treasures and a set of excellent fakes. When he was warned about the upcoming raid, compliments of Mr Striker here, he moved one lot out and another lot in. Apparently, his boys had a busy day. I've heard that he has a fortified warehouse in South Melbourne somewhere.'

Ruby laughed. 'I would have loved to have seen Mr Messenger's face.'

'According to a couple of Customs officers who were at the raid, it was priceless,' said Reggie. 'He's not well-liked in his own department, so they took delight in his comeuppance. On Messenger's recommendation, Customs had sent two experts in Egyptian antiquities down from Sydney to assess the loot. When they broke into Swithins' place, they went from one exhibit to the next, examining each and declaring them fakes. You can imagine the ructions this is causing in Sydney. The Comptroller-General of Customs wants Messenger's head on a plate. The word is that he is going to be demoted—stripped of his officer status—and assigned to opium raids. If he doesn't resign first.'

'He deserves everything he gets,' said Ruby, frowning. 'Bashing Dusty and putting him in hospital.'

Horace's face darkened. 'I have no sympathy for your brother. I suppose you're aware that he's ruined my political aspirations?'

Ruby turned on the gangster. 'Dusty was doing his job. You can't expect me to support you over that issue. You're undermining the democratic process.'

Striker scowled. 'What democratic process? You're being naïve, my girl.'

Reggie stepped in, sensing that the conversation was moving into dangerous territory. 'So, Horace, what are your political plans now that Nick McArdle has headed back to Sydney?'

'Politics is too unpredictable and dirty,' said Horace, recovering his equilibrium. 'I'll stick to gambling, brothels, and bootlegging.'

'What about the Mayor?' asked Reggie.

'He's disappointed that the ploy to insert Nico didn't come off, but he admitted to me that he thought his nephew was erratic and untrustworthy. It's not been a good week for the Swithins. First the raid, then Nico.'

Ruby ventured the question that had been on her mind for some time. 'I have to ask. How do the Swithins feel about me? I suppose they know the truth?'

Horace nodded. 'They were shocked and angry at first. They felt that you'd deceived them, pretending to be Miss Kitty and putting Messenger onto them.'

'Well, I did.'

'I visited them after the raid, and we had a nice quiet chat. I explained about Miss Kitty's death and how you'd been convinced it was murder. Without your intervention, I told them, I would never have discovered Stanley's killer. I also explained that you were the one who forewarned me about Messenger's raid and thereby saved the Mayor's collection from being seized and him being prosecuted. That calmed them down a bit. The Mayor needs me as a friend, you see, so he knows better than to hold a grudge against you. That would be unwise.'

Reggie picked up his hat. 'Now that Gascoigne has been exposed and Messenger sent packing, I think that this young lady can relax now. It's ended well. The Mayor can keep his precious collection without the risk of being raided a second time.'

'True,' agreed Striker. 'It would be a foolhardy Customs officer who tried that again.'

The conversation came to an end. There was silence as Reggie and Ruby stood, preparing to leave Horace Striker's office. The gangster got up from behind his desk, glanced briefly at the photograph of Stanley Duggan, and walked around to face them. He hesitated, then leaned forward to shake

Reggie's hand.

'Good work, Mr Crime Reporter. You've taken a load off my shoulders. I won't forget this. Just leave me out of whatever you write from now on.

'And as for you, Miss Ruby, I hope this isn't the last I see of you. You'll always be welcome at The Stockade. Not your brother, but certainly you.'

Ruby stepped forward and kissed Striker on the cheek.

'Thank you, Horace. I will always be grateful to you.' She smiled. 'I'll tell Dusty to leave you alone too. At least, for a while.'

Horace Striker chuckled, then returned to his desk. 'Hare will show you out.'

* * *

Outside, on the street, Ruby touched Reggie's arm. 'Before we go, what did Horace mean about Gascoigne's punishment being appropriate?'

'Are you sure you want to know?'

Ruby nodded. 'I'm sure.'

'We received a most unusual report in the newsroom last Monday. A couple of fishermen were sitting on the end of St Kilda pier when they noticed a motor boat further out. It cut its engine, and then a box was lowered into the water.

'One of the fishermen was curious. He got out his binoculars. The box, he said, was decorated with strange carvings, brightly coloured. He watched it float for a few minutes, and then it turned on its end and sank beneath the surface. The boat started its engine and headed back to shore.'

'What's that got to do with John Gascoigne?'

'I spoke to the fisherman myself. He swore that the box was a sarcophagus, an Egyptian sarcophagus.'

Ruby was silent, digesting the implications of the sighting. 'You don't think—'

'I do. The word is that Mayor Swithins is missing a sarcophagus, one of his collection of fakes. As Horace Striker said, the punishment fitted the circumstances.'

Reggie smoothed his moustache then looked at her intently. 'What's next for you?' he asked.

'I'm going to burn the notebook. Get rid of the evidence.' She took a deep breath. 'There's something I need to tell you. There was a lot of money under the floorboards.'

'Eight thousand pounds altogether, wasn't it?'

'You know about it, then?'

'Dusty told me.'

Ruby laughed. 'He would tell you.'

'What do you plan to do with it?'

'I think I'll buy some new furniture and decorate my house the way I want it. Make it my own.'

Reggie nodded approvingly, then added, 'Can I have the Chesterfield? It would suit my place.'

'Of course. I owe you so much.'

'What about the rest of the money?'

'I'm going to give four thousand pounds to the Melbourne Museum, to establish an antiquities collection. I think that's *fitting* too.'

'Do you think that's wise? You don't want to spend some on a holiday or an automobile?'

'I've made up my mind, Reggie. It's the right thing to do.'

The crime reporter nodded slowly. 'If that's what you want, then you'll be pleased to know that Silas will be managing the money. Apparently, the museum administrators have been doing a background check into Mr Gascoigne over the last few months. Certain irregularities have been found. Now that he's gone missing, they've asked Silas to take over temporarily, but they also suggested his position would be made permanent once Gascoigne is officially removed from the position. Now, what are you going to do with Katherine's Egyptian jewellery?'

'That will become part of the exhibit, but not yet. It's my birthday next month. I'll celebrate with a gala Egyptian party at The Stockade, if Horace approves, and wear it one last time. And I'll buy you a new suit to replace the one that Gascoigne ruined.'

'From Zink and Sons. Oxford Street, Sydney?' His eyes brightened. 'Or Savile Row?'

'Whatever you like.'

'I hear that Wattle Path is having a gala event tomorrow night. Would you like to go with me?' Reggie asked, looking at her intently.

'Just as friends. Nothing more?'

'More than just friends. And I'll teach you the tango.' He took her hand and raised it to his lips.

She nodded. 'The new Ruby would love that.'

A Note from the Author

I have retained Australian spelling, punctuation and word usage, where possible.

Acknowledgements

Writers Victoria has been instrumental in my development as a writer. Dr Kate Ryan's editing skills helped me polish the manuscript and prepare it for publication.

Researching the historical and social background to this book has been aided by the National Library of Australia's research portal, *Trove*, using their digitised newspapers from the past. In particular, I drew on reports in *The Argus* and *The Age* to research the gangs of Fitzroy and Richmond, as well as the world-wide obsession with all-things Egyptian after Howard Carter's discovery of Tutankhamun's tomb.

My sincere thanks must go to the Dames of Detection—Harriette Sackler, Verena Rose, and Shawn Reilly Simmons—of Level Best Books, for their continued faith in me as an author. I am extremely fortunate to have them as the editors and publishers of my work. I also wish to acknowledge the support of the other Level Best authors, who have advised and assisted me.

My love and gratitude go to my two children, Trevor and Angela, and their partners, Lauren and Sam, for their support and encouragement. My grandchildren, Ellie and Maddie, give added joy to my life.

I appreciate the support of Kate Becker, from Thesaurus Booksellers, Brighton, for being my partner in crime at my author talks, and Cheryl and Andrew, from Beaumaris Books. Congratulations also to the winner of the Victoria Golf Club's 'Name a Character' charity raffle, Toula McArdle, who features in 'A Deadly Game'. I hope she enjoys her new persona. Thanks also must go to my good friend, Suellen, who suggested that there was still life in Reggie, and that I should continue to develop him as a character. Good advice! And where would I be without my friends, as well as my golfing buddies at the Victoria Golf Club, who have shown such a keen interest in my writing?

Finally, there is my wonderful husband, Bob, who has patiently supported and encouraged me throughout this foray into becoming a novelist, as well as reading and re-reading my manuscripts. Thanks sweetheart.

About the Author

Laraine Stephens lives in Beaumaris, a bayside suburb of Melbourne, Australia. With an Arts degree from the University of Melbourne, a Diploma of Education and a Graduate Diploma in Librarianship, she worked in secondary schools as a Head of Library. On retirement, Laraine turned her hand to the craft of crime writing.

SOCIAL MEDIA HANDLES:
  Laraine Stephens | Facebook

AUTHOR WEBSITE:
  https://larainestephens.com

Also by Laraine Stephens

The Death Mask Murders: A Reggie da Costa Mystery

Deadly Intent: A Reggie da Costa Mystery